CHAOS AND AMBER

CHAOS AND AMBER

BOOK TWO OF THE NEW AMBER TRILOGY

JOHN GREGORY BETANCOURT

ibooks

new york

www.ibooks.net

DISTRIBUTED BY SIMON & SCHUSTER

This one is for
KIM

ACKNOWLEDGMENTS

The author would like to thank Byron Preiss for making this project possible; his editor Howard Zimmerman, who has done a superlative job through a sometimes grueling schedule; and Theresa Thomas, Warren Lapine, Lee F. Szczepanik, Jr., and L. Jagi Lamplighter Wright, for providing commentary, criticism, and advice on the early drafts.

ONE

beron!"

Over a roaring wind, I heard a distant calling of my name. I had been dreaming of sailing a small boat across a churning, wind-swept sea; the dream clung to me, and I could not easily shake its tendrils away.

Where was I? My eyes were closed, but I sensed no light beyond them. Could it be nighttime, or was I in a dark room? I heard what might have been either the rush of wind or the beating of a thousand wings around me. My skin prickled all over with goosebumps, and I felt at once cold and hot, wet and dry.

When I tried to sit up and open my eyes, however, I could not. I found my lack of strength vaguely troubling. But it was so easy not to care, to let myself slide back into the dreaming—

"Oberon! Wake up!"

Ships. I had just begun to dream of ships for a second time when that nagging voice broke in again. The motion around me—a gentle rocking as from waves—reminded me of a ship's deck . . . but there came no susurrant lap from the waves, no cries of gulls nor smell of briny sea.

No, not a ship, I decided, trying to focus my attention on the problem. Also not a horse; no stamping hooves nor neighs nor smells of dung and horse-sweat. A moving carriage, perhaps? That almost made sense. My father had a magnificent carriage, like a giant pumpkin made of spun glass. I remembered my first and only ride in it; we had passed through dozens, maybe hundreds of nightmare worlds. But that didn't explain why I felt both hot and cold. It didn't explain a lot of things.

What *was* that roaring noise?

And why couldn't I open my eyes?

"Oberon!"

I tried to turn my head toward that distant voice but couldn't quite figure out where it came from. Above me? Below? I had gotten turned around; every direction felt wrong, as though I teetered on the edge of a cliff, about to fall. I shivered, and an impulse to flee came over me. I didn't like this place. I didn't like the sensations of being here. I had to get out, now, before something horrible happened.

Once more I tried to rouse myself from sleep. With that effort, colors suddenly pulsed in my head; lights sang and danced before my closed eyelids, and strange tastes and smells and textures flooded my senses. The flavors of lemon and salt and roast chicken and straw all mixed together, the smells of mud and sweat and honey—

If I dreamed, I dreamed strangely. Yet, somehow, I knew I was *not* dreaming . . . not *quite*, anyway. This was something else, something strange and unnatural and unpleasant.

"Oberon!" that distant voice bellowed. *"Get your lazy ass out of bed! The king needs you! Now!"*

The king. Yes, King Elnar needed me. I was one of his lieutenants. I tried to reach for my sword. It must be time to muster the men—

No, that was wrong. King Elnar had died a long time ago . . . it now seemed a lifetime past. A sour, discordant note crept into the sounds in my head; the dancing lights pulsed, bright and dark, dark and bright. I reached for the memory, found it, shuddered at the sudden chill it brought. Yes, I remembered too well . . . remembered how King Elnar fell at the hands of hell-creatures in Ilerium. I had seen his severed head stuck on a pole in the mud outside of Kingstown, a warning and a trap for me when I returned there unexpectedly.

"You killed me!" I had heard his accusing voice say, impossibly coming from that severed head on the pole. "Traitor!" it called. "Traitor. . . !"

I'd opened my mouth to argue, but the words disappeared in a sudden roar of wind. In my mind, I pressed my eyes shut, refusing to see, but the image lingered. And I knew he had been right.

King Elnar, the entire population of Kingstown, and countless thousands of soldiers—all had died because of me. Hell-creatures had invaded Ilerium to find and kill me because my father was a Lord of Chaos, commanding powers I could barely begin to understand.

Now, with King Elnar gone, I no longer served anyone but myself. I didn't have to listen to his accusing voice. I didn't have to wake up. I didn't have to do anything I didn't choose to do.

"Oberon! On your feet!"

I tried to answer, to tell the voice to go to hell, but I could not make my body obey. That vaguely bothered me. Had I been drugged? Had I been sick or grievously injured? Everything I remembered—

could it all have been some nightmare or wild fever-dream?

It all seemed so clear. I remembered my Uncle Dworkin, who had swept back into my life after ten years' absence. Dworkin had saved me from a band of hell-creatures, announced himself as my true father, and carted me off to a magnificent castle on another world . . . a castle full of people who claimed to be my half-brothers and half-sisters. Aber and Freda . . . Locke and Davin and Blaise . . . too many for me to take them all in at once.

And I *was* one of them; I had known it the moment I saw them. We all shared many traits with Dworkin; clearly he had sired us, though with different mothers. I had never suspected my true heritage, but now I recognized the truth of it: Dworkin really *was* my father.

In Juniper Castle I had learned I was born to a noble line of sorcerers. My family had its roots in a place called the Courts of Chaos, the center of the universe, where magic was real. As I understood it, all other worlds were mere Shadows cast by the Courts.

These sorcerers used something called the Logrus, which was a kind of shifting pattern or maze—I wasn't quite clear on how it worked or what it looked like, since different people described it in different ways. All I knew was it granted them miraculous powers, including the ability to move between Shadows and summon objects from distant places. I hoped to be able to travel through it myself, but it seemed I didn't have the ability to do so. I was a magical cripple as far as my family was concerned . . . even though I had already learned to do a little bit of magic on my own. I could change my appearance for short periods of time when I tried.

Unfortunately, our family was at war with an unknown enemy. This mysterious foe had been tracking down and murdering all of Dworkin's offspring, and when he (whoever he was) discovered me in Ilerium, I had become his next target. That was why Dworkin returned and rescued me. My father had gathered all his surviving children together in Juniper, his castle stronghold, guarded by a hundred thousand soldiers under the command of his eldest son, Locke.

Unfortunately, an even larger army of hell-creatures showed up to wipe us all out, and an epic battle ensued. We carried the first day, but at a terrible cost. Our army was decimated, Locke died, and dark sorceries had cut off everyone's access to the Logrus. With no magical means of escape remaining, it seemed we were about to lose. Home, fortune, life; everything.

Fortuitously, it turned out I had a different sort of magic within myself . . . a Pattern—different from the Logrus and yet related to it. Calling on its power, and with Dworkin's guidance, my siblings fled into other Shadows, scattering like dust in the wind, hopefully to places where they would remain safe from harm . . . at least for now. With our enemy's attention and troops focused on Juniper, we had at least a short time to be safe.

Dworkin decided to return to the Courts of Chaos to seek help. Who had attacked Juniper? Who was trying to destroy Dworkin's bloodline? We needed to find the answers.

I had accompanied him, along with my half-brother, Aber. I liked Aber best of all my siblings; he was the only one who seemed to have a sense of humor, and he had been the only one to really take me in and make me feel like I belonged. Aber had been the one who most helped me understand how everything and everyone in our family worked.

A voice broke in on me again, over the sounds of wind:

"Oberon! The king! Rally to the king!"

"He's dead," I tried to say, but it came out a faint mumble.

"Did you hear that?" the voice asked. I did not think its owner was talking to me. "He tried to say something."

"Oberon!" said another voice, lower in pitch, stronger. I recognized it instantly. It belonged to my father. "Listen to me carefully, my boy. You must wake up now—*right now!* Don't hesitate. *Do it!"*

I was mad at my father, I decided. He had dragged me from my safe, cozy life in Ilerium, where I'd known my place and my duty. I had been one of King Elnar's lieutenants, and I had been happy. This whole nightmare—armies attacking, people trying to murder me and destroy our whole family—it was all Dworkin's fault. Before his death, my brother Locke told me the truth of it: Dworkin brought all of this down upon himself through an unfortunate affair with King Uthor of Chaos's daughter.

"Oberon! Look at me!"

Something hit me in the face. I heard the slap, felt it like a white-hot brand across my right cheek. Rage crystallized within me. I forgot the rush of wind in my ears, the darkness and the confusion. Nobody hits me and gets away with it.

I was like a drowning man struggling up through thick, heavy waters. Rage buoyed me upwards. Distantly, I heard a groan. It was an awful, pitiful sound, not the sound a man—a warrior—should have made. When I realized it came from my lips, I tried to stifle it.

And at that moment I opened my eyes.

Dworkin, my father, loomed over me, a short, almost dwarfish man of indeterminate years. He had a look of intense concentration on his face, as though studying some specimen of scientific interest rather than his own son.

I tried to speak, but no sound came out. The breath wheezed in my throat.

"Wake up, I said!"

My father slapped me a second time, hard. My head whipped back from the force.

Both cheeks stinging, I gritted my teeth and turned my head back to face him. My ears rang. The whole room seemed to be whirling around.

As he raised his hand to strike me again, I grabbed his wrist and held it back.

"Don't—" I growled, "or I'll—break your—arm!"

He smiled toothily. "Ah. About time."

I released him and he lowered his arm.

Moving my head made the room swim drunkenly around me. I spotted my half-brother Aber standing behind and to the side of Dworkin, studying me with clear concern. He seemed to be swaying like a tree in a windstorm.

Turning my head farther, I discovered I lay on my back on a high, narrow bed. Slowly, half groaning, I shifted to the other side. It seemed to take forever. The bed sat in a small, dimly lit room. My eyes didn't want to focus on the far wall. It appeared to be made of blocks of red stone flecked with green. A phosphorescent yellowish-green light oozed from between the stones and trickled up toward the ceiling, where it pooled.

I pressed my eyes shut, then rubbed them with my fists. No, I definitely was not ready to see yet. But Dad wanted me awake, and I assumed he had a damn good reason. He'd better, or I really *would* break his arm. And maybe his neck.

Sucking in a deep breath, using every ounce of my strength, I managed to sit up. That was a huge mistake. The room pinwheeled around me, doing its best imitation of a drunkard's stagger. My insides convulsed in response, but disgorged nothing. I had no idea of how long it had been since I'd last eaten.

"Where am I?"

"Home," Aber said. "Our family's estates in the Beyond." At my puzzled look, he went on. "Close to the Courts of Chaos. You know."

I didn't know, but my head felt ready to explode, and I couldn't muster much enthusiasm to care. The roar in my ears returned. Groaning, I pressed my eyes shut and willed everything back to normal. It didn't work.

We must have been out on some drinking binge last night: too much ale, maybe a fistfight or two, hopefully a pair of comely barmaids well bedded. I had awakened from many worse things over the years.

The only thing was, I didn't remember any of it.

"How do you feel?" Dworkin asked me.

I hesitated. "Not quite dead."

"Do you know where you are?"

The last thing I remembered—

"The Courts of Chaos," I whispered.

"The Beyond is a Shadow of the Courts," said Dworkin, "so close to Chaos that the . . . ah, *atmospherics* are almost identical."

I had hated the Courts of Chaos even before I'd come here with my father and Aber. I'd seen the Courts distantly, through one of my sister Freda's Trump cards. Trumps had the power to open doorways to other worlds. Just gazing at the Courts—strangely shaped buildings, lightning-filled sky, stars that moved and whirled around like fireflies—made me physically ill. Looking back, I should have known coming here would be a mistake. I should have refused to go when my father told me he planned to go to the Courts of Chaos for help.

But I hadn't refused. I hadn't said a word. I'd gone with him because, despite a lifetime of lies and deceptions, he was still my father, and I felt the full weight of my responsibility as his son. Duty and honor had been drilled into me since I was old enough to know what they meant. He'd made sure of that.

Before Juniper could fall, we had used his Trump to get away. In the Courts of Chaos, blood dripped up, stones moved like sheep across the ground, and somewhere, a serpent in a tower made of bones worked dark sorceries to destroy our family.

If the Beyond truly was like the Courts of Chaos, that explained the walls, which now seemed to pulsate gently as they wept their phosphoric light. Overhead, the high-beamed wooden ceiling began to flicker like candles seen through a paper lantern.

Unbidden, a moan welled up from deep in my chest.

"Steady," said Aber.

"Keep him talking," Dworkin said to Aber, then turned and

crossed to the other side of the room. I couldn't see what he was doing at the table, nor did I particularly care at that point. I wanted to curl up and go back to sleep.

Aber sat beside me on the edge of the bed. He had been my one true friend in Juniper, and I had immediately sensed a real camaraderie between us. Now he seemed to drift in and out of focus as I gazed up at him. The brown of his hair began to drip like the walls, colors running down his face. I hesitated. It was him—but not quite. He had horns. His features were heavier, thicker, almost a parody of the young man I knew. And yet . . . the other Aber . . . the Aber I knew in Juniper . . . seemed to be there as well, superimposed on this one. He seemed to flicker back and forth between the two.

Quickly I looked away. Hallucinations? Madness? Maybe it was an effect of being so close to the Courts of Chaos. Maybe it was me and not him at all. I had no way of knowing.

TWO

hy are we in this place . . . ?" I whispered, feeling my insides knot and twist like a serpent swallowing its own tail. "I don't . . . understand . . ."

"Dad's trying to figure out what's wrong with you," he said softly, looking me in the eyes. "Don't go to sleep. It's important. He doesn't want to lose you."

Lose me? What did that mean?

"Get me—out of—here!" I managed to gasp.

"It's more complicated than that," he said. "We can't leave. Someone is trying to kill us, remember, and we have to find out why. And Dad's just been summoned before King Uthor. He has to go. You don't ignore the King of Chaos."

"This place—hurts—"

His brow furrowed. "Maybe you just need to get used to it. You know, like on a ship."

"Sea legs . . ." I whispered, thinking of boats, as the world moved around me.

"Yeah. Chaos legs." He chuckled.

I tried to rise and found some leverage with my elbows, but couldn't keep my balance. I fell in the wrong direction. Aber grabbed my arm and helped pull me upright.

Why did everything want to go *up* instead of *down*? And why did *up* keep moving to the sides? If it would all stop for a minute, I thought I'd be able to get my bearings. My head began to pound.

"Steady."

Without being asked, Aber rose, took my legs, and swung them around and over the side of the bed. Big mistake; I almost passed out as the room seemed to twist down and away, moving out from under me.

I gasped. This couldn't be happening, couldn't possibly be real. The room was strangely shaped. No corners met at right angles—walls curved and the ceiling sloped in an architect's nightmare. It was also sparsely furnished: a tall lookingglass, the bed on which I now sat, a table pushed up against the far wall, and two heavy wooden chairs whose high backs had been carved with the likenesses of dragons.

"Let's get you up," Aber said.

"Wait—"

Reaching down with my feet, I touched the floor with the tips of my toes. Hard, bare, no carpet, just wood that had been polished smooth as glass. It seemed fine. I frowned. So why couldn't I get my balance? Why was everything moving?

Aber glanced over his shoulder at our father. "If you pass out again, Dad will skin you alive."

"But—"

"Don't be a baby about it! Just get up!"

I glared, but shut up. He didn't understand. Well, I'd just have to show him. It wasn't possible for *anyone* to stand here with the floor moving so much.

"Stand up!" he said. "On your feet, Oberon!"

"Help me—"

With a sigh, Aber draped my right arm over his shoulder and heaved. He was stronger than he looked, like everyone in my family, and he got me up with little trouble considering I must have weighed a hundred pounds more than he did.

Leaning on him, I stood unsteadily. The room kept shifting. The corners moved. The floor kept trying to slide away from under me. Without Aber propping me up, I would have fallen.

"There you go," he said, cheerful as always. "First things first. Chaos legs. See?"

He let go. For a second, it wasn't so bad. I steadied myself on his arm and actually thought about trying to walk. Maybe I could make it a few feet.

Then the walls spasmed with reds and yellows. The floor heaved. I felt myself falling and seized his arm hard enough to make him yelp.

"No—you—don't!" He staggered under my weight, bracing himself.

A fierce humming noise filled my ears. The room spun and slipped, and I felt myself going over backwards. Aber quickly caught my shoulders and lowered me back to the floor with a grunt.

I hugged the broad wooden boards, feeling the universe spin, praying that everything would stop moving soon. What sort of place *was* this? I couldn't even stand up here.

Pressing my eyes shut, I tried to block this place from my mind. I willed myself back to Ilerium. It had worked once before, after all.

But it didn't now.

"Want to try standing again?" Aber asked.

"No!"

"At least sit up," he said. "You can do it. Try."

"Maybe . . ."

Taking a deep breath, I eased myself up and braced my feet against the floor. The walls seemed to slide around me like they weren't fastened down. But at least I was sitting now.

"Better," Aber said. I noticed he was rubbing his arm where I'd grabbed him. "We'll take it slowly."

"I need sleep," I growled. "Then I can wake up from this nightmare!"

"You'll get the hang of it. Give yourself time."

Time? I had always been able to walk, even when I was so drunk I could barely see. But I could tell he wasn't going to let me rest.

"Give me a hand—I'll try again."

"Are you sure?" Aber said, hesitating. He rubbed his arm again. I must have really hurt him.

"Sorry about your arm," I said. Sighing, I looked up at his face. He flickered: horns, no horns, horns. I had never felt so dizzy and disoriented.

"Don't worry," he said. "Accidents happen. I heal fast, and I'm happy to carry a grudge." He chuckled. "I'll get even when you least expect it, dear brother. Maybe you ought to sit still for a while."

Slowly I began to crawl toward the bed. It felt like a trip across a constantly moving sheet of ice—tipping first one way then another, with me hanging on desperately and trying not to slide away. Maybe

I could use the bed to balance myself. Mostly I tried not to think about throwing up.

As I reached the bed and began to climb back onto it, Dworkin hurried over, grabbed a fistful of my hair, and yanked my head back. I felt my eyes roll in panic as colors and lights burst like fireworks around me.

"Let go!" I cried. It came out more like the howl of some haunted beast.

Shoving his face close to mine, he peered into my eyes like a physician studying a new patient. I smelled wine on his breath and knew he'd been drinking. That wasn't a good sign. He'd drunk himself into a stupor in Juniper when faced with overwhelming problems. With a comment of, "Interesting," he let go.

I fell flat with an *oomph* of lost air. Then I curled up in a ball on the floor. My breath came in shudders. I wanted to pull the universe in on top of me.

"Do not go to sleep," Dworkin told me firmly.

I peered up at him through a haze.

"Why?" I whispered

"Because you will die."

I groaned. "I'm too stubborn to die."

"Then you are a fool, my boy."

"Send me back to Juniper!" I begged. "Or Ilerium. Anywhere but here!" I would rather face an army of hell-creatures alone and unarmed than put up with this Shadow of the Courts of Chaos for another minute.

"Quiet, Oberon," he said. He began to pace. "I need to think."

As the room began to steady once more, I forced myself to roll over toward the bed. I leaned back against it, watching him. As long as I remained motionless, barely breathing, the room seemed almost steady.

"Can I do anything to help?" Aber asked.

Dworkin said, "Try this."

As I watched, he reached into the air and, seemingly from nothingness, pulled down a large reddish-brown clay pitcher. That was another one of those Logrus tricks. Wine? Something stronger, hopefully. I needed a drink right now. I needed it desperately. I wasn't sure I could keep it down, but I welcomed the chance to try.

Aber accepted the pitcher with his left hand, then reached down, grabbed my shirt, and hoisted all two hundred and forty pounds of me to my feet as though picking up a kitten. When he released me, I teetered unsteadily. Colors leaped and pulsed around me; my vision dimmed, then brightened, then dimmed again. The scream of wind in my ears grew wild and discordant.

"Whiskey?" I gasped. "Brandy?"

"Afraid not," Aber said.

"What—?"

"See for yourself."

Without warning, he raised the pitcher and dumped the contents over my head.

I gasped. It was cold water. *Very* cold water. Water so icy it shocked and numbed my entire body.

Stunned, I didn't move, couldn't breathe. I just stared at him, feeling like a whipped dog thrown out into the pouring rain in the dead of winter just in time to be kicked by a runaway horse.

"Now," said Aber, "we're even." He grinned mischievously at me.

Folding my arms, I silently cursed all siblings to the worst of the seven hells. Fathers, too. A special torture-pit must be reserved for the gleefully malevolent. Dworkin had doubled up with laughter.

So I glared at both of them and waited for their composure to return.

"Remember, Oberon," Dworkin said sharply, catching his breath. He leaned toward me, one stubby finger leveled at my eyes. As I focused on him, his entire body seemed to waver like a flame in a strong breeze. "No sleeping. If you go to sleep, there is a good chance you will never wake up."

I gave a low growl of displeasure. I wasn't sure if I meant it for him or Aber.

"We need to talk," I said to Dworkin.

"Not now." He returned to the table, gathered up half a dozen scrolls scattered there and hurried out the door.

"When—" I began.

The door slammed before I could finish. I looked at Aber.

"Off to see the king," my brother said with a half sigh. "I told you he'd been summoned, remember?"

"Why?"

"Dad petitioned for an audience. It took a while. Everything has its proper time and ceremony. And I'm afraid Dad isn't held in very high regard at the Courts. None of us is."

What rot. I saw the truth. The delay was a deliberate insult. . . . King Uthor's way of letting us know we weren't important enough to merit his attention. We would have to change that. Being here was the first step. Making ourselves important would be the second.

Right now, though, I felt like crawling into bed, pulling the covers over my ears, and hiding from the world for the next ten years. Fathers and their advice be damned, if I could just get rid of Aber. . . .

"You should go with Dad," I suggested.

"Hah! He would never let me." A sour note crept into his voice. "I'm not like you . . ."

"He didn't ask me."

"No, he wouldn't. Not with you being sick. He would have taken Locke, though. He was always the privileged one. The favorite son. And now there's you, of course. As soon as you're well, you'll take Locke's place."

"If you're not happy with your place here, do something about it."

He chuckled. "What do you suggest? Should I murder my way to the top of the family? Make sure I'm the last male heir, so he has to depend on me whether he likes it or not?"

"No. But I'm sure there's something . . ."

"Uh-uh. Dad doesn't like me. That's not going to change." He smiled a bit at my expression. "I *do* have a plan, though, and I *am* doing something to help. I don't stand around all day whining about my place in the family, you know."

I gave him a searching look, but he didn't elaborate. I changed the subject.

"I don't suppose you have any intention of letting me go back to sleep?"

"Nope." He focused on me and grinned wolfishly. His horns were back. "One must take these small pleasures as they come. Just try, and I'll empty a lake on your head!"

"You're a sadist!"

"I'll take that as a compliment."

I gave him a half-hearted glower. "Then how about a towel? And maybe some dry clothes."

"Well . . . not just yet, dear brother. I've been ordered to keep you awake, and that's what I'm going to do. I don't want you *too* comfortable just yet."

Dripping, cold and miserable and thoroughly wide awake now, I stumbled to one of the dragon-backed chairs, sat heavily, and glared at him. At least the room wasn't moving so much anymore. Maybe there was something to his "Chaos legs" theory. Or the ice-water had shocked the worst of the disorientation from me.

"I *am* going to kill you, you know," I promised. "Don't think this is over."

He gave a thoroughly evil chuckle.

"First you have to catch me," he said, "and I don't think you're up to it."

At that remark, I rose and took a step toward him. The room jumped and shook. My skin seemed to be on fire. Winds howled in my ears.

I ignored everything and took another step. No matter what it cost, I wouldn't let him get the better of me. That was the difference between us. No one *ever* got the better of me.

"You ought to sit down," he said hastily.

"No." I gritted my teeth and took another step. Then another.

"You're going to fall."

"You'd be amazed at what I can do," I said, "when I put my mind to it."

One foot at a time. I took another step. Everything around me swayed. That howling noise, like wind but a hundred times louder, filled my ears.

Chaos legs, indeed.

I reached for him.

Aber gulped.

THREE

I don't know if it was the shock of the cold water or just getting up out of bed and moving around, but it came to me suddenly, as I was advancing with malicious intent on my brother, that I had stopped paying so much attention to the strange noises, pulsing colors, and seemingly random movements of the universe around me. Instead, by focusing all my attention on fratricide, I found myself at least beginning to compensate for the distractions around me. With effort, I *could* stand and walk on my own—if awkwardly and unsteadily. A small improvement, but an important one.

Aber suddenly laughed, then reached into the air, felt around for a second, and plucked a large white towel seemingly from nothingness.

"Here." He threw the towel in my face. "You're no fun when you're wet."

"About time you realized it."

I shook my head like a dog caught in the rain, mindless of the way the room suddenly lurched and dipped, just to spray him with droplets. A petty revenge; I quickly regretted it.

"Hey!" He shielded his face.

That gave me some small satisfaction. Then, as I began to blot myself dry, he flopped down on one of the chairs, watching me like a hunter studying an unfamiliar beast. Somehow, I got the impression he didn't trust me not to keel over dead or unconscious at any moment. Well, he had me up, and now I had no intention of resting. Sick or not, I had to find out what I'd missed. We hadn't come here for me to waste time sleeping.

"How long was I in bed?" I demanded.

"Three days."

"Three!" I stared at him, scarcely able to believe it. "Impossible!"

He shrugged. "We've been busy. Dad finally decided you weren't going to wake up on your own, so we spent the last three hours talking to you, shaking you, and yelling at you. You only started to respond when he told you some king needed you. Not King Uthor, I guess?"

"King Elnar. I served him in Ilerium." I shook my head, then winced as it suddenly throbbed; the room whirled around me, then steadied a bit when I stopped moving. "I barely heard you. I was dreaming. I thought I was sailing on a ship."

"A ship? Why?"

"This room—this place—it all feels like it's moving. It still does. But it's not, is it? It's me?"

"Afraid so, Oberon."

I sighed. When I stayed still, the room largely stopped jumping around. Turning slowly and carefully, making no sudden movements, I found the floor seemed to glide subtly underfoot, as though trying to shift with or against me depending on which way I turned. Cold and damp and sick and altogether miserable just about summed up my condition. But for now the worst of the dizziness had passed, and with it at least some of my desire to strangle Aber.

Feeling less like a drowned dog, I threw the towel back at his head. He caught it, tossed it aside, and made it disappear with a snap of his fingers as easily as he had appeared it.

"No sleeping," he warned me again.

"Not much chance of that with *you* on guard. How about some food?" I felt a yawning emptiness inside. "And wine. Lots of wine."

"Are you sure that's wise?"

I hesitated. He was probably right.

"Okay, skip the wine. I'm starving. If you can find it, I want something plain. Bread, cheese, maybe a meat pie—whatever you can scrounge up on short notice."

He hesitated, glancing toward the door. "The dining hall is downstairs. Dinner won't be served for another two or three hours. Do you think you can make it?"

"I . . . I think I'll eat here." I wasn't ready for stairs just yet.

He reached into the air and pulled a dinner tray from nothingness, then set it on the table. Bread, cheese, a sharp knife, and a large glass of what looked like cider of some kind.

"Thanks. Join me?"

"Not yet. I—"

He broke off as a bell sounded outside. It rang three times, then grew still. From the way his brow furrowed, I didn't think it was good news.

I said, "What's the alarm for?"

"Visitors."

"The unwelcome kind?"

"I . . . don't know." He rose, took a step toward the door, paused. "Don't go to sleep," he said ominously, "or else. There's plenty more water where that pitcher came from. I'll be back in a couple of minutes."

"I won't go back to sleep," I said with a chuckle, trying to appear innocent. "After three days of it, lying down is the last thing on my mind right now."

"Hmm." He gave me a suspicious look, then shut the door. I heard his footsteps receding on the other side.

The food did look good. I carved a large chunk off the cheese and chewed it slowly. Sharp and well aged, with a slightly smoky aftertaste, it was quite delicious. I took another bite. No sense waiting for my brother if he wasn't going to eat.

The bread, warm and crusty, went well with the cheese. The cider didn't appeal to me much—it had always struck me as a child's drink unless properly laced with spirits—but it washed everything down satisfactorily.

I finished everything, then sat back, feeling full and vaguely content. No sounds came from the hall, and the bell did not ring again.

Then I heard a distant banging sound, followed by a couple of softer bangs. Doors? Windows opening to air out some long-unused parlor?

Much as I hoped for a simple, harmless explanation, doubts crept in. What was happening down there? Where had Aber gone? Why hadn't he come back?

As I listened for Aber's returning footsteps outside the door, my apprehension grew. I hated being sick and disoriented. I was used to being in control of every situation, a leader and not some helpless invalid. If anyone attacked us, I would not be able to leave this room, let alone protect Aber or fight my way clear of the building.

I strained to hear over the constant low hiss of wind. No clash of weapons nor screams from dying guards reached me. If we were under attack, wouldn't I hear *something*? Our visitors had to be friendly. Probably neighbors paying a social call; after all, Dworkin hadn't been here in years. Wouldn't everyone want to stop by, say hello, and catch up on all the gossip for old times' sake? That must be it. As host, Aber couldn't get away. Nor would he want to let them know about my illness. We couldn't reveal our weaknesses to anyone here.

A long silence stretched. The wind rose slightly. I picked at the crumbs on my plate, gulped the dregs of the cider, and waited impatiently. Doing nothing had always been hard for me. The chair creaked slightly as I shifted. Not so much as a whisper came from the outside.

It had been at least half an hour. Aber wouldn't have left me here this long unless something had happened. Who were these mysterious visitors? What did they want?

I heard a crash like that of breaking glass, fairly close, and stood. Guests didn't go around breaking windows. Something was definitely wrong.

It couldn't hurt to take a look outside. After all, nobody had told me I *couldn't* leave the room—just that I couldn't go back to sleep.

Bracing myself against the arms of the chair, I rose. The room wobbled a bit, but steadied when I remained motionless for a couple of heartbeats. Where was my swordbelt? There—hanging on a peg to the left of the door.

Half walking, half gliding across the shifting floor, I made my way safely to the other side, took my swordbelt down, and fastened it around my waist. The calm before battle settled over me. If I was to die, I would die like a man, with a blade in hand. My sword's cool silvered hilt felt comfortable and reassuring as I rested my palm upon it.

And then everything suddenly began to tilt to the left; I braced myself against the wall and pressed my eyes shut. *Stop it, stop it, stop it!* Slowly, equilibrium returned.

Like an old man, I eased my way over to the door, straining to hear over the dull distant rush of wind. For a second I thought I heard angry voices, but couldn't be certain.

Lifting the latch, I pulled the door open smoothly. Good; Aber hadn't barred it from outside. Clearly he didn't think I'd be foolish enough to go exploring on my own.

I carefully peeked out into a long stone corridor that seemed to be oozing reds and browns. As with my room, all the angles seemed wrong. Doors opened at irregular intervals on both sides, with what might have been oil lamps burning in sconces every few feet between. Light dribbled in faint golden trails toward the ceiling, where it pooled.

My head swam as I tried to take it in. Aber and my father seemed to have no trouble walking around; what was their trick? Perhaps it had something to do with the Logrus. I felt a rising sense of depression; I didn't think I'd ever get used to this place.

Thankfully, no hordes of hell-creatures rushed to attack me. In fact, I saw no one at all. If that bell had signaled the arrival of guests, they were still downstairs. I listened for a long time, but heard nothing—no banging, no breaking glass, no angry voices. Had I imagined them? I didn't think so, but in this place, I really couldn't be sure.

While the floor tried to push me into the wall, I braced myself and waited for my sense of balance to return. It did, but slowly.

This place was insane. The sooner we left, the better off we would be. I didn't see how I could possibly help anyone here.

The hallway appeared to dead-end thirty or so feet to the right, which meant Aber must have turned left. The passage curved out of sight in that direction.

I hesitated. I needed a plan. What exactly did I hope to accomplish with this little expedition? Did I want to check on Aber and these mysterious visitors?

No, not yet. If my brother had run into trouble, I was in no condition to help him. In fact, I'd probably make things worse by needing rescue myself. And if—as I half suspected—some of our neighbors had dropped in, I did not want to reveal my weakness to them. Better to let everyone wonder what had become of me.

The thing to do was reconnoiter. I wouldn't go far; no sense in getting lost. Perhaps I could find my father's rooms . . . there might be something there that could help me.

Keeping one hand on the wall, I turned—and found myself face to face with one of the most beautiful women I had ever seen. I took a deep breath. Her black hair shimmered with bluish highlights. Her eyes held the honeyed color of molten gold. Her skin, pale as milk, held the faintest of blushes at her cheeks—save for a small beauty mark on the left. From her high, finely drawn cheekbones to her delicate chin to the sensuous fullness of her deep red lips, I had never seen anyone like her.

Where had she come from? One of the other rooms on this floor?

"Hello!" I said.

She looked startled for a second, then dropped her gaze to the floor and curtsied. "You are . . . Lord Oberon?"

"Yes." From her demeanor, she had to be a servant. I felt a pang of disappointment. "And you?"

"Rèalla, my lord."

"Do you know what that bell was about?" I asked.

"Bell?"

"Didn't you hear it?" I said.

"No, my lord."

"It sounded not long ago—maybe fifteen minutes."

"I did not hear it, my lord. Perhaps it happened when I was in the wine cellar."

"So you were just downstairs?"

"Yes, my lord."

"Are there any . . . problems down there?"

She looked at me strangely. "Problems, my lord?"

"Yes—I heard some odd noises."

She shook her head. "No, my lord. Everything is fine."

That was good news. I allowed myself to relax a bit and glanced over my shoulder. Still no sign of Aber, though . . . probably stuck playing the genial host. For once, I welcomed his absence. Something about Rèalla fascinated me. I could have spent the rest of the day looking at her.

She went on, "You are wet, my lord. Do you need dry clothing? I am sure something can be found—"

"That's all right," I said with a chuckle and a half shrug. "I'll dry soon enough. Right now, I'm having trouble finding my way around—" A sudden wave of giddiness washed over me. Against my will, I staggered half a step, startling her. I caught myself against the wall, thinking I must look like a clumsy idiot.

"Are you ill, my lord?" she asked.

I sucked in a deep breath, trying to hide my weakness. I wanted her to see me as I saw myself—tall, strong, brave. Not a cripple who couldn't walk ten paces without falling down.

"A bit dizzy, is all," I said. "I was sick, but I'm over the worse of it."

"Here. Let me help you."

She leaned forward to assist me, hand poised, and I caught her scent—a light, sweet musk. The hallway began to spin slowly around me. I breathed her in, deeply, my heart racing. I tried to stay calm.

"Which way," I said in as smooth a voice as I could manage, "are my father's rooms?"

"Lord Dworkin's?" Her gaze flicked up to my face for a second, and I saw mild surprise there. "Two floors above us, my lord."

"Show me the way."

"It is forbidden—"

The floor shifted unexpectedly under my feet, and I staggered again in the other direction, catching my balance on her shoulder.

Her muscles tensed and quivered beneath me, shifting like liquid beneath her skin. It was a very strange sensation, unlike anything I had felt before. It made me regard her more carefully. She *looked* human—but something made me hesitate. Human bones and muscles do not move that way.

"Is something wrong, Lord?" she asked.

"No." I shook my head and smiled. It had to be my screwed-up senses playing tricks on me. She was a beautiful woman—nothing more.

The floor tilted. I staggered to the left.

"Lord Oberon?" she cried, seizing my arm and holding me upright. "What's wrong?"

"I am . . . still a little dizzy. Help me. I need to lean on someone or I'll fall."

"Shall I take you back to your bedroom—"

"It's not necessary." I hesitated, polishing the lie. "I just need someone beside me so I won't fall. If you don't want to help—"

"No, my lord," she said quickly. "Lean on me. I will help you. Where are you going?"

"Up to my father's rooms."

I leaned on her shoulder as lightly as I could. Again I felt her muscles jump and quiver under my hand. It seemed readily apparent to me that she didn't like my touch, but she put up with it.

Slowly and carefully, she turned around and helped me walk toward the dead end. Just before it, we came to a narrow, spiraling set of wooden steps deep in a shadowed alcove. I had taken it for a doorway. The steps led to upper and lower floors.

"This was the closest way to the upper floors," she said half apologetically.

"It's fine, Rèalla."

I paused. From below I heard a distant murmur, like half a dozen voices talking, and a faint clink-clink-clink of pottery being stacked or moved about. "The kitchens?" I asked.

"Yes, Lord Oberon. They are just below us."

I sniffed, but only caught Rèalla's musky scent. Odd—shouldn't dinner preparations have been well under way? Perhaps smells worked differently here, too. I tried to imagine them pooling on the floor or ceiling, like the light.

That sound of breaking glass must have come from the kitchens, I decided. Some servant dropped a platter . . . of course the cook's angry voice would have followed, berating him for his clumsiness. There was a simple explanation for everything I had heard.

Turning slightly, I gazed up the stairway into darkness, toward my father's rooms. Only one person at a time could go up or down— if I had to leave fast, this was the way I'd go.

Grasping the hand rail firmly, I began to climb. Rèalla followed.

I concentrated on the steps, taking them one at a time. Every few feet they seemed to twist and shift beneath me, but by keeping one hand on the rail and the other on the wall, I made it safely up to the next floor. When I peeked out, the hallways was empty. Light pooied on the ceiling from a couple of small lamps. Didn't the architect who had designed this place believe in windows?

"What's on this floor?" I asked.

"Personal rooms," Rèalla said. "Lord Aber is the only noble-born here at the moment . . . besides Lord Dworkin, of course."

"Of course." The rest of my family was either dead or scattered to remote Shadow worlds. The ones that we could account for at all.

Returning to the stairway, I began to climb toward the floor above. The steps ended at a heavy wooden door. The center panel held the carved face of a man with horns, his mouth open as if about to speak.

I knocked for form's sake, knowing my father was out, then pushed it open to reveal a long, dark corridor pungent with the scents of mold, strange herbs, and other things I could not begin to identify. I eased myself inside. Shelves covered with odd looking trophies filled the wall opposite me—huge glass spheres, stuffed animal heads, human skulls, mummified cats, and a jumble of phials, scrolls, tubes, and magical paraphernalia I could not begin to identify. A thick coat of dust lay over everything, though it had been recently disturbed toward the far end by someone's recent passage. Probably Dad checking out his treasures after getting back.

"Nobody cleans in here?" I asked with a chuckle.

"It is not allowed," Rèalla said in hushed tones. She had not left the steps. "We should not be here, my lord. I will be punished when Lord Dworkin finds out."

"Nonsense. I'm with you. Since I told you to bring me, there was nothing you could do about it. My father will understand."

It all reminded me of Dworkin's private rooms in Juniper, only from the odor of decay these had long been neglected. How long had he been away from here? Not just years, but decades from the look of things.

"My lord . . ." An anxious note crept into Rèalla's voice.

"He's not here," I said, trying to reassure her, "so there is no reason for us to stay. Let's go back down." I knew I could find my way back here again, and next time I could do it unassisted.

"Yes, Lord Oberon." Rèalla seemed relieved. Turning, she led the way back down the stairs. I followed gingerly, breathing deeply of her musk, trying desperately not to call on her for help. And I wanted very much for her to see me as a whole, strong man.

"Thank you," I told her as I walked unsteadily back into my room. "I . . . hope I will see you again, Rèalla."

"I am sure you will, my lord," she said, with a shy little smile and a half curtsy. "Whenever you need me, call and I will come."

"Thank you. Oh . . . about those dry clothes? See if you can find some for me. I'm the same size as my brother Mattus. Look in his room."

"Yes, my lord."

As she hurried back upstairs, I sank into my chair and gazed down at the empty food tray. My stomach growled; second helpings were definitely in order. Maybe I should have asked for more food instead of dry clothes.

I glanced at the open door. What had happened to Aber? Never around when you needed him . . . and I still wanted to find out about those mysterious visitors.

Yawning, I leaned forward on the table, then put my head down on my arms. I couldn't help it; exhaustion washed over me. Although an inner voice screamed warnings, I let my eyes close, and then I found darkness.

FOUR

old water sluiced over me.

Gasping, sputtering, I leaped to my feet, knocking over my chair. The world jumped and swayed, and I almost fell.

It was Aber. He had poured another pitcher of water on my head and now stood back, grinning at his handiwork.

He said, "I didn't think you'd give me a second chance to do that."

I glowered. He looked entirely too smug.

"I'm going to strangle you," I said, and then I began shivering.

"You were warned!" He wagged a finger at me. "Sleep at your own peril, brother."

I snarled, "I wasn't asleep!"

"Hah! Towel?"

"Please."

He pulled one from the air and tossed it to me. For the second time that day, I dried myself off and wished him an unpleasant fate. At least Rèalla would be bringing me dry clothing soon.

"Just wait," I said. "If I ever figure out how to use that Logrus thing . . ."

"Be my guest." He picked up the chair I'd knocked over and set it next to me. I sat down again. "But it isn't going to happen, and you know it."

I sighed; he was right. I accepted it now. Members of our family all had a certain Pattern inside them, some kind of mystical design that allowed them to master the Logrus. Unfortunately, the pattern inside me was so distorted, according to Dworkin, that I would never be able to master the Logrus. Trying would kill me, as it had killed Dworkin's brother and several others in our family.

Suddenly I remembered what had called Aber away.

"What about that bell?" I said. "Did we have company?"

"Company? Of a sort." He sighed. "A dozen of King Uthor's soldiers stopped by. They're searching the house for something. They should be up here soon."

I raised my eyebrows in surprise. "Searching for what?"

"I don't know. They wouldn't tell me. But it must be pretty important."

"You should have thrown them out!"

He chuckled. "You don't do that to King Uthor's men if you want to live. It would be . . . impolite."

I struggled to my feet. "Get me downstairs. I'll throw them out myself!"

"Sit down. You're being foolish."

I glared at him. "Is it better to let strangers ransack everything?"

"In this case, yes. That's what Dad would do."

"And you left them alone? To do whatever they want?"

"Sure. Why not? I have nothing to hide." He shrugged. "Besides, you're far more important than the house—and it's a good thing I came back here to check up on you, too. No telling how long you were asleep."

At least he placed as high a value on me as I did on him.

"You said I was unconscious for three days," I said softly. "Tell me what I've missed."

"What's the last thing you remember?"

I paused, thinking. "We were in Juniper. Dad drew new Trumps, and everyone left . . . except the three of us."

"That's right. Then what?"

In my mind I began to relive our mad exodus from Juniper. There had been a tremendous battle fought outside the castle, with me and two of my half-brothers each commanding a third of the army. I recalled the terrible price we had paid for victory that day . . . my brothers Davin and Locke had died, and command had fallen on me.

With the army badly outnumbered, I saw the situation was hopeless. It was then that an idea occurred to me. Dworkin claimed the Pattern within me was different than the Logrus-pattern he and everyone else carried. Since everyone's access to the Logrus had been blocked by magical means, I had him draw a magical Trump using the Pattern within me as its starting point.

This new type of Trump worked. We found it could open a path to other Shadow worlds without difficulty. Suddenly we had a way out of Juniper.

I had him scatter my half-brothers and half-sisters to distant Shadows, where no one but he and I would know they had gone. Under the assumption that a spy had been telling our unknown enemy where to find—and kill—us, they were ordered not to come back to Juniper or to the Courts of Chaos. I only hoped they would be all right.

Then, when only Dworkin, Aber, and I were left, Dworkin showed me the last Trump he had made. It showed a nightmare scene that made my skin crawl. I hated the place at first sight, hated the Courts of Chaos and everything like them on some deep level I could not as yet understand . . . and yet I had agreed to go there. *Here.* The Beyond.

Dworkin and I would have used the Trump and gone through immediately, but Aber stopped us.

"We can't slink back to Chaos like whipped dogs," he said, folding his arms stubbornly. "Ours is an ancient family, and we are due respect for our station."

"What do you expect?" I demanded, half joking. "A parade?"

"Yes!" he snapped back at me. "That's *exactly* what I expect!"

It wasn't so much a parade as an entourage. It took us less than an hour to round up every servant in the castle, plus two dozen sturdy men-at-arms. Then, another hour to empty his bedroom of everything he wanted—plus Dworkin's rooms, with their experiments, machines, and other weird things he had built or collected through the years.

Finally, with our numbers swollen to more than a hundred strong, Dworkin used the Trump and began sending people through. Aber went first, then the guards, then the servants with their various burdens, until finally only the two of us remained.

"After you," Dworkin said, waving me forward.

Taking a deep breath, I stepped through quickly, before my un-nerving fear of the place could stop me. I remembered nothing of what happened after that. Just a stride forward, a sense of falling, the sound of rushing winds, and then . . . darkness.

"That's it," I told Aber. "Dad used the Trump, we all walked through to . . ." I frowned. "I don't remember."

Aber clasped my shoulder, growing serious. "You collapsed as soon as you set foot here. Just folded up without a word. I thought you and Dad had been attacked on the other side, and everyone drew their weapons and rushed to help, but then Dad came through and he looked fine. He wasn't even breathing hard. He didn't want to lin-ger outside, so a couple of guards picked you up and carried you into the house. They brought you up here."

I chewed on my lip, then nodded. It sounded true.

"Go on," I said.

He shrugged. "At first we thought you were dead, but Dad ex-amined you and said it was more like a very deep sleep. Your heart beat slowly and faintly. You were barely breathing. Sometimes you'd stir and cry out a little, but it was never more than that. Dad thought you were trying to wake yourself up, but couldn't."

"I don't really remember much," I said truthfully. I tried to think back to my dreams, but could not summon them now; some-thing about a ship . . . roaring winds . . . sailing on a distant sea . . .

I shivered. No, my dreams were gone now, and I did not want them back. I had not enjoyed them.

"So that's all," Aber said with a little shrug. "We settled in again at the house. Servants had been keeping everything ready for our return. It was just a matter of picking up where we'd left off twenty years ago."

"Twenty years!" I echoed in disbelief. The time shocked me. Aber looked no more than twenty-five, and he acted more like sixteen. "How old are you, really?"

"Twenty-three." He grinned at my bewildered expression. "Time runs differently in Shadows. As far as I'm concerned, I was here seven months ago."

"I begin to understand," I said.

If seven months in Juniper equaled twenty years in the Beyond and hence the Courts of Chaos, that explained a lot. For every month of training for our troops, our mysterious enemy had had three years to build his own forces. No wonder we had been outnumbered and outmaneuvered. Despite all our planning, we could never hope to fight off an opponent who had so much more time to prepare. Rather than the series of lightning attacks I had experienced, our enemy had been slowly, carefully, and methodically picking us off at his leisure.

"Go on," I said to Aber.

"That's about it. We took turns tending you. Dad went out periodically to renew his alliances with other families. Then King Uthor sent for Dad this morning, and before he left he decided we had to try to wake you up."

"And it worked."

"Right. And now that he's gone, the king's troops are searching our house."

"But *why*?" I wondered. "Why draw Dad away first? What are they looking for?"

"They wouldn't say." Aber sighed helplessly. "I wish I knew. I'd give it to them."

"That might be the worst thing we could do."

"Maybe. Or it might end all this craziness. I'd give a lot just to have my boring old life back again."

"Me too." I found I meant it. Much as my newfound family and their magical powers fascinated me, I couldn't remember a single moment of happiness since Dworkin had swept back into my life.

Iron-shod boots thumped down the hallway outside. King Uthor's men had reached this floor, it seemed. I took a deep breath. Doors banged open. I heard furniture being thrown about, then something made of glass shattered noisily.

"Listen carefully," Aber said, a note of anxiety creeping into his voice. "You must be calm. Stay in your seat. Don't show any fear or weakness. They will report back on anything or anyone who seems odd or out of place. Promise?"

I swallowed, one hand rising to caress my sword where I'd left it on the table. My every impulse told me to stand and fight, to force these intruders out. They had no right to be here. They had no right to search our house. And yet, in my current state, I knew I wouldn't stand a chance against them.

"Promise me!" Aber said again, urgently. He rose, looking at the door. "They will be here any second!"

Gazing up at him, I saw how afraid he was. I felt my own apprehension grow, too. Better to play it safe for now. A foolish death benefited no one.

"Promise me!" he demanded.

I took a deep breath, then nodded. "I'll do as you say. I'll stay in my seat no matter what they say or do."

"Thank you." He moved behind me, putting one hand on my shoulder reassuringly. "You made the right decision."

King Uthor's men were close now. I could hear them just outside, talking softly.

An unpleasant prickling sensation began at the nape of my neck and spread down my back and arms. I couldn't make out the words, but those voices—those guttural tones—I recognized them!

They threw open the door to my room, and my worst fears were confirmed. Two hell-creatures, like the ones who had destroyed Ilerium, like the ones who had destroyed Juniper, swaggered inside.

FIVE

hey wore beautifully silvered chain mail, the chest emblazoned with a red crown. Their slitted eyes glowed pinkly behind their high-plumed steel helmets. Although nasals and cheek guards concealed most of their features, I spotted a faintly iridescent pattern of scales around their mouths and chins.

Growling in anger, I half rose from my chair. The room began to tilt and slide around me.

"Easy," Aber said in a calming voice. His hand already on my shoulder pushed me back into my seat.

"Who are you?" one of the hell-creatures demanded of me. His voice was a gravelly croak.

I glared up at him but had a hard time restraining myself. Hell-creatures! Here in the Courts of Chaos . . . in our own house! They had destroyed my home and slain my king in Ilerium. They had destroyed Castle Juniper and murdered who-knew-how-many family members. And now my brother wanted me to sit here calmly and let them tear this place apart, too!

I glowered and thought hard about going for my sword. Unfortunately, I was in no condition to take them on, and I knew it. They would have cut me down before I made it to my feet.

"This is my brother, Oberon," Aber said hastily, when I didn't answer.

"He is not listed in your family's genealogy."

"Not yet," Aber said quickly. "He will be."

I did not move, did not speak, only stared in tense silence. My heart pounded; a cold sweat began to trickle down my back.

Dismissing us with a casualness that bordered on contempt, the two hell-creatures turned to my bed. They drew knives and cut through the sheets and blanket, then ripped into the mattress. I leaned forward, watching with interest as they pulled out the goose-down stuffing and throw it into the corner. Then they removed their gauntlets and began sifting through the feathers carefully, feeling for—what? Something small, certainly, if they required bare hands to find it.

"Are you sure you don't know what they're doing here?" I whispered to Aber, studying them carefully.

Aber shook his head. "Like I said, they wouldn't tell me anything downstairs. Just that they were here on King Uthor's orders, and I was to cooperate or I would be arrested."

"What about Dad? Has he seen King Uthor yet?"

"I don't think so."

I thought about that for a long moment. It seemed to me we needed to know more.

"Let me try something." To the hell-creatures, I said in a loud voice: "What are you looking for? Maybe I know where it is."

They both ignored me.

"See?" Aber said quietly.

"Hey!" I said, more loudly. "Are you deaf?"

The one who had addressed me before turned his head slightly. The pink eyes met my own.

"Shut up, *d'nai*," he said. I did not know the word, but from the sneering delivery I recognized it as an insult. "We will tell you when to talk." Then he turned back to the goose down and continued his search.

Rage billowed through me. Sick or not, I couldn't ignore the slight. Slowly, my hand moved toward my sword, which still lay on the table before me. If I could draw it before they noticed—there were only two of them here—

Aber's hand on my shoulder became a vice, pinning me to my chair. He leaned forward.

"Do nothing," he said very softly in my left ear. "These are King Uthor's men. If you interfere, they will hurt us both. Maybe even kill us. Don't throw our lives away."

"They are hell-creatures!" I whispered.

"They are *lai she'on*."

I hesitated. "What?"

"An ancient race that has served the Lords of Chaos from the beginning of time. Do not draw your weapon or they will kill us both."

Gritting my teeth, I withdrew my hand from my sword's hilt. No, I wouldn't throw away both our lives. But when I could stand and hold a weapon properly again, I silently vowed to make this particular hell-creature take back his words.

Aber relaxed his grip on my shoulder.

The hell-creatures—*lai she'on*—whatever—finished their search of my room by dumping the chamber pot on the floor. They kicked it out of the way, gave a sneering look in our direction, then trooped out into the hall.

"Bastards," I muttered.

"We're all bastards in the Courts. I think it's a requirement," Aber said, blithely making light of the situation.

I snorted. "Shouldn't you be with them?" I asked, eying the door uneasily. It sounded like they were doing quite a lot of damage. "Supervising, or something?"

He shrugged. "I gave them the master key to the house. They don't need me. They can get in anywhere they want."

"I meant to watch what they're doing."

"I'm sure they wouldn't like that."

"If they find whatever they're looking for, don't you want to know what it is?"

"Sure." He drained his wine and refilled his glass. "But they're not going to tell me, and if they find it, for all I know they'd kill me to keep me from seeing it."

"You do have a point," I admitted.

"Besides, Dad isn't a fool. If he has something valuable that everyone wants, he knows enough to put it where only he can get to it."

"How?"

"There are ways," he said, nodding knowingly.

That wasn't exactly helpful. I sighed, shaking my head. This whole mad family of mine could be infuriating at times. None of them ever gave me a straight answer when I wanted one.

"Lord Aber?" said a familiar voice from the doorway. "Lord Oberon? May we proceed?"

I glanced over and saw Anari, an elderly man in red-and-white livery who had managed our household in Juniper. He had come here with us, I remembered. A half-dozen other servants stood behind him, all armed with mops, buckets, and other cleaning equipment.

"Please," Aber said.

Anari motioned his forces forward, and everyone hurried inside and began to clean up—gathering the bedding, mopping the floor, straightening the furniture. One of them carried off the empty mattress casing while two more gathered all the goose feathers into new sheets and blanket, then dragged them out into the hallway.

"I guess I'm not going back to sleep anytime soon," I said wryly. Not that I could sleep with hell-creatures, these *lai she'on*, loose in the house, even ones who weren't specifically trying to kill me. "What do you think Dad will do when he finds out?"

"Oh, I don't think he'll mind." Aber nudged me, then gave a pointed glance at Anari and the other cleaners. "We have nothing to hide, after all."

"True," I murmured. No sense giving the servants more to worry and gossip about. *Lai she'on* searching our rooms were bad enough.

My brother said, "I think this calls for a drink."

For once, I agreed wholeheartedly.

Reaching into the air, he produced a bottle of red wine with a flourish. The label showed a pair of red stags running through a dark green forest. He uncorked it, produced two goblets by similar magical means, handed me one, and poured us both large portions.

"Cheers." I raised my glass in a toast.

"To mysteries," he said. Our glasses clinked.

"May there be fewer of them!" I added.

We both downed the wine, grinning at each other, listening to the ongoing noises of destruction from outside. Doors slammed; furniture crashed. Then I heard boots tramping directly over our heads; apparently they had moved upstairs.

Thus, the ransacking of our father's house continued.

By the time the sounds of searching had faded to distant cracks, bangs, and crashes, several hours later, we were on our third bottle of the red stag wine.

"What's directly over us?" I asked. My tongue felt thick; my words slurred slightly.

"Third floor. Living quarters. My room, I think."

I felt a jolt of alarm. "They're probably going through your Trumps and everything else you brought back from Juniper."

He smirked. "Oh, I don't think so."

"Why not?"

"They're tucked away. Safe."

I chuckled and allowed myself to relax. "Like Dad would have done with whatever they're looking for."

"Exactly."

More boots tramped overhead, and porcelain shattered noisily. Then a thump shook the whole house.

"Show me," I said.

"What?"

"Where your Trumps are."

"More wine?" he said.

"Sure."

He refilled my goblet for what seemed the twentieth time.

I said, "You're not going to tell me."

"Nope."

Silence fell. I found myself straining to hear, anticipating the next noise. It didn't come.

"They must have gone up to the fourth floor," Aber said finally. "That one is all Dad's. He keeps his old experiments there."

"Experiments?"

He chuckled. "That's what you'd call it if you want to be kind. It's mostly junk. Bits and pieces of magical stuff. Things he's researched and thrown aside. It will take anyone else years to figure out what most of it does."

"They'll probably smash it all."

"Probably," he agreed.

"Don't you care?"

He shrugged. "It's no great loss. He'd moved all the good stuff to Juniper, anyway. So it's already in their hands."

Already in their hands? Did he know more than he was saying?

I asked, "So you think these hell-creatures are the same ones who took Juniper?"

"*Lai she'on*." He frowned. "Yes. Maybe . . . I don't know. Don't you think so?"

I shrugged, recalling our father's magical carriage. Then I

thought of all the other devices in his workshop, all the tubes and wires and strange glowing glass balls. It had been a lifetime's accumulation of magical items, and I was certain Dad would feel its loss keenly. When I envisioned the fall of Juniper Castle, with hell-creatures storming into the deserted corridors and rooms, I easily saw them smashing the things he had built.

None of the *lai she'on* attacking Juniper had worn crown symbols, however. Of course, they could have been disguised . . . a painted emblem is the easiest thing in the world to hide.

Another, more distant crash sounded.

"Fourth floor?" I asked, eying the ceiling.

"I think so."

I leaned back and drained the last of my wine. Perhaps the search wouldn't take much longer. I certainly wanted it over and these hell-creatures gone.

"Let me fill your glass."

Aber produced another bottle of that excellent two-stag red. When I held out my goblet, he poured, and we continued our drinking, a comfortable silence stretching between us.

Every once it a while, a distant thump spoke of the continuing search above us.

"I wonder what Dad is doing right now," I said at one point. Had he been seen by the king? Been attacked and murdered on the way?

Something worse?

Surely we would have heard if something had happened to him . . . wouldn't we?

Aber said, "I bet he's having more fun than we are."

It was probably the wine, but I found that offhanded remark incredibly funny. Somehow, I just couldn't see our father having fun, regardless of the situation.

Where *was* he now? I hated not knowing.

After that we drank in silence.

Somehow, I had a feeling our father had walked into a trap when he went to that audience with King Uthor. It seemed too convenient. The summons had gotten him out of this house and left Aber and me off guard here.

How long had it been? I had no way of telling time, no reference to day or night in this strange, windowless house in this accursed world. He had certainly been gone for hours . . . far too long for a simple audience. In Ilerium, King Elnar's audiences seldom lasted more than ten or fifteen minutes . . . though he sometimes kept petitioners waiting for hours.

What had happened to our father?

I could only hope he was waiting in some antechamber for the King Uthor's nod.

SIX

he time passed with annoying slowness. It felt as though everything and everyone—myself included—had paused it mid-step, in anticipation of something momentous.

At one point Anari returned with two men, who silently restored the now-mended mattress to the bed. A woman followed with fresh sheets and a blanket. When she spoke to Anari, they both used hushed, almost reverential tones. And they kept glancing surreptitiously in our direction.

Neither Aber nor I deigned to notice them. We were both pretty drunk. They left, and an almost eerie silence spread over the house.

"Do you think the hell-creatures . . . the *lai she'on* . . . are gone?" I finally asked.

"No. Anari will tell us." He sighed. "They must be on the fifth floor."

"What's there?"

"Servants' quarters."

After we finished our fifth bottle, I finally decided I had drunk too much. I felt happily numb, and though everything had a comfortably blurry shine, I couldn't tell if it was me or the wine or our location that caused it. My senses had become so screwed up since entering this place that nothing looked or felt or smelled quite right any more. Fortunately, thanks to the wine, I didn't particularly care.

Aber, too, had begun to slur his words, and several times he laughed to himself as though at some private joke. To be good company, I laughed along. Every once in a while we would exchange trivialities:

—"Do the walls look like they're bleeding to you?" (Me.)

—"Not really." (Him.) "Is that what you see?"

—"Yes." (A hesitation.) "But they're not bleeding like they were an hour ago."

—"Oh."

I sat back, pondering everything around me with the deep sense of wisdom that can only be found in an excess of alcohol.

"You know what we need?" I said.

"What?"

"Windows."

He actually fell off his chair, he laughed so hard.

"What's so funny?" I demanded.

"Windows. There aren't any."

"Why not?"

"It's safer."

"How do you know if it's morning or night?"

"You don't. There's no such thing here."

"Doesn't it get dark?" I asked.

"Not in the sense it did in Juniper."

I thought about that for a while. It seemed impossible, but my whole life since leaving Ilerium had seemed that way.

"How late is it?" I finally said, stifling a yawn.

"Very." With a sigh, he rose. "Come on, I'll show you to your room. I imagine it's been searched and cleaned up by now."

I looked at him in surprise. "This isn't my room?"

"This little cell?" He chuckled. "What kind of hospitality do you think we offer family members? This is just a spare room where Dad stuck you. You'll have a proper suite on the next floor. Come, I'll show you."

He rose unsteadily. I did, too.

The room rolled around me, and the sound of wind—which had died down to a murmur like distant surf—rose to deafen me. By leaning on his shoulder, I managed to keep my feet, and together we staggered out into the hall.

"You can have Mattus's rooms," he grunted, bearing up under my weight. "It's not like he needs them any more."

That reminded me—what had happened to Rèalla? Probably drafted to help with the cleanup. I didn't blame her for not fetching me dry clothes. Priorities, priorities . . .

Aber led the way out to the hall, turned left, left again, then twice more left. It should have us put us back where we started, but somehow we found ourselves facing broad stone steps leading both up and down. Sconces held oil lamps whose light bubbled steadily upwards to pool on the ceiling.

I glanced behind us. The corridor seemed to narrow and coil in on itself. All the angles were wrong here, I reminded myself. Corners weren't square. I wouldn't be able to track my position mentally as I moved about.

"Think you can make it?" he asked.

"With you to lean on? Sure!"

With him supporting me, we ascended to the next floor.

Still no windows, I noticed, like Aber had said. For some reason, it began to bother me—though it was probably just as well that I couldn't see outside. I remembered my sister Freda's Trump, which showed the Courts of Chaos. Merely looking at the image had unnerved me. A sky that writhed like a living thing, stars that darted and swirled in seemingly random patterns, and giant stones that moved across the land on their own, while colors pulsed and bled. I should have been happy not to have to gaze out onto such nightmare landscapes.

And yet not having windows made me feel trapped, somehow. It was one of those games you just can't win.

As we climbed, I never lifted my hand from the railing. The steps started to slide out from under me, but I paused a few seconds, pretending I needed to catch my breath, before continuing. Aber, drunk and staggering a bit himself, never even noticed.

Finally, we reached the top. More bleeding walls, more sconces with oil lamps that bubbled their light up to the ceiling. Strangely enough, it had all began to feel normal.

My brother turned left sharply five times, but instead of ending up back where we started, we were suddenly facing a new hallway lined with tall, ornately carved wooden doors.

"Here we are!" he announced with a grand sweep of his arm. "Mattus's suite is ugly, but he never had any sense of style. It ought to do!"

He halted before the first door on the left, then rapped sharply on the wood.

"Hulloo!" he called. "Wake up!"

"Why—" I began.

I had been about to ask why he would knock on a dead man's door, but a large face carved into the central wooden panel began to move. It yawned, blinked twice, and seemed to focus on Aber.

"Greetings!" it said pleasantly. "This room belongs to Lord Mattus. State your business."

"Just visiting," Aber said. "Do you remember me?"

"I do believe it's Lord Aber!" the door said, squinting a bit. I wondered if it might be near-sighted. "You have grown since last we spoke. Welcome, welcome, dear boy! I can talk to you, but Mattus left strict instruction that you cannot, under any circumstances, enter his room without permission, or I will be—and he made this quite clear—rendered into toothpicks."

So Aber wasn't welcome here! Somehow, it didn't surprise me; no one in my family seemed exactly trusting. They were to the last more likely to stab you in the back than put in a kindly word.

"I have bad news," Aber said in a serious voice, ignoring the slight. "My brother Mattus is dead."

"No! No!" the face in the door gasped. "It cannot be!"

"I'm afraid so."

"When? Where?"

"It happened some time ago, and far from here."

The face gave a wrenching sob. "He did not suffer, I hope?"

"No. It was fast."

That, actually, was a lie. Mattus had been tortured to death in a tower made of bones. But I saw no sense in correcting Aber's story . . . the face in the door seemed quite emotional, and I wasn't up to dealing with weeping woodwork right now.

The door sighed, eyes distant, remembering. "He was a good tenant. The sixth generation of your family that I have guarded, in fact, since my installation here . . . . By the way, is there a seventh generation yet? Someone who might, as it were, inhabit these rooms?"

"Not yet," Aber said. "At least, not that I'm aware of."

The door finally seemed to notice me. "And who is this? Do I notice a family resemblance?"

Aber motioned me closer, so I took a step forward. The face squinted at me. I examined him just as closely. Large nose, broad lips, high cheekbones—almost a caricature of a man's face. But it had been kindly drawn and had a sympathetic if somewhat sad expression.

Aber said, "This is Oberon, my brother."

"Oberon . . . Oberon . . ." The carved forehead wrinkled. "He has never been through me before."

"That's right. This will be his room now."

"So fast they go, so fast . . ." It actually seemed about to cry. That was something I didn't want to see.

Taking a deep breath, I asked, "Do you have a name?"

"I am but a door. I do not need a name. But if you must call me something, Lord Mattus calls . . . called me . . . Port."

"Port," I said. It fit admirably well. "Fine. I'll call you that, too." I turned to Aber. "Anything I should be aware of? Warnings? Special instructions? Useful advice?"

My brother shrugged. "He's just a door. He'll guard your rooms, let you know if anyone wants in, and lock himself—or unlock himself—as instructed."

"Then, Port, please open up. I'd like to see inside."

"Sorry, good sir, but I cannot."

"Why?" I demanded.

"Because," said the door, a trifle archly, "I have only your word that Lord Mattus is dead. I was not carved yesterday, you know. Lord Mattus warned me not to trust anyone here under any circumstance. After all—and I mean no disrespect, good sirs!—some person or persons might come along, falsely claim that Lord Mattus is dead, state that they are the new tenants, and ask for entrance. You must see the unfortunate situation in which I now find myself placed."

I scratched my head. "A good point," I said slowly, looking at my brother. "I don't have an answer."

"Then," said the door, "Move along. I don't approve of loitering in the hallway."

I drew my sword. It had been a long day; my patience was at an end.

"Open up," I said, "or I'll carve a new entrance through your heart!"

SEVEN

 hate to be the voice of reason," Aber said, "but that won't be necessary, Oberon."

The door glared at me. "I should say not! There are spells laid upon me to prevent just that sort of trespass!"

"Not only that," said Aber, "but I have the key."

He turned over his hand. A large iron key sat there; he hadn't been carrying it a moment before, so he must have pulled it through the Logrus. "You don't need his help, dear brother. You can let yourself in."

"Thanks!" I said.

"What would you do without me?"

He held out the key, and I accepted it gingerly. It was as long as my hand and as thick around as my index finger, and it was much heavier than it looked. A strong blow with it might well do serious damage to someone's head.

"You're sure it's for this door?" I asked.

"Yes."

"Where do I stick it?" I asked, turning to study Port's features. He didn't have any obvious keyholes. "In his mouth? Up his nose?"

"Certainly not!" Port said, glaring up at me. "Perhaps you ought to stick it in one of *your own* orifices to see how it feels!"

"I wasn't asking you," I told him.

"No need to ask," Aber said. "It's a magic key. Just holding it is enough. Tell him you want inside."

"That's all?" I asked skeptically. I looked at the door. "Let me in, please."

"Very good, sir!" Port said unhappily, and I heard a series of clicks as a hidden lock unlocked itself.

Very convenient! I liked the idea of coming home drunk late at night, telling the door to let me inside, and having it lock up after me. Magic definitely had its good points.

"How does it work?" I asked Aber.

"Simple. Whoever holds the key gets inside."

"It's a rule," Port added. "All doors have to follow rules, you know."

"And there's a master key, too?" I asked, remembering what Aber had said. "To all the doors in the house?"

"Yes, but only one. It's Dad's. He keeps it stashed in his bedroom, in a box under his pillow."

I shook my head. "That doesn't sound very safe."

"The bed, the box, and the key are all invisible, unless you know how to look."

"And you know the trick."

"Yes."

"Care to share it?"

"Another time."

Somehow, I didn't think that time would ever come. Clearly he could lay hands on the master key when needed—as, indeed, he had done this afternoon, when he gave it to the hell-creatures so they could search our house.

"And," Aber added with a chuckle, "if invisibility isn't enough, Dad has certain *things* keeping an eye on his rooms, too."

From the way he said "things" I got the sensation they weren't necessarily human. Monsters? Familiars? Even Port could have done the job; I imagined him making gleeful reports on trespassers.

"Then," I said, "I think I'll leave his rooms alone."

"Good idea."

"What now?" I cleared my throat and looked down at the key, which I still held. "Do I carry three pounds of iron with me for the rest of my life, or will Port accept me as his new master now?"

"I *am* right here," Port said a bit stiffly. "You don't have to keep talking about me in the third person!"

Ignoring him, Aber said: "He would probably accept you—"

"I do!" said Port.

"—but there is a ritual to go through, just for form's sake. It should make certain."

"What is it?" I asked.

"Repeat these words: 'I am the holder of this key. I am the master of this room. You will harken and obey.'"

I did this thing.

"Okay," Port said with a sigh. "Lord Mattus is dead. I formally accept it. Let all present bear witness: I am now Lord Oberon's door, and these are now Lord Oberon's rooms. I will guard him and obey him in all things. So let it be."

"Thank you, Port," I said.

His brow furrowed as he gazed up at me. "I am doing my job, Lord Oberon. It's a rule."

To me, Aber said, "Return your key to Dad when he gets here. He keeps them all locked up in his study for situations like this. You have no idea what a pain it is when you lose a key and have to replace a magical door."

I chuckled. "Stubborn, I bet, even in the face of reason and axes?"

"That about sums it up."

"It's a rule," Port said. "I must obey my master and protect his interests at all times."

"All right," I said. "I'll make sure I remember."

I took a deep breath, and the walls began to wobble. Mattus's suite—my suite now—lay at hand. What would I find? A collection of fine weapons? A store of powerful magical items? Gold, silver, gems—an emperor's treasure trove?

I felt my pulse quicken with excitement. I knew next to nothing about my half-brother Mattus, except we had about the same height and build, and his taste in clothes mostly matched my own. What would his rooms say about him?

Reaching out, I gave the door a push. It swung open easily, revealing a good-sized chamber. The high-canopied bed looked invitingly soft. Two lamps, one by the door and one by the bed, bubbled their golden light toward the ceiling. A small, tidy desk had been pushed up against the wall to the right. To the left sat an intricately carved washstand with basin and pitcher, a full-height looking glass in a white-painted oval frame, and a large wardrobe made of red and black woods decorated in intricate geometric pyramid patterns. Two plain, non-magical doors, one large and one small, both closed, led to other rooms.

A twinge of disappointment went through me. Clean and neat, Mattus's bedroom struck me as singularly uninteresting. Nothing about the place spoke to my brother's likes and dislikes, nor to his own powers or personality. Anyone could have lived here, man or woman, child or doddering elder.

"Were these rooms searched by the hell-creatures . . . by the *lai she'on*?" I asked Port. If all of Mattus's furniture had been destroyed, this mismatched assortment could have been thrown together quickly as replacements.

"Yes, Lord Oberon," Port said. "After their departure, I took the liberty of permitting the household staff to repair the damage. I did not think Mattus would object."

"Was there much damage?"

"They cut open the bed and tore out both the mattress and pillow stuffing. That was all."

I nodded; so much for my furniture theory. "The *lai she'on* were looking for something. Did they find it here?"

"I do not believe so, Lord Oberon. At least, they did not take anything from this room with them. I would not have permitted it."

"Good for you. Stick up for your beliefs."

"It is a rule."

Feeling the floor glide underfoot, I wandered into the room. Everything looked tidy, from the carefully brushed carpets to the well scrubbed floorboards. Yet the furniture had that hand-me-down look of cast-off pieces hastily thrown together. Considering how Aber could pull pretty much anything he wanted from thin air using the Logrus, I was amazed. Mattus should have lived like a prince; apparently, he hadn't cared to do so.

I looked more closely at the desk. The inkwell, made of a clear cut glass, showed no signs of ever having held ink. The spotless blotter and stack of crisp new writing paper both looked as though they had never been touched. I held one sheet of paper up to the bubbling light and noticed an intricate watermark, a rampant lion.

Of course, I reasoned, hell-creatures could have destroyed the inkwell and ruined the paper; these could all be replacements brought in by servants when they cleaned and straightened. And yet I didn't think so. These items *felt* right, as though they belonged here.

To Port, I said, "Mattus did not spend much time in here, did he?"

"Alas, but no, Lord Oberon. Not since childhood. He spent most of his time off on adventures."

I nodded, knowing he had gone off exploring the Shadow worlds. That's what I would have done in his place. This room was a place to sleep when he visited family and friends, nothing more. Home, for him, must have been some distant kingdom . . . just as Juniper had been our father's home and Ilerium had been mine.

"Yes, it's all yours, and congratulations," Aber said from the doorway, sounding bored. He stifled a yawn. "You seem better. Over whatever caused your attack, or unconsciousness, or whatever it was."

I agreed. "I'm sure I'll be all right now."

"Go to sleep. I'd sure Dad would let you now. We're going to have a busy day tomorrow, I think."

"Soon," I said.

"Then I'll take my leave, if you don't mind. My suite is across the hall and down a bit. Ask any door for directions, if you need me. They know every room in the house."

"Not so, Lord Aber!" objected Port. "I only know this floor . . ."

I chuckled. "I imagine they see a lot."

"Sir!" said Port sternly. "You are talking about me in the third person again!"

"Sorry." I sighed; I couldn't believe a door would reprimand me. "No offense meant, Port. I'm used to doors being inanimate objects."

"Entirely understandable, and thank you, sir."

"Don't spoil the woodwork," Aber said. "Next he'll be asking you to wax and polish him."

"Lord Aber!" Port sounded aghast. "I would never do such a thing!"

I chuckled. "I think Port and I will get along." I glanced at my door. "You must have quite a few stories to tell, Port!"

"Doors do not gossip, Lord Oberon!" Port protested. "We value our owners' privacy too much."

"Another rule?"

"Just so."

"We'll see. Get a few goblets of brandy in you, and I'll bet—"

"Sir! Doors do not drink!"

I gave him a knowing wink. "I won't tell anyone!"

Port continued his protests, to no avail. Aber had to laugh.

I opened a door into a sitting room—containing several sofas, a pair of comfortable looking chairs, and not much else—and a smaller door into what appeared to be a servant's bedchamber. Then, finishing my circuit of the bedroom I joined my brother in the doorway. This suite would do nicely, and I found Port both useful and amusing. All told, quite acceptable.

"Thanks for everything," I told my brother.

He slapped my shoulder. "Sleep lightly, Oberon."

"Is there any other way?"

"Not here. And don't forget my warning—"

"Trust no one?"

He grinned. "Right!"

"Present company excepted, of course."

"Of course." Suddenly he turned and called out, "Boy!"

My valet from Juniper Castle, Horace—a young man of thirteen or so with close-cropped black hair and a shy demeanor—came bounding over to join us. He must have followed us up the stairs and been watching quietly from the side. I'd been too drunk to notice him before.

"Here, Lord Aber, Lord Oberon!" Horace said in a high squeak of a voice.

Aber said, "Oberon is feeling better, but he needs to be watched closely. Stay up with him tonight. Call me if anything happens. Do you understand?"

"Anything?"

"Anything unusual or dangerous . . . anything that threatens his life."

Horace gulped. "Yes, sir."

"If you fail in your duty," he went on in a severe voice, "*you* will be held responsible for anything that happens to your master. By me *and* by our father."

"Yes, sir," he said.

"Nothing will happen," I told Aber firmly. If not for the wine, I thought I could have walked unaided and mostly kept my balance. "At this rate, I'll be back to my old self in a day or two."

"I hope so, but I'm not taking any chances," Aber said firmly. "Dad doesn't like me the way he does you. If anything happens to you, he'll gladly skin me alive. *After* I skin your valet."

Horace gulped audibly.

"Stop it," I said. "You're scaring him."

"I meant to."

"He's just a boy."

"Don't make excuses." Aber hesitated, looking toward his own room. "Maybe I'd better sit up with you after all. If you think there's any danger—"

"No, no. Go to your own bed." I made quick shooing motions with my hands. Those movements made the floor tilt alarmingly. "I can tell you're exhausted. More exhausted than me, even. It's been a long day for all of us. Go to bed, I'll do the same, and we'll have breakfast with Dad in the morning. We can all catch up then."

Still he hesitated.

"I'll be fine," I assured him. "I'm over the worst of it."

He finally nodded, gave a last stern look at Horace, and trooped down the hall toward his door.

Turning, I wandered back into my bedroom trailed by Horace, who shut the door behind us. When I glanced over my shoulder, I found Port's face on the inside now, staring at me with a deliberately noncommittal expression. He cleared his throat, and I got the impression I'd forgotten something.

"What is it?" I asked.

"Do you wish to leave instructions for me, sir?"

"Wake me in the morning?"

"I am *not* a clock," he said a bit archly. "I am a door. I do not tell time, whistle on the hour, or wake people up. What I *meant* was—who should I let into your rooms?"

"Oh, I don't know." I hesitated. "Aber, my father, Horace here, servants when they need to clean." Then I chuckled, thinking of Rèalla and how she would look in my bed. "And, of course, any beautiful half-dressed women who happen along."

Port smirked. "Except for Aber, whom Mattus did not trust, those were almost exactly the same instructions your brother left with me."

I cocked my head thoughtfully. "Do you know why he didn't trust Aber?"

"Not exactly, Lord Oberon. I believe it involved a woman, however, though I am not aware of the exact details."

"Did he leave you any other instructions?"

"Your sister Blaise was allowed in at any time, day or night."

I found that odd. For some reason I had mentally lumped

Mattus into Locke's camp, with the soldiers. My half-sister Blaise, obsessed with spying and wielding household power, struck me as someone who wouldn't have any ready followers in our family.

"Do you know why?" I asked.

"No, sir."

"What about Freda?" I asked. I liked my sister almost as much as I liked Aber, and I wondered where she stood with Mattus.

"I had no special instructions regarding Freda."

"Could anyone else come in at will?" I asked.

"No, sir."

"Was there anyone else deliberately excluded, the way Aber was?"

"No, sir."

Well, it had been worth a try. Aber and Mattus not getting along . . . probably it had been nothing more than sibling rivalry. There had been a lot of that before, during, and after my arrival in Juniper. Having two powerful, conceited, and supremely arrogant brothers in love with the same woman would certainly lead to trouble.

Yawning, I unbuckled my swordbelt and set it on the desk. Horace had turned down the bed while I talked to Port. If the mattress and pillows had been ripped apart by the hell-creatures, seamstresses had mended both as good as new; they looked soft and comfortable. I plopped down, feeling soft feathers yield beneath my weight.

Horace hurried forward to help me with my boots.

"What do you think of this place?" I asked him as he pulled off my right boot.

He hesitated, and I could tell he did not want to speak his mind.

"Go on," I said. "I want the truth."

"Sir . . . I do not much like it."

He bent to his task and got my second boot off as quickly as the first. He carried them to the door and set them outside to be cleaned.

"Why not?"

Hesitantly, he said, "Nothing is quite right."

I nodded, knowing what he meant; I felt exactly the same way. A vague sense of *wrongness* permeated everything. Angles that didn't match my mental geometry, stones that oozed colors, lamps that dribbled their light to the ceiling . . . it was all very strange and quite unsettling.

The large lookingglass, turned slightly toward the bed, caught my eye when I began to unlace my shirt. Finally, when I saw my reflection, I understood everyone's concern. My features were gaunt and pale, my hands trembled, and dark circles lined my eyes. I looked like I'd just been through the worst campaign in the history of warfare. Even so, a few days' rest would fix me up. I always healed quickly.

With a sigh, I pulled off my pants and threw them to Horace—who hung them over the back of the desk chair, along with my shirt—and slid between clean, crisp sheets.

I snuggled in. This was the good life. Soft pillows, a comfortable bed, a roof to keep out the rain . . . yes, for a soldier like me, even this weird, mixed-up world offered luxuries. All I needed was a beautiful woman beside me—preferably a lusty widow—and my life would be complete.

Horace went into the next room and returned with a three-legged stool. He set it down at the end of the bed and perched on top. With his elbows on his knees and his chin cupped in his hands, he proceeded to stare at me. This would be a long night for him. I saw him give a little sigh.

"Take heart," I said. "I don't think we'll be here very long." When our father found out the house had been searched in his absence, I had a feeling he would be angry enough to abandon the Courts of Chaos.

"Yes, Oberon. What should I do if something happens?" he asked. "Should I call Lord Aber, as he said?"

"Nothing will happen."

I saw him sigh.

"But if it does," I went on, "try your best to wake me first. Only call Aber as a last resort. After all, I don't want him to skin you alive."

"Me either!" He looked relieved.

I closed my eyes. It had been a long, difficult day. Between my sickness, the lateness of the hour, and all the alcohol I had drunk, exhaustion overwhelmed me.

I slept.

I dreamed . . .

. . . and felt the dream slide away toward madness.

EIGHT

Movement all around me.

Not a boat this time: a curious sense of drifting in all directions at once, as if I soared, birdlike, high above my body. This sensation had come upon me a number of times before, some distant part of me recalled. It was neither sleep nor dreaming, but a sort of vision . . . or a visitation . . . by my spirit to another place. Whatever I saw next would be real, I knew, but happening far away. And I would be powerless to interfere.

With a growing sense of foreboding, I opened my dream-eyes and looked down. I soared high above a land of ever-changing design and color. Large, rounded stones moved like sheep through high green grass. To the left, trees walked on their roots like men, gathering in circles to talk to one other. I saw no signs of human life.

Overhead, a dusky red sky seethed with movement. A dozen moons rolled like balls across the heavens. I saw no sign of a sun, and yet it was not dark.

On I flew, crossing over vast expanses of grass until I came to a tower made of skulls, some human and some clearly not. Here I slowed, drifting like a phantom cloud, unseen and untouchable.

I had been to this place before. Here, in several other such visions, I had witnessed my brothers Taine and Mattus being tortured and (at least in Mattus's case) killed. It hadn't been pleasant.

When I stretched out my hand to touch the tower, once more my fingers passed into the wall of bones as though through fog. It was exactly like the last time. I knew I could be nothing more than an observer here.

Taking a deep breath, I allowed myself to drift through the wall and into the tower. Shadows flickered within. As my eyes adjusted to the gloom, I made out a familiar looking stairway built from arm bones and leg bones. It circled the inside wall of the tower, climbing into a deeper darkness, descending into a murky, pulsating redness.

I drifted down, and the redness resolved itself into a circle of burning torches. A square slab of rock, shaped like a sacrificial altar, lay in the center of the room. Deep shadows lay before it, and I sensed an unseen presence there, watching and waiting.

My heart began to pound and the breath caught in my throat. Why had I been summoned here this time? What power had brought me to this place?

I tried to wake myself from this nightmare vision, tried to force my eyes open in the real world, but it didn't work. Stubbornly, I remained anchored to this place. Apparently I was not yet done here.

Then I heard the sounds of tramping boots to one side. Four hell-creatures in silvered armor entered through a small doorway. Unlike the ones who had searched our home, these did not have crowns blazed on their chests . . . but that seemed to be the only difference. Between them they dragged a human—a naked, filthy man with thick iron chains on his legs and arms. Only the slight shuffling movement of his feet as he tried to walk gave any indication of life.

Long, tangled hair and a matted beard obscured his face, and his head hung limp.

I tried to see who it was, but couldn't tell. He appeared half dead, and what I could see of his body through the dirt made my skin crawl. Festering sores and wounds, some old but many more that were recent, covered every inch of his arms, legs, chest, and stomach.

Without saying a word, the four hell-creatures flung him down on the slab of stone. I had to give this fellow credit—when they began to fasten his chains to huge iron rings, he still struggled despite his condition. Unfortunately, he no longer had enough strength to fight much. They shoved him down and finished their job, then stood back at attention.

From the shadows at the far side of the chamber, where I had sensed a presence before, came a huge serpentlike creature that must have been twenty feet long. Though it slithered on its belly, it held its front end erect. Its almost human torso had two scaled, vaguely human arms that ended in broad taloned hands, one of which held a silver-bladed knife.

"Tell me what I want to know," the creature said softly, its body weaving left and right, left and right. "Spare yourself, son of Dworkin. Earn an easy death . . ."

The man on the table had the strength to lift his head a bit, but he made no reply. As his hair fell back, I saw sunken blue eyes and a familiar white dueling scar on his left cheek, and only then did I recognized him: my half brother Taine. I had dreamed of Taine twice before, and the last time had been less than a week ago as I reckoned time . . . but from his appearance, he had been here for months—maybe years.

I swallowed. No, these were not dreams, despite their nightmare quality. These were true visions. This was *real*. I remembered how Aber told me that time in different Shadow worlds moved at different speeds.

The serpent-creature writhed forward, beginning to chant, the words ancient and powerful. I only half understood them, but they set my skin crawling. Quickly I shut my mind to the sound.

Though I longed to do something to help poor Taine, I knew I had no form here, no arms to take up weapons nor muscles to swing them. I could be nothing more than a silent spectator to whatever horrors unfolded.

The silver blade flashed down, opening new cuts on Taine's arms and legs and chest. Thin blood began to flow, but instead of dripping toward the floor, the drops lifted into the air and hung there, spinning slowly, starting to form an intricate crimson pattern.

I *knew* that design. I recognized it at once: it matched the Pattern within *me*, the Pattern that was somehow imprinted on the very essence of my being. I summoned that Pattern to my mind now and compared it to what was being sketched in mid-air.

No, they were not the same. They were cousins. Close, but not quite a match . . . the Pattern in the air was flawed and broken, possessing several odd turns and twists that did not belong there. And a small section on the left simply fell apart, becoming a random series of drops.

And yet I sensed that, flawed thought it was, an immense power radiated from it. A power which made my whole body tingle with pins and needles.

"Show me the son of Dworkin!" the serpent-creature called again. "Reveal him!"

Taine lay still, probably unconscious. His blood no longer flowed. A thin line of drool fell from his mouth to the altar's stone.

But I knew the serpent had not been speaking to him. It spoke instead to the Pattern in the air.

Slowly the droplets of blood began to spin, around and around, faster and faster. They took on a shimmering, silvery quality, then grew clear, becoming a window.

Drifting forward, I peered through it with the serpent. We gazed into darkness.

No, not darkness, but a dark room . . . a room where a man lay on a high-canopied bed, deeply asleep. A room where a boy stood over the man, trying desperately to shake him awake.

My room. *My* body.

The serpent-creature breathed, "Yes-s-s . . . he is the one. . . ."

An odd prickling sensation spread up my neck. I had to do something. I had to find a way to stop it. If the serpent-creature attacked me while I was lying in bed, I had a feeling I wouldn't be able to get back.

The serpent began to chant again. A strange cloud began to gather in front of the mirror. Tendrils began to reach toward the window.

Could it be some poisonous vapor? Something else entirely? I didn't know, but it could only mean harm for me. It grew darker, more solid. One tendril passed through the spinning window and reached toward the bed.

A jolt of horror and fear went through me. I had to stop it. If I didn't do something, I knew I would not live through this night.

NINE

looked frantically around the room. Except for the serpent, its guards, my brother, and the altar slab, it was empty. Then my attention suddenly fixed on the Pattern hanging in the air before us. I saw the Pattern's flaws now, and I knew where it went wrong. And, as I stared at it, I saw through the droplets of blood a series of dark threads that seemed to be holding everything together.

Yes—maybe I could destroy the window. If the serpent couldn't see me, its spells wouldn't be able to get through.

Slowly I moved closer, circling the Pattern, studying the threads. Yes . . . those threads had to be the key. If I could break them and close the window . . .

Using my spectral form, I reached out and touched the nearest thread. It had a strange texture, not quite solid but not quite liquid, either. My fingers suddenly burned from the contact, as though I'd touched a hot iron, and I jerked them back.

The image of my room grew clearer. The largest part of the mist—its body?—began to ooze forward. It was much larger than the spinning window, and slowly, like water pouring through a drain, it began to squeeze through the opening.

If I didn't act fast, I'd be too late. Reaching out, ignoring the pain, I began seizing threads with both hands and ripping them apart. They broke with surprising easy, though at each touch I felt a sharp shock of pain from my fingertips to my elbows. Ignoring it, I worked as fast as I could.

Half of the mist had entered my room. Fortunately, the serpent still had not noticed me or what I was doing. Its attention remained fixed on my bedroom, its chanting, the mist, and whatever dark sorcery it worked against me.

"No more," I whispered, half to myself, half to the Pattern, willing this thing to be done. More threads snapped and parted. They came apart more easily now. My hands were numb and I barely felt any pain. *"You are undone. You are free. This creature holds no power over you."*

Only a dozen more of the threads remained unbroken. A few spinning droplets of blood came loose from the Pattern. They flew off and struck the walls, splattering silently against the bones. Luckily neither the serpent nor its guards noticed.

Working faster now, I broke the rest of the threads.

When I finished, the window into my room seemed to ripple and churn, and then the image disappeared. The dark mist, sliced in half, began to fly wildly around the room, twisting and writhing like a thing in agony. I heard a high-pitched scream that went on and on and on. It *had* been alive. And I had hurt it.

"What—" the serpent-creature said, its chanting halted.

Suddenly my brother's blood flew everywhere, striking the serpent-creature and his guards in a red shower. Hissing, they all drew back. The Pattern, bloodless, hung motionless in the air now. It shone with a clear bright light like a powerful lantern.

Reaching out, I redrew its shape. Its lines moved under my fingers, uncoiling where it was wrong, bending and reshaping. Suddenly it came together again, whole and correct. I recognized it as a true representation of the Pattern inside me.

Its glow increased. A clear blue light filled the tower. I could see every bone in the wall distinctly now. Still the blaze grew. Individual scales stood out on the serpent's monstrous body as though etched in stone.

Through the Pattern I saw my room again. Horace bent over me, shaking my shoulders frantically. Don't bother, I thought. Nothing could possibly wake me until I returned to my body.

"Close that window," I told the Pattern. I didn't want the serpent to see me, in case it had any more tricks. *"Don't show my room."*

The image of my bedroom disappeared instantly. I felt a sudden swell of pride. It had worked!

Hissing, dripping with my brother's blood, its long tail lashing, the serpent reared back. It searched the tower with its glowing red eyes.

"Who is here?" it screamed. "Show yourself!"

The four hell-creatures drew their swords and turned, looking for me. But I remained invisible to them.

Brighter and brighter the new Pattern flared, glowing like the sun at noon. I reached out and seized it with my hands. With the black threads gone, it no longer hurt. Instead, a feeling of power and well-being came over me. Blue sparks began to stream up my hands and arms, surrounding me, bathing me in a cool blue light.

Holding the Pattern, I faced my half-brother Taine and the hell-creature guards. Hissing, they shielded their eyes and staggered back.

I hurled the Pattern toward the first of them. The hell-creature stood transfixed, unable to move, unable to run, as the Pattern grew huge.

"Kill!" I shouted. It was half command, half wish.

As though obeying my will, the Pattern touched the nearest hell-creature, and in that instant his skin sagged, his flesh seemed to wither, and his eyes lost their glow. Like a dried leaf, he crumpled to dust.

"Now, the others—"

As if it understood my words, the Pattern moved again. The three remaining guards tried to flee, but didn't get far. It touched them, too, and as it did, they became dust.

I felt a surge of pride and power. Finally *I* was doing something real. Finally *I* could deal with a threat against my family and myself.

"Now—the serpent—" I commanded.

The glowing Pattern began to move toward him.

"Son of Dworkin," the serpent said, in a low and gravelly voice. It was now looking straight at me. A coldness touched my heart. "You are revealed. Your magic is like a child's. Be gone!"

Then it unfolded its hands and made a quick motion, almost like throwing a dart at a dartboard. A wall of darkness raced toward the Pattern—toward me—growing huge. I turned too late, and it seemed to blot out everything.

Gasping, I sat up in bed. For a second, I didn't know where I was or what had happened. My head pounded. I felt feverish and disoriented.

Aber. He was bending over me. I saw concern in his eyes.

"Oberon?" he demanded. "Are you all right?"

"Yes." Panting, I lay back. Beneath me, the sheets were soaked with sweat. "I . . . I think so. I just need to catch my breath."

"What happened?"

"I had another vision. I saw Taine and the serpent-creature again."

Horace stood just behind Aber, peering around at me. He was pale, and I saw the scarlet imprint of a hand on his left cheek. Aber must have backhanded him for letting his guard down—or for waiting too long in calling him.

I looked around the room, but saw no sign of that dark mist. It must have been killed or destroyed when the window closed.

"How long has it been?" I asked.

"At least two hours," Aber said, sitting on the edge of the bed next to me. He folded his arms and sighed. "You started moaning in your sleep, Horace said, so he tried to wake you. Finally, when he couldn't, he came to get me."

I nodded.

"Leave us," I said to Horace. "Wait in the next room. Aber and I need to talk privately. If I need you again, I'll call you."

"Yes, Oberon." He ran out.

Much as I liked Horace, I did not yet know how far I could trust him to guard my privacy. From certain things that had happened in Juniper, I knew we had spies among us . . . possibly even a family member. I didn't want servants hearing about these visions. That serpent-creature knew a lot about magic, and I didn't want it to figure out how I had come to its tower.

After the door had shut behind the boy, I turned back to my brother. Quickly I told him all I had seen and done in the tower of bones. When I got to the part about changing the Pattern and using it to kill the hell-creatures, he just sat there with his mouth open, fascinated and, perhaps, more than a little awed.

I felt a surge of pride once more. This time I really *had* done something to strike against our enemies. If only I knew more about this Pattern and how it worked . . .

"You did well," Aber admitted when I finished my story. He had an odd look in his eyes. "This Pattern seems to have a power greater than we realize . . . perhaps nearing that of the Logrus."

"And Taine is still alive, though I don't think he's going to last much longer," I said. "He looked terrible. He's really been abused. Do you think we can rescue him? Is there anything you can do to find out the location of this tower?"

"I hope so. I'll try contacting him with a Trump as soon as I get back to my room. Maybe I'll be able to reach him now that we're home. I don't think he's very far from here."

"That's what Dad said the last time." Taking a deep breath, I sat up, remembering. "Dad's audience with King Uthor—what happened? Is he back yet?"

"Not yet."

I chewed my lip. "It's been too long. Something's wrong."

"We don't know that. Maybe he's still talking with the king. Or . . ."

"Or what?"

Aber swallowed. "Maybe he's been arrested."

"If so, wouldn't someone tell us?" I said. "Besides, why should he be arrested? As far as we know, he hasn't done anything."

"I suppose you're right. But I've never heard of the King's guards searching someone's house . . . especially not a Lord of Chaos's house. They wouldn't do it without cause."

"No, they wouldn't." I mulled that over. "There must be a reason. But what?"

"Something Dad's done—"

"Or something he's suspected of," I said.

We looked at each other.

Neither of us had an answer.

TEN

We talked for another hour, trying to work out what Dad might have done to incur the king's wrath, but we made no real progress. It could have been anything . . . from insulting the wrong woman at a dinner party to swiping King Uthor's wooden leg (assuming he had a wooden leg, which I very much doubted—but we had a good laugh over it).

Despite all our theories, we both kept coming back to the guards who had searched our house. What had they been looking for? Something small . . . something easily hidden . . . something Dad shouldn't have had.

What could it be?

My instincts told me the answer was important. It might well be the key to understanding everything that had happened to our family, from the murders of so many of our brothers and sisters to the attack on Juniper Castle.

"We might as well sleep on it," I finally told Aber, since we didn't seem to be making any progress. "Maybe the answer will come to us."

"I guess."

"And you'll try to reach Taine with his Trump?"

"Right away. And what about you?" he asked. "Will you be safe now?"

"I think so." I sighed, eyes distant. "I don't think the serpent-creature will try anything else tonight."

"I'm sure he won't. He'll deal more cautiously with you from now on. After all, you might surprise him with another magical attack, and next time you might kill him."

"It wasn't anything deliberate. I was lucky."

"Luck is all it takes." He gave a shrug. "Sometimes it's better to be lucky than skilled. Something is still troubling me, though."

I nodded. "Our enemies know too much about us. And I don't like that serpent spying on me in my own bed in my own room in this house. How long has it been doing that? Does it know everything we've been talking about?"

"I don't like it, either," he admitted. "It doesn't make me feel safe here."

I stood and began to pace like a caged tiger. "Is there something you can do to protect us? Some charm or spell to keep prying eyes out?"

"Spells can be set up to shield us. I'm sure Dad could do it, and easily. Freda, too."

I chewed my lower lip thoughtfully. He hadn't volunteered his own magical talents to protect us. What did that imply? Uncertainty . . . or weakness?

"That's no help," I said. "Dad and Freda aren't here, and we need protection immediately. For all we know, that serpent is watching us *right now* and plotting his next attack."

"If so . . ." He made a rude gesture toward the ceiling.

I couldn't help myself; despite the gravity of the situation, I chuckled. But it still didn't change the situation.

I asked, "What about you? Can you do anything to protect us?"

Aber hesitated. "It's not the sort of thing at which I'm skilled."

"Give it a try," I urged. "It can't hurt."

He sighed. "All right."

"Will it take long?"

"Maybe an hour to prepare everything, set up the spells, and lay them over the house. Maybe a little more if I run into problems."

"Is there anything I can do to help?" For some reason, I longed to see more real magic . . . perhaps because I had managed to use some myself. If I could learn to control this Pattern, to master its power the way the serpent in the tower had mastered the Logrus, I might stand a fighting chance against it.

"No. It's fairly delicate work, and it will require all my concentration."

"So I'd be in the way," I said, with a twinge of disappointment. "All right. I'll stay here."

"That's probably for the best." He said it with clear relief, as though I might inadvertently mess up his work. "Better for you that way. It's fairly meticulous Logrus manipulation—setting up magical trip-wires, in case we have magical prowlers. That way we'll be alerted if someone comes snooping."

"Let me know when you're done. If you run into problems or need my help, don't hesitate to call." I grinned and gave a wry attempt at humor. "I might not be able to use the Logrus, but I have a strong back. Give me a heavy box and I'll carry it for you."

"No boxes involved, I'm afraid."

He seemed distracted—probably already laying out the spells in his mind—and when he gave a curt nod and stood, I did not object. Best to get the spells in place before the serpent tried again to kill me—or any of us. I knew it would be back if we didn't act swiftly.

Aber headed for the door, paused, looked back.

"Don't forget—have your valet watch you while you sleep," he said, "just in case."

"All right."

After the door closed, I turned to the desk and sat heavily, mentally reviewing everything that had happened in the tower of skulls. What else should I have done? What else could I have done?

I hadn't told Aber this, but the Pattern I'd reshaped had obeyed my commands . . . as though it *understood* what I'd told it to do.

How could that be possible?

It had almost seemed *alive*. And, when I touched it, it made me feel whole and strong, better than I'd felt in years. I *still* felt that way, I realized, flexing my fingers and staring down at my hands, remembering the feeling of power that had surged through me. Even the slight stiffness in my left thumb, due to a months-old battle injury, had disappeared.

Not only that, but the floors and walls no longer seemed to be moving. Everything around me seemed normal . . . or as normal as it could be, in a world where nothing obeyed the laws of nature I had grown up with.

Rising, I began to pace the length of my room again. I felt trapped and restless. Clearly, I wasn't ready to go back to sleep.

Opening the door to the next room, I checked on Horace and found him curled up on a small bed in the corner, still fully dressed. He was already asleep, poor kid. Easing the door shut, I went back to the door to the hallway.

"Shouldn't you be in bed, Lord Oberon?" said Port, gazing up at me. "The hour is late and you look terrible."

"I thought you were a door, not a doctor."

"I am allowed to offer commentary and advice as needed. You ought to rest."

With a sigh, I said, "Thanks. I don't need advice right now, though."

"Very good, Lord Oberon." He had a slightly snippy tone. "Henceforth I will keep my advice to myself." His face disappeared, leaving an empty wooden panel in the door.

"I didn't mean to offend you," I said. But he didn't reappear. Well, screw him and his opinion—I didn't need to get into arguments with inanimate objects.

I had thirty minutes to kill while Aber set up his magical tripwires. I didn't want to fall asleep and miss the results, so I dressed, pulled on my boots, and went out into the hallway. Might as well explore some more, I thought.

I prowled the length of the hall. Each door had a different face carved into its middle, all with eyes closed, seemingly asleep. I did not knock on any of the doors. Port had been loud and talkative. I didn't want to mess up Aber's work by distracting him.

The hallway dead-ended. To the left, in a small dark alcove, a narrow servant's stairs wound up and down. It had to be the same one I'd explored earlier with Rèalla.

I headed down. What I really needed now was a drink—and something stronger than wine. With a house this big, at least one of the rooms ought to have an ample supply of liquor.

Two floors down, I went to the end of the corridor, turned right, then right again, then a third and a fourth time. My mind told me I had come full circle and back to my starting point, but I found myself in a cavernous hall at the foot of a broad set of marble stairs.

Two guards, both of whom I recognized as men we'd brought from Juniper, snapped to attention as soon as they spotted me. They stood by a pair of huge iron-shod doors at the far end of the hall. Not much chance of an attack coming from that direction, but it never hurt to be prepared. While I didn't know either one of them by name, I gave a quick wave. They grinned and saluted. My presence definitely seemed to raise their spirits—the hero of Juniper, the only son of Lord Dworkin who had been able to defeat the hell-creatures and drive them back. Yes, I would definitely be a rallying point for our troops.

"Any idea where they keep the drinks around here?" I asked as I approached them.

"Do you mean the wine cellar, sir?" one of them asked.

"I was hoping for something stronger."

"Try this." He pulled out a small metal flask and offered it to me.

I unstoppered it, and the smells of a strong sour mash rose. I took a tentative sip.

Whatever it was, it burned going down. I gasped, eyes watering. I'd only tasted rotgut this bad a couple of times. If it didn't cause blindness and insanity, it sure felt like it ought to.

"Do you like it, sir?" the guard asked, grinning. I noticed his two upper front teeth were missing.

"Awful! Simply awful!" I grinned back, then took a bigger swallow. It went down a bit easier this time. "Quite a kick. What's in it?"

"You don't want to know."

"Thanks. Here you go." I held out the flask.

"Keep it, sir. I'll have plenty more in a few days."

I raised my eyebrows. "You make it yourself?"

"Yes, sir! Two weeks old, and that's as good as it gets!"

I laughed. "Thanks, I will keep it." I gave an approving nod. "I'll return the flask when it's gone."

"Much appreciated, sir."

After that, I wandered off down the hall, opening doors and taking small sips. I discovered a salon with comfortable looking couches and chairs, a library filled with racks of scrolls and shelves of books, a map room, and several closets. A couple of narrow corridors seemed designed for servants. No one except those two guards seemed up and about at this hour.

Aber had to be nearly done with his magic by now, I figured, so I climbed the marble steps back up to the third floor, found my bedroom door, and Port let me in without my having to ask. My valet was nowhere in sight—still sound asleep, I assumed—so I sat down at the desk to wait for Aber. Idly I opened both drawers, but except for quills and a small blade for sharpening them, they were empty.

After a few minutes had passed, Port's voice interrupted:

"Sir. Lord Aber is here."

"Thanks." I rose and went out to the hall to join him.

"It's done," he said. He looked exhausted; the spells seemed to have taken a lot out of him. "I don't think anyone will be able to spy on us now without setting off alarm bells."

"Good. And Taine?"

"I tried, but . . ." He shrugged. "No answer."

"He might still be unconscious," I said. "He wasn't in good shape." He might also be dead . . . those injuries were enough to kill any lesser man.

"I'll try again tomorrow morning."

I nodded. "Good."

"We both might as well turn in," he said. "We've had enough excitement for one night. The guards are supposed to call me if Dad comes back. Do you want me to wake you if he does?"

"Yes."

"All right. And," he went on, "don't forget to have Horace watch over you while you sleep, just in case."

"All right. I'll wake him," I promised.

He bade me good night and returned to his room. I went back into mine, found Horace sleeping in his little room off mine, and shook him awake. Then I told him he needed to watch me again while I slept. To his credit, the boy didn't protest, but immediately went out and took his seat on the stool.

I stripped and climbed into bed, and the second my head touched the pillow, I slept.

This time I dreamed strangely. There was a chanting voice saying something in a language I almost but not quite understood. Shadows moved around me. Someone—a dim figure, but I had the impression of unblinking round eyes—sat on my chest, making it hard for me to breathe.

"Hell-creature!" I heard myself snarl, and I reached instinctively for a sword that wasn't there.

"Shh, my lord," a familiar woman's voice said.

"Helda?" I asked.

"Sleep, Lord Oberon," the voice said.

I groaned. My head hurt. The pressure on my chest grew. I couldn't tell if I was dreaming or awake. Could this be another vision? Some premonition of danger to come?

A face loomed out of the twisting shadows. I blinked rapidly, trying to focus my eyes. Black hair, pale skin, perfect white teeth, a grave expression—

"Rèalla?" I whispered.

"Lie back," she said. Soft hands pushed me down onto the bed. "You are still sick," she said, and she began to rub my chest. Her hands were warm as blood. I felt myself relaxing, sliding back toward sleep.

"It's this place . . ." I whispered.

"Yes," she said, "it is." Then she pressed a small goblet to my lips and poured. "Drink this, my lord. It will make you feel better."

It was warm brandy, and it had been spiced with something like cinnamon. The taste did not excite me, but liquor was liquor so I gulped anyway. What the hell. If I had to dream, I might as well enjoy it.

The brandy had a bitter aftertaste. She had added something else to it. An herb? Some medicine? I didn't know, but almost immediately I felt its effects. My vision clouded, and I felt myself sinking down, down, down, borne away on a river of darkness.

I slept the sleep of the dead.

The next time I awakened, I felt . . . different. Weak and light-headed. That was the first thing. And the second . . . complete disorientation.

I lay on my side, staring at the wall and the desk. All the confidence and strength I had felt the night before had fled, and now the world drifted around me. The bed seemed to be rocking like the deck of a ship at sea. The walls slowly oozed colors, and the faint light from the lamp on the desk, its wick turned low, dribbled up to pool on the ceiling.

I blinked and tried to sit up, but I couldn't do it. With a sigh, I fell back on the pillow. A gentle touch steadied my arm, then moved to caress my cheek.

"Horace?" I asked, voice rough from sleep. What would he be doing in my bed?

"Do I look like a boy?" asked a woman's soft voice from beside me.

ELEVEN

I sat up suddenly, then gulped as the room pitched unexpectedly to one side. My head swam. Moving only my eyes, I followed a pale hand to a slender arm, white as alabaster, which led to a shapely elbow, then to the soft curve of a shoulder, then to a delicate neck, and finally to a face so beautiful it still took my breath away.

I knew her. The woman who, only yesterday, had shown me the way to Dworkin's floor . . .

It took a moment for the fuzziness of my thoughts to clear. I never forgot a beautiful woman's name, and hers finally came to me.

"Rèalla?" I said.

"Yes, Lord Oberon." She smiled and stroked the line of my jaw with her fingertips. Her scent, strange and spicy, made my heart begin to race.

She lay next to me under the covers. Her gold eyes met and held mine for a heartbeat, then coyly turned downward. I noticed her slightly parted lips, behind which lay perfect pearls of teeth, her delicate nose, slightly upturned, and high pale cheekbones, which accentuated the lines of her face. I had seen few women who equaled her beauty.

"What are you doing here?" I asked softly, dumbfounded. A

beautiful woman was the last thing I would have expected to find next to me when I awoke.

"I would have thought that obvious," she said, snuggling closer and laying her head on my chest. "After all, you did want me here . . . didn't you?"

"Yes," I whispered. It was true. I had wanted her since the moment I saw her in the hallway.

I peeked under the sheet. She was naked, as I expected—and, if it was possible, even more beautiful from the neck down. I lowered the sheet and grinned back at her. I had awakened to many worse things over the years.

"So . . ." she giggled. "Here I am."

"Then you must be a goddess . . ." I began with a smile.

"I am no goddess, Lord."

"Then you're here in disguise?"

That line usually made a woman blush, and with Rèalla it did the same, a rose color blossoming across her cheeks and neck. I saw the twist of a smile at the corners of her perfect red lips.

"You are sweet, my lord."

"Call me Oberon."

"As you wish, Oberon."

I swallowed hard, trying to think back to what had happened last night. Had we done anything? I remembered lying down alone; Rèalla certainly hadn't been here. The last thing I'd seen was Horace as he sat on his stool at the foot of the bed, watching me.

Surreptitiously, I glanced around the room, but I didn't see the boy anywhere. Where had he gone? Probably back to his room as soon as Rèalla got here. He had enough sense to know when he wasn't wanted or needed.

But . . . more pressing . . . why didn't I remember anything of last night?

I frowned, thinking back. Maybe I *did* remember. Somehow, I had a vague impression of her having been here with me . . . of her body pressing tightly against mine . . . her lips hot on my mouth and chest . . .

And then the ghost of last night fled. I knew nothing more about it . . . could not even be sure she had actually been here with at all. Everything had a distant, confused quality, like a half-remembered dream.

Could I have been asleep when we made love? Or maybe I had been drunk. Vaguely, I remembered sipping brandy from a cup in her hand . . .

And then the memory passed and it was just the two of us in bed again. She continued to stroke my face and nuzzle against my chest. Putting my arm around her shoulders, I drew her close. I felt warm and comfortable, and I hoped this moment would never end.

"You are not like the rest of your family, Oberon," she told me. "There is a kindness in you . . . a warmth . . . *mmm.* I do like it, very much."

"About last night, Rèalla . . ." I said, brow furrowing.

"You do not remember it," she said with a light laugh. "I know. Do not worry."

"Was I that drunk?"

"A little drunk, perhaps . . . but I gave you a sleeping draught.

Before, when I first came to you, demons plagued your sleep. You moaned that the room was moving, and you cried out that we were being attacked—"

"Nightmares," I guessed. "Hallucinations."

"Yes, Oberon." She sighed. "You said hell-creatures were attacking us . . . and you called me Helda."

"Helda!" The name went through my with a jolt. Helda . . . my lovely Helda, who had been murdered by hell-creatures in Ilerium. She had been an innocent victim. If not for me, she would still be alive today.

"That is right."

"I'm sorry, Rèalla," I said, trying to remember. Very little of it came back to me. "I don't remember . . ."

"Shh, it's not important." She gave a little shudder. "Let us talk of more pleasant things."

"Of course." I gave her a light kiss on the forehead. "Thank you."

"It was nothing." With a long, sharp fingernail, she traced a pattern in the bristle of hairs on my chest. I found her touch sensuous. The smell of her, the musk she exuded, surrounded me like perfume. I breathed deeply, head swimming. "I was told to watch over you," she continued, "in case you . . . needed anything."

"Anything at all?"

She smiled in reply, and reading an invitation in that smile, I kissed her lips, her cheeks, and then her eyelids. Her long lashes fluttered against my skin like the wings of a trapped butterfly.

"And now?" I asked. "What do you think I need most?"

"This."

Without warning, she leaned over and kissed me, long and hard and passionately. I responded without hesitation, pulling her closer. The world and my family and the Courts of Chaos be damned, right now I wanted her as much as she seemed to want me, and nothing else mattered.

Some time later, as we lay exhausted atop a tangled mess of bedding, I felt a deep contentment spreading through me. Rèalla still nestled against my shoulder, her breath warm and soft on my cheek, and I realized how much I had missed a woman's touch and companionship. It made me feel less alone in this world, more a part of something greater than myself. I sighed, sated, happy on some deep level.

"You are more than well, I think," Rèalla said finally. She slipped like water from my grasp and left the bed.

Rolling over, I propped myself up on one elbow to watch. She had draped her robe and undergarments across the desk's chair, and now she reached for them.

"Not so fast!" I said.

"What, Oberon?" she asked, puzzled.

Swinging my legs to the floor, I leaped forward, caught her arm, and pulling her gently back to the bed. I kissed the insides of her wrists and elbows, gazing up at her beautiful face.

Smiling, she swayed closer, breasts at my eye level, enticing, teasing me, her scent filling my nose and throat with a heady perfume.

Inhaling deeply, I pulled her down on top of me. I had to have her, could not live or think or breathe without her, and for a second time we became a tangle of hands and tongues, fingers and mouths.

This time we made love slowly, the haste of first-time lovers satisfied. She was even better when we could relax and explore each other's bodies fully. Few women had ever excited me as she did, not even my beloved Helda. I never wanted to leave Rèalla's arms again.

At last, breathless, she pushed me away with a happy laugh, gave me a final kiss on the cheek, and began to dress. I admired her from the bed, counting myself lucky she had been the one chosen to look after me. My father had good taste in women, it seemed.

And, I guessed, Dad must have returned if he'd sent her to me. Sucking in a big, contented breath, I sprawled back on the pillows. A glow of happiness filled me. With Dad back, a beautiful new lover, and my health almost completely restored . . . yes, things were definitely looking up.

When she finished dressing, Rèalla blew me a kiss, then started for the door.

"Must you go?" I asked, watching her. She might have come to me as a nurse, but she was more than that now. I did not surrender my lovers willingly.

"You are an animal!" she said with a laugh. "Are you never satisfied, my lord?"

I chuckled, then patted the mattress beside me. "Come back and see!"

"I cannot. The morning is here. I have many duties."

"Who cares? Stay with me! I'll make it all right." I gave her a wink. "I do have some influence here, you know."

"I know, Oberon. But even so . . ."

Standing, I took her in my arms and kissed her long and passionately. She responded, and we stayed that way for a long minute.

Finally she broke away.

"I will come back tonight, if you wish . . . now please, Oberon. I must go." Smiling a bit wistfully, she pulled free from my arms. "It is long past time."

"If you must . . ."

With a reluctant sigh, I let her go. It had been too long since I had been with a woman like her, a woman I could grow to care about . . . even to love. And, somehow, I knew we would never again capture a moment this peaceful, this perfect. They were far too few in my life.

She hesitated in the doorway, gazing back at me. "Until tonight," she said.

I took her delicate white hand and gave it a lingering kiss. "I need extra care. You can tell my father that."

"There is no need to lie, Oberon. You are as fit as any man here. I will return soon . . . as long and as often as you will have me."

"I would . . . I will!"

She smiled again, then eased the door closed. I caught a glimpse of Port's disapproving face in the woodwork, but he quickly vanished. An unwilling voyeur, no doubt—he could hardly leave when our lovemaking grew noisy, after all.

I felt more amused than anything else.

"Port?" I said.

His face appeared, the expression still reproving.

"Yes, Lord Oberon?" he said.

"You are to say nothing about Rèalla's visit here to anyone, and especially not to my brother or father. Is that understood?"

"Are you sure that is wise, Lord Oberon?"

"Oh, yes." I chuckled to myself. It was more than wise, it was beneficial . . . I knew my father and brother wouldn't approve of my bedding the servants. Rèalla's and my relationship would have to remain private, at least for now. That seemed the wisest course.

"Very good, Lord," Port said unhappily. "Was there anything else?"

"Do you know if my father returned last night?"

"No, Lord. He does not sleep on this floor."

"Very good. That will be all."

With a frown, Port's face vanished into the wood again. I had no doubt that he would follow my instructions to the letter.

Yawning and scratching, I turned to the looking glass and studied my reflection. The first thing I noticed was a strange red welt on my chest, just above my heart. Odd . . . I hadn't noticed it last night before bed, nor had Rèalla or Horace commented on it.

Frowning, I leaning closer for a better look. It had a single blood-red dot in its center, like the mark a bee's stinger would leave. When I touched the welt, it felt hot, but not painful. An insect bite? It had to be. But what kind of insect would leave a mark like that . . . or that large?

Though no more color had come back into my cheeks and my skin remained a pasty white, overall I felt stronger today than yesterday, and much less like a man on his deathbed. My hands barely shook, and when I walked about, the floors and walls no longer seemed to move against me. Yes, I was definitely doing better.

As for the bite mark on my chest—well, I wasn't in Ilerium any more. Who knew what sort of insects lived in the Courts of Chaos? If the welt bothered me later, I'd ask Anari to find a poultice for it.

At the wash stand, I filled the basin with tepid water from the pitcher, made a lather with the block of soap, and scrubbed myself clean from head to heels. When I toweled dry, I felt a lot better, more like a civilized person again. A straight razor sat next to the wash basin, and I stropped it on a little leather strap hanging from the right side of the stand. Then I made a second lather with the soap and shaved off my four-days' growth of beard with minimal blood loss. After my experiences in Juniper, where a demon disguised as the castle barber tried to slit my throat, I planned on doing my own shaving.

Next I opened my wardrobe and explored the contents. Several dozen suits of clothing hung inside, and boots, shoes, and neatly folded undergarments sat on the floor. He seemed to favor dusty blues and grays. Finally, after much thought, I selected a pair of soft gray deerskin pants with a matching shirt embroidered with a gold phoenix on the chest. That's how I felt right now, reborn from the ashes of my old self. Gold braid decorated the cuffs and collar, and I thought it added a distinguished look.

As with the last set of Mattus's clothes I'd appropriated, this one fit me admirably well, as though it had been made to my exact measurements. When I examined my reflection in the looking glass, I gave a nod of satisfaction. Rèalla had me interested in my appearance again, and biased though I might be, I had to admit I cut quite a handsome figure.

Satisfied, I went to Horace's little room and found him snoring softly in his own bed. So much for watching over me last night. Aber would skin him alive if he found out the boy had deserted his post. Just as well Horace had—I didn't particularly need or want an audience for my love-making.

"Time to get up," I told him. "Horace? Horace?"

He snored on, oblivious. Poor kid, he was completely exhausted. He'd probably been up most of the night looking after me. Good thing Rèalla had come along to relieve him.

Even so, I needed him up now. Duty called, and he had to learn what that meant. In the army, I'd missed more than my fair share of sleep. You got used to it.

I bent and shook his shoulder.

"Horace!" I called. "Wake up!"

It took a minute, but finally he opened his eyes and sat up, looking groggy and confused. He yawned widely.

"Sorry, Oberon!" he said, staring up at me through bleary, dark-rimmed eyes. "I must have fallen asleep."

"Are you sick?" I demanded. "I couldn't wake you."

"No, Oberon," he said with another yawn. "I tried to stay up with you last night to make sure nothing happened, like Lord Aber said." Then he gulped, and I knew he remembered my brother's threats.

"I appreciate your effort," I said, "but it wasn't necessary for you to stay up all night. I didn't have any more problems, and I feel much better today."

"If I may say so, sir, you still look sick."

"It's not how I look, it's how I feel."

"Yes, sir." He hesitated. "Did you carry me in here? I do not remember falling asleep. The last thing I remember, I was sitting on the stool, watching you . . ."

"Don't worry about it." I smiled to myself, realizing the truth: Rèalla must have carried him to his bed before waking me. Good thing he *did* fall asleep; I didn't need to be guarded from beautiful women. "You did fine," I told him. "I'm more than satisfied."

"Thank you, sir!" He seemed greatly relieved.

"Have you explored the house yet? Do you know the way to the dining hall?"

"Yes, sir."

"Get dressed. You have five minutes. Then you can show me the way."

Happily, breakfast here seemed to be quite a subdued affair, in a relatively normal room and with relatively normal food. From the lamps flowed a thick golden stream of light that covered the ceiling, but I was rapidly becoming used to it. It seemed as much a part of this place as the angles that did not quite mesh with my perceptions.

Apparently I was the first one up today; though large trays of food sat ready on the sideboard, they hadn't been touched yet. Lifting the lids, I peeked into each. About half the food was recognizable. I helped myself to eggs, chops of some kind, and small honeyed rolls. To drink, pitchers of iced juices sat to one side, but I motioned a serving girl over and instructed her to find me a bottle of red wine, and this she did immediately.

Just as I was settling in at the head of the table, Aber strolled through the door.

"Good morning," I said.

"Hi," he said. "Bad night?"

"Why does everyone keep asking that?" I said, thinking of both Horace and Port. "I couldn't have slept better."

"You look awful."

"I feel better, though."

"That's good."

I thought of Rèalla and hid my smile behind a bite of a honeyed roll. She, more than anything else, had to be responsible for my quick recovery. Nothing like love to raise a man's spirits.

Licking my fingers, I changed the subject. "Have you seen Dad this morning?"

"He's not back yet," Aber said. He began heaping his plate with egg-shaped purple fruits, tiny pink berries, and some kind of stringy cheeselike dish.

"What! Are you sure?"

"I'm quite sure."

I couldn't believe it. He must have returned—hadn't he sent Rèalla last night to tend to me?

And if he hadn't . . . who had?

Aber joined me at the table, taking the opposite seat. He seemed his usual cheerful self.

"He must be here," I said firmly. "You missed him." That had to be the answer.

"I checked this morning. I thought he might have used a Trump to get back late last night, but his bed hasn't been slept in, and neither the doors nor the guards saw him come or go. He hasn't come back."

No audience with a king would last so long, I knew. Something had happened. Something had gone wrong.

TWELVE

took a deep breath. "He's been gone too long."

"Probably."

"Aren't you concerned?"

"I am," he said. "At least, a little." He looked at me seriously. "You don't think he'd abandon us here, do you? I know he's not particularly fond of me, and I forced myself on you both for the trip here. But if he saw things going badly, do you think he'd run off into the Shadows and leave us here?"

"I don't know," I admitted. After all, everything I'd grown up believing had been an elaborate lie. And he had lied to me repeatedly in Juniper. I *thought* he cared about me—about us all—to try to protect us. But would he abandon us if it was the only way to save himself?

I took another bite of my honeyed roll, trying to work through the problem. Our father had powers I couldn't as yet even imagine. He might be anywhere now, from just outside the dining room door to hidden in a secret castle a thousand miles away . . . or he might not even be on this world. He could just as easily be hiding on a different Shadow where no one would ever find him.

Would he abandon us? If things went badly, would he leave us sitting here, alone and unknowing, while he struck off on his own for safety?

I remembered all the trouble he had gone through to rescue me in Ilerium. It would have been safer to leave me there, to let me die at the hands of the hell-creatures. And yet he had risked his own life to rescue me—and the life of his favorite daughter, my half-sister Freda. Those were not the actions of a man who would abandon his offspring.

And yet, pressed for time, feeling threatened, I could also see him dumping Aber and me here. If he convinced himself we'd be safe in the Beyond—why not leave us here? He might be my father, and he might be a powerful sorcerer, but he had lied to me for the last twenty years about my life. Everything I'd ever believed about the universe had been wrong. I realized now that I didn't know him, not really, nor could I predict his actions.

Could he abandon us? Yes.

Would he abandon us? I didn't know.

"Besides," Aber went on between bites as he dug into a plate of steak and eggs a servant set before him, "we don't know that anything happened to him."

I said, "Then where is he?"

"Maybe he's visiting with friends at the court."

"I thought he didn't have any."

"Oh, he must have a few . . . even if they aren't openly supportive. Maybe he's trying to rekindle old alliances."

"Did you try his Trump?"

"Are you crazy? The last time I did, he nearly bit my head off. I ruined some sort of delicate experiment. He made he swear I'd never do it again."

I chuckled. "*I* made no such promises. After breakfast, I'll try to reach him."

"Better you than me."

"Maybe he found an old girlfriend after his audience . . ."

"More likely an old wife."

I raised my eyebrows. "How many has he had?"

"By my count," Aber said, "at last six from the Courts and two from the Beyond . . . though I've heard at least one wife didn't last out the wedding night, so perhaps she shouldn't count. And who knows how many in Shadows. Your mother among them, I assume?"

"Nope."

"Bastard."

I didn't ask which one of us; it was literally true in my case, figuratively true in Dad's, and on occasion entirely true of us both.

"When he gets back," Aber said, "you can ask him for an exact count. Assuming he's kept track."

I gave a snort. "He's lied to me my whole life. He's *still* lying to me, as far as I can tell. I can't trust anything he says."

"True." Aber shrugged. "Everyone in the family knows his hold on the truth is slippery at best. It's part of his charm."

I sighed. "So we're back where we started. We don't know where he is, what happened during his audience with King Uthor, or when he might come home."

He shrugged again. "That about sums it up. I don't think you ought to try to contact him yet, though."

"If you have a better plan," I said, "I'd like to hear it."

"Unfortunately, I don't."

After that, we ate in silence. I noticed Aber studying me from the corners of his eyes, and I began to shift uneasily in my seat. I had never enjoyed close scrutiny. It always made me nervous.

"All right," I finally said, after putting up with it as long as I could. I set down my fork and looked straight at him. "You've been staring at me for ten minutes. What's wrong?" I patted the top of my head. "Am I sprouting antlers or something?"

"I keep thinking about that vision you had yesterday," he said, "and how you killed the *lai she'on* guards. That sounds like a Logrus trick. And when the serpent knocked you back to your own body—he used primal Chaos."

"What's that?"

"An essential force. It's dangerous to summon and hard to control, without practice and patience. It's something he would not have done except as a last resort."

"Dangerous—how?"

"You can control it, up to a point, but it almost has a power and a will of its own."

"Treacherous?"

"Yes. If it gets away from you, it will destroy everything and everyone it touches, feeding on death, growing larger all the while. If it gets big enough, it can destroy an entire Shadow."

I gulped. "And the serpent threw this stuff at *me*?"

"Luckily your physical form wasn't there. You would be dead now." He studied my face. "Clearly he fears you. That trick with the Pattern . . . what other powers might you have, I wonder?"

I gave a dismissive wave. "None that I know of."

"Maybe you *should* try to master the Logrus," he mused. "If you could control it . . ."

"Thanks, but no." I shook my head. I knew without doubt that the Logrus wouldn't work for me. "I think Dad told the truth when he said the Logrus would kill me if I tried to enter it. I'm not willing to risk it."

"I could speak with the keeper on your behalf. Maybe he has a different test. If he thinks you can safely enter the Logrus, why not try it? After all, you said Dad lied to you about everything. Maybe he lied to you about the Logrus, too."

"I'm not ready to try it."

He shrugged. "It was just an idea."

"Don't get me wrong, I appreciate it. I'm just not ready to risk my life yet."

"Fair enough." Wiping his mouth on a napkin, he pushed his plate to the side. A serving girl whisked it away. "You look better. Are you up for a trip outside?"

"You mean here? Or a visit to King Uthor's court?"

"Here. We'll take it slowly. What do you say?"

I hesitated. Something made me want to say "No," but I finally nodded.

"I'll give it a try."

After all, I couldn't hide indoors for the rest of my life. If Chaos was to be my new home, I'd have to get over my fears. How bad could it be?

He gave a nod. "Good."

I finished my own meal in a few bites, but Aber seemed in no hurry to leave. I sat back, and all the questions in the back of my mind began to pour out. I actually felt sorry for my brother as I began to grill him about the house (five floors, 186 rooms at last count—though apparently it fluctuated according to the season), what had happened those three days I'd been unconscious (not much—our father had gone out periodically to meet with friends and allies, returning only to check on me and grab a few hours of sleep), and the nature of Chaos (which seemed even more confusing the longer he talked about it).

"Maybe we should pay King Uthor a visit . . ." I suggested, as my questions ran out.

"He would never grant the likes of us an audience."

"You never know. And even if we don't get to see him, we might learn something . . . like where Dad's being held."

He looked surprised. "Do you think he's been arrested?"

"I don't know. We ought to find out, though. Even if he hasn't been arrested, he might be in danger. I don't think he'd abandon us here willingly."

"King Uthor might arrest *us* if we go poking around."

"Why? We don't know anything, nor have we done anything wrong." Suddenly I grinned. "Or have you been holding out on me? Are you and Dad involved in a conspiracy against the crown?"

He pulled a sour face. "You know better than that."

"I didn't think so. But it would have made things simpler. I could turn you both in, claim my reward, and take over the family lands and titles."

"Spoken," Aber said bitterly, "like a true member of our family.

Unfortunately, it's never going to happen. Dad knows better than to trust me with a conspiracy. I'd end up spilling the whole plan to the first person who asked." He shook his head. "I've never been terribly good at keeping secrets. That's more Freda's department."

"Freda? I would have guessed Blaise . . ."

"Blaise likes to brag too much to keep secrets well. Freda, though . . ."

"What about her?"

"She used to help Dad with his experiments. She'd never say what they were doing together. It drove Locke and Blaise crazy!" He chuckled, eyes distant, as he remembered happier times. "They both thought they were missing out on something grand. But no matter how much they begged, Dad wouldn't let them into his workshop."

I smiled at my mental image of a frustrated Locke and Blaise. They, along with Freda, had been locked in a struggle for top position in our family. All three of them thought much too highly of themselves, as far as I was concerned.

"And you loved it," I said.

"Yes!" He laughed. "You would have, too, I think."

"Oh, I know I would have."

He cleared his throat. "Getting back to the problem at hand . . . Even if we knew what illicit activities Dad was involved in, I don't think turning him in would help us at this point. Our enemies want us dead . . . dead to the last member of our family."

"True," I admitted. "But we're not really in a position of strength now. With strong allies, we might be."

"Well," Aber said after a thoughtful pause, "if I wanted to ally myself with someone strong, I'd start with King Uthor."

"You're assuming he's not behind the attacks."

"Do you think he might be?" he asked in surprise.

I shrugged. "I don't know enough to decide one way or another. I can only say the hell-creatures—"

"*Lai she'on,*" he said.

"—who searched our house looked a lot like the ones guarding Taine in my vision. And they looked like the hell-creatures who invaded Juniper and Ilerium."

He gave a dismissive wave of his arm. "All the *lai she'on* look much the same. They are bred for it."

"We aren't talking about facts, we're talking about possibilities. Just take it for granted that King Uthor is behind the attacks on our family for a minute. Where does that leave us?"

"If that's true," he said, "we're really screwed. King Uthor is the most powerful man anywhere. If he's our enemy, we might as well line up and let him slit our throats."

"Don't be fatalistic."

"Easy for you to say. You don't know what you're talking about. Or what we would be up against. On the other hand, I don't believe he's behind the attacks."

"No? Why not?"

"Because he wouldn't need to be sneaky about them. He could simply proclaim us enemies and order our deaths. Chaos is more than a place . . . it is a power. Unleashed it in its primal form, it can devour whole worlds."

I shrugged; it sounded like an exaggeration to me, but I had no way to judge. "All right. Let's consider the other possibility . . . what if it *isn't* King Uthor behind the attacks?"

"Then he'd have every reason to protect us. We are, after all, loyal subjects."

"Exactly! Now, what if—by not firming up our alliance with him—we miss the chance to save our family and ourselves?"

"You argue too well," Aber complained. "You almost make it sound possible."

"It *is* possible."

He sighed. "King Uthor would take one look at me and either burst out laughing or eat me alive. He doesn't need allies . . . allies need him."

"You never know until you try."

"I think we're better off staying away from court."

"Any particular reason?"

"No . . . it's just a feeling I have."

"King Uthor has no cause to arrest us," I pointed out. "Neither you nor I have done nothing wrong. And we have a good reason for going—to look for our father. Who can argue with that?"

"I can," he said. "Think about it. What if the attacks have all been part of a blood feud? In which case, he'd have every right to kill us out of hand just for showing up and annoying him."

I mulled that over. "It can't be so easy for him to kill people. Kings don't slaughter nobility. They wouldn't be kings very long if they did."

He shifted uneasily. "Well, no. Technically, he'd have to follow court etiquette. You'd be insulted, then challenged to a duel by one of his champions."

"And killed?"

"How good are you with a trisp?"

"A *what?*"

He chuckled. "I thought so. It's a traditional weapon, kind of like a cat's claw, but larger, and its blades extend. You attack with a trisp and defend with a fandon—which, I assume, you've also never used?"

"A fandon? No, I've never seen or heard of it."

"You haven't missed much. Except for tradition, I think everyone would have abandoned them centuries ago in favor of swords."

"So I'd be killed with a trisp?"

"Sliced to bits." He chuckled grimly. "Me too, for that matter. I can never keep my fandon up properly. The way the stones move—"

"Wait!" I said. "Stones? That move?"

"Right. You stand on them. They float, but they respond to subtle movements of your feet. Up, down, left, right—you keep your stone moving and keep your opponent off balance."

"You're making all this up," I said accusingly. Weapons I'd never heard of—and now we had to fight on floating stones?

He shrugged. "It's true. There are traditional ways of doing everything here. Dueling with trisp and fandon is the recognized way to settle disputes."

Despite my skepticism, he did not seem to be joking with me. Maybe these weapons were real after all. I mulled over the possibilities. Fighting in mid-air with weapons I'd never used before . . . I wouldn't stand a chance. Maybe a visit to King Uthor's court should be held back as a last resort.

I remembered our father's phenomenal skills with a blade, then Locke's offhand comment that Dad wasn't terribly good by Chaos standards. What tremendous fighters must these Lords of Chaos be!

"Come on," Aber said, rising. "First let's see what happens when you go outside. I'm tired of being locked indoors. Fresh air will do us both some good. And maybe Dad will show up in the meantime."

I had no choice but to agree, so I rose and followed him. With an unerring sense of direction, he passed through a maze of hallways that seemed to twist in upon themselves. Finally our passage dead-ended at a heavy wooden door, which he pushed open.

I stared through the doorway at a broad, sand-covered court-yard. On the other side, a hundred yards away, rose a stone wall per-haps thirty feet high. The wall extended to either side as far as I could see, apparently circling the house. Guards in uniform patrolled the top of the wall, and more guards drilled with swords and shields fifty yards to the right, at the far edge of the courtyard. The steady tramp of boots and the ring of steel on steel, of sword on sword, made it a familiar, welcome sound.

Then I made the mistake of looking up. Ye gods! The sky un-nerved me—if sky you could call something that churned like a storm-tossed sea. Twisting colors, a splash of drifting stars, sudden spikes of blue lightning, and half a dozen moons all moving in dif-ferent directions made my head swim. Gazing upon it sent waves of nausea and dizziness through me, and against my will I felt my body start to drift. The roar of phantom winds rose to fill my ears.

"Hey!" I heard a distant voice shouting. "Oberon! Look at me! *Oberon!*"

It was Aber. I forced my attention to him and focused on his concerned face. Grabbing his arm, I steadied myself. I felt sick, off balance, disoriented.

"I hear you," I said. "The sky . . ."

"If it's too much for you, say so!" he said. "We don't have to stay outside long. But I think it's important for you to get used to it."

"Yes." I nodded; that made a lot of sense.

Pointedly, I did not look up. The universe grew steady once more and the roar of wind in my ears lessened.

Aber started forward briskly, out of the house, into the court-yard. I followed. Sand crunched under my boots, and the air carried strange spicy scents like nothing I could identify.

"What do you think?" he asked, indicating the whole of the house and sky with a sweep of his arm.

Gulping, I lowered my eyes and concentrated on the ground at my feet. Out here, what had looked like sand turned out to be some-thing else. The whole courtyard seethed with movement underfoot, as sand and stone shifted constantly, like a mass of crawling insects. And yet neither Aber nor I sank into the ground. We walked nor-mally, as though we stood on solid land.

Aber, grinning like a madman, threw wide his arms.

"What do you think?" he cried again, gazing up at the sky. "Isn't it splendid? Doesn't it make your heart race and your senses quicken? Can you *feel* it around us?"

"You're insane!" I gasped out. "It's a nightmare!"

THIRTEEN

Aber laughed at me.

"So—this is—what the Courts of Chaos—are like?"

"Just about," he said. "In the Beyond, we're quite close . . . I can feel the pull of Chaos, like a current moving through the air. You should be able to sense it, too."

I just stared at him, bewildered. "What do you mean, sense it? I don't quite understand."

"Close your eyes."

I did so. I felt myself swaying, and the ground seemed to slide down and away from me.

"Ignore your senses," he said. "No sight, no sound, no smell nor touch nor taste. You should feel a slight tugging inside . . . as though you're standing in a river while the waters push through your body."

I remained still, scarcely breathing. My heart beat in my chest. Air whispered through my nose and throat. That low, throaty roar of phantom winds sounded distantly in my ears.

Then, gradually, I became aware of a curious sensation . . . a gentle pull not so much on my body as on my spirit, as though some unknown force tried to draw me closer.

I turned with it, trying to find the direction it wanted me to go. Yes—I had it now. It was unmistakable.

I opened my eyes and pointed toward the gate.

"That way."

Aber looked startled.

"No," he said. "That's not right."

"What do you mean?" I demanded. "I can feel it! It's pulling me."

"You have it backwards." He pointed in the opposite direction. "The pull toward the Courts of Chaos goes that way."

I turned and stared in the direction he indicated, back toward our family's towering house. No, I was certain I didn't want to go back there. Turning, trying to find where the pull was strongest, I found myself facing the gate again. The Courts of Chaos definitely held no pull for me. Clearly this psychic tug came from something else . . . something in the other direction.

I told him as much.

"I don't understand," he said, frowning. "But then, there's a lot I don't understand about you, Brother."

Shrugging, I said, "Sorry. What you see is all there is."

"I think not." His eyes narrowed, studying me. "There is more to you, I think, than you even know yourself. But let's talk of other things now. Come on, I'll show you around the grounds. The gardens are nice."

"Nice?"

"If you like rocks."

Chuckling, he led the way, and I had a feeling he was about to play another of his famous practical jokes on me. We followed the wall to the right, away from the drilling men-at-arms. The house loomed over us, huge and windowless, oozing bright colors from every seam and joint.

A few blackened, twisted treelike plants grew from the soil, and their branches moved even though no wind blew. They seemed to sense our passage, and several times I jumped when branches whipped close to my face. Aber just ignored them and kept walking.

Rounding a corner of the house, we came into sight of the "garden"—a penned area where rocks roamed through knee-high grass at will, looking like petrified sheep. The rocks ranged from head-sized to bigger than a man, and now and again they banged into one another with loud crashing sounds. Benches set around the pen made it seem like rock-watching might be considered pleasurable here.

Aber went right up to the fence and leaned on it, staring out across the field. He seemed to recognize some of the rocks and actually began pointing out his favorites:

"That's Jasmine. And that one's Teal."

"You've *named* them?" I stared at him like he'd lost his mind. He had to be playing a joke on me. Who had time for such nonsense with our family being murdered and our father gone missing?

He seemed to realize how I felt, since he sighed and shrugged and wouldn't look me in the eye.

"It's not for everyone," he said. "You have to be sensitive to their presence to appreciate the beauty. It's like . . . it's like poetry!"

I rolled my eyes. "Then it must be an acquired taste," I said. "But don't feel bad. I only have one use for poetry, and that's to help get beautiful women into my bed."

"You're just like Locke." Sighing again, Aber turned and walked on alongside the fence.

"No need to be insulting!" I hurried to catch up. "Or should I take that as a compliment?"

Flatly, he replied, "There's more to see ahead, around the corner."

"Not more rocks?"

"No . . . fountains, Pella's flower garden, a petrified dragon."

"A dragon!" I felt my heart quicken. They were creatures of legend. I'd heard stories of them my whole life.

"Yes, Locke killed it years ago. It took twenty mules and twice that many men to cart it back here. But it's a trophy worth keeping."

"How did Locke kill it?"

"He showed it a medusa's head."

Awed, my estimation of Locke went up yet another notch. I'd known my brother was an able military officer and a skilled swordsman, but I'd had no idea he'd gone adventuring.

"All right," I said. "I have to know. How did he get a medusa's head?"

"I'm not really sure . . . he said something about a labyrinth and a golden fleece."

I shrugged.

Aber went on, "Want to see what my mother looked like? There's a statue of her there, too. I'm told it's a good resemblance."

"Sure." Statues, at least, I could appreciate. But a dragon, even a petrified one, couldn't be missed.

My sudden enthusiasm seemed to cheer him up. As we walked, he kept gazing into the rock pen. Boulders small and large drifted in an intricate dance. He honestly seemed to enjoy them, like a falconer admiring his birds or a hunter showing off his hounds. And why shouldn't he? In Juniper he had been trapped in a house filled with squabbling siblings and a paranoid drunkard of a father, a mysterious enemy had been systematically murdering family members, and we were under siege from an army determined to slaughter us all to the last one. Here, at least for the moment, we appeared safe. He could relax and be himself.

"Hey! Look at that!" He stopped short and pointed at the two largest hump-backed rocks, which now circled each other like wolves in the center of the pen. "They're going to fight!"

"A fight?" I stopped and regarded them. "How can you tell?"

"Experience! Watch!"

Sighing, I leaned on the fence beside him. The two boulders wheeled and spun and circled in an intricate dance, drew apart, then suddenly raced towards each other faster than a man could run. When they struck with a loud *crack!*, rock chips and dust flew into the air. Then, as they drew apart, I noticed that the larger of the two had a crack running down its middle. It split in two, and each half moved off in a different direction.

Aber groaned in disappointment. "They don't usually hit that hard," he said. "One usually backs down."

"They look dangerous," I said.

"Not really. If you're careful. You can even ride them, if you want. It's fun."

I shook my head. Strange as the house seemed, everything inside looked normal by comparison. A deep sense of melancholy spread through me. I longed for Ilerium or Juniper, where I knew the rules and nothing fantastic waited around each corner to jump out at me.

Deep-blue lightning flickered overhead, bright enough to draw my attention. Then bright tongues of blue light split the sky, and a growl of thunder rumbled close at hand.

"A storm?" I asked.

He hesitated, looking up. "I don't know. I've never seen anything quite like this before."

"Maybe we'd better get inside," I suggested. The dragon could wait; since it was petrified, it wouldn't be going anywhere. Besides, I remembered the attack on our forces in Juniper. It had started with a storm. Our enemies had directed lightning bolts down on top of us, shattering the upper floors of Juniper Castle and killing dozens of people.

"I think we'd better," Aber said. Turning, he headed back toward the courtyard. I hurried to keep up.

Then a finger of lightning lanced down from the sky, hitting the ground twenty feet away. Sand peppered my face and hands. I threw up my arms to protect my eyes.

"Run!" Aber screamed.

I turned and found him sprawled on the ground. The force of the lightning had knocked him down. "We're being attacked! We have to get inside!"

I hurried to him. "Attacked—here?"

"Yes! Now go on, get inside!"

"Not without you." Instead, I pulled him to his feet. Together we sprinted for the door.

More lightning flickered over head. Thunder growled in warning. One bolt lashed down at us, but it struck the rock-pen, splintering the little wooden fence. As though sensing their chance to escape, the rocks inside began to drift toward the opening.

Side by side now, we pounded past them, circling the house. The doorway came into sight.

I let Aber pull ahead, then darted to the side. My instincts and military training told me to spread out the distance between us and move unexpectedly. That would make it harder for whoever was aiming the lightning bolts to get us both. And if he did manage to strike home, better to kill just one of us.

Before I'd taken half a dozen steps, blue lightning leaped down from the heavens. It moved faster than I could react, crackling with energy, and it struck me with a blow like a hammer to the head. Surrounding me, burning across my skin, filling my eyes with a shining blue light, I reeled to the side. Everything around me looked weird and distant.

Then I sucked in a breath—and felt the flames coil and burn inside my chest.

FOURTEEN

ain—nothing but pain—pain wrapped in more pain—

I thought my lungs would burst. I couldn't breathe, couldn't move, couldn't think. I tried to scream, but no sound came out.

—fires searing me, burning into my flesh—

Just ahead, I saw Aber starting to look back. He began to turn, but it happened so slowly, it almost seemed as though he wasn't moving at all.

Gods, the pain!—Make it stop!—

Aber's mouth gaped open as he shouted something to me. Crackling thunder filled my ears; I couldn't hear a word he said.

My arms—my head—my eyes—

Everything glowed from a crisp blue light that seemed to radiate away from inside me. Shadows, sharp and black, stretched dark fingers away in all directions. A sense of inevitable doom pervaded everything and everyone around me.

Pain!—

My sight began to dim. I couldn't be dying here, not now. . . . It wasn't fair—I wasn't done yet—

Dark.

*   *   *

Consciousness returned slowly.

A hush had fallen over everything and everyone. I had a sense of dislocation, as though I watched myself from a great distance, and yet I could see nothing but white in every direction. Detached from my body, like an observer looking through someone else's eyes, I peered into the whiteness for answers.

Though my life might be nothing more than a speck of dust on a game-board of cosmic proportions, my thoughts remained clear and sharp. I remembered the lightning. I remembered the pain, though it had vanished. An eerie calmness, like nothing I had ever felt before, began to settle over me.

A laugh, high and musical, broke the silence.

"Who's there?" I called.

A blur of white passed a hand-breadth from my eyes, then a brilliant light dazzled me. I blinked furiously and shaded my face with my hand.

That light—it moved and breathed, it ate and drank with me. Yes, it had eyes, whatever it was. But no human ever gazed out through them, these windows to the soul, so pure and perfect they made my heart ache just to be near.

"Why are you here?" the voice said. It seemed to come from below, then above, then below again.

"First, tell me where I am," I said.

"Here, with me," said the voice.

I licked my lips. "Am I the first one?"

Again, the laughter. "No. There have been others."

"Where am I?"

"With your mother."

"Then . . . I am dead?" I licked my lips. "These are the Seven Heavens? My just reward?"

I sensed puzzlement.

"Where am I?" I asked again.

"Good-bye . . ." said the voice. "Good-bye . . ."

"No!" I called. "Wait! Mother, I—"

Somehow, the world shifted. Suddenly everything was different. Sounds rose—the rumble of thunder—shouts of men—

I lay facedown, my left cheek pressed into the sand. I felt it moving, crawling about like something alive.

Opening my eyes, I blinked at a sudden rush of color. Blues and browns and reds and greens blurred together like paints in a rainstorm.

My eyes did not want to focus, so I concentrated on a couple of pebbles a few inches in front of my eyes. They whirled and danced in intricate patterns. As I stared, they slowly grew sharp and distinct once more.

Not dead . . . that was the first and most important thing.

An acrid, unpleasant odor surrounded me, like burning flesh. I coughed a bit.

"Lord Aber?" distant voices called. "Get him up! Hurry! Inside!"

When I tried to push myself up, though, I found my arms didn't want to obey. I fumbled, didn't have the strength to continue.

What had happened?

Lightning . . . lightning had struck me.

Somehow, I had lived through it. I blinked again, took a deep breath, and sat up in a single motion. Coughing wracked my body.

Boots crunched on the sand in front of me. Hands seized me, lifted me, began to carry me.

"He's alive!" someone called.

I wondered—did he mean me or Aber?

It took every ounce of strength, but I raised my head and tried to see what was happening. Tears blurred my vision. I couldn't see anything much.

"Aber?" I croaked.

A dark, unmoving shape a few yards ahead might have been him.

No, he couldn't be dead. Moaning, I longed to crawl into a hole and pull the opening shut behind me. No, not Aber—my one friend here—

I began to crawl. Sharp, knifelike pains stabbed my knees and hands. My back ached terribly, and my chest burned. My eyes watered so much I could barely see, and my tears streamed onto the ground.

The dark shape ahead of me wasn't moving. If anything had happened to my brother, I didn't know what I'd do.

I had to pause to catch my breath. Spots jumped and flitted before my eyes. My ears rang.

But I was alive.

Just a few more feet and I'd reach my brother. Had he been hit, too, or had the lightning bolt jumped to him from me?

An acrid smell, like burnt flesh and clothing, suffused everything. I prayed it wasn't coming from him.

Suddenly the guards who had been exercising across the yard reached me, running full tilt. Without asking, four of them picked me up and carried me toward the house at a trot.

"Aber—" My voice came out a feeble croak. "Get Aber—"

"They have him, Lord Oberon." The voice sounded distant, as though he stood at the far end of a long tunnel.

Somehow, I managed to focus on the speaker, a young officer with close-cropped blond hair and a slightly hooked nose. He supported my left shoulder as they carried me toward the house at a trot.

"Dead?" I whispered.

His lips moved, but I couldn't hear the words this time. My hearing seemed to be cutting in and out.

Then I started coughing and couldn't stop.

"—lightning hit you, sir," he was saying. "Jace went for the company doctor. Don't try to talk, sir. You're both safe."

"Aber—" I said.

"Can you hear me—Lord Oberon? Lord Oberon?"

"Yes . . ." My voice sounded like a frog's croak. "Is Aber—is he dead?"

His voice sounded louder this time. "Alive. Don't try to talk, sir. He hit his head. He's going to need stitches, but he should be all right."

"Thanks."

My brother still lived—that was all I needed to know. I allowed myself to relax.

They reached the door to the house and carried me inside. I hated feeling like a cripple, but didn't have the strength to object.

The young officer and his men set me down carefully on the floor next to the wall. They all crowded inside, out of the storm, out of harm's way.

My hearing definitely seemed to be returning. I heard crashes of thunder now, though it still sounded flat and far away.

Stripping off his jacket, the young officer folded it into a make-shift pillow and slipped it under my head.

"What's your name?" I asked him.

"Captain Neole."

I began coughing again. The smells of burnt flesh and fabric grew stronger in the close, confined space. After a minute, I realized the smells came from me.

When I turned my head, I saw that Aber now lay beside me. Blood slicked the right-hand side of his face and pooled on the floor under him. A cold panic swept through me. He wasn't moving. Maybe Neole had made a mistake—

I pressed my eyes shut as a coughing fit struck.

The next thing I knew, a white-haired old man was bending over me, his weathered face creased with worry. I must have blacked out again; he hadn't been there a second ago.

He was the castle doctor—I recognized him from Juniper. I had seen him after the first great battle, the one in which Locke and Davin had fallen.

"Lord Oberon? Can you hear me?" he demanded, clapping his hands in front of my face to get my attention.

"Yes . . ." I whispered.

He held up a pair of fingers.

"How many?" he demanded.

"Two." I began a new round of coughing.

"You'll live, I think."

He moved over to Aber, knelt, and felt my brother's pulse.

"Well?" I demanded.

"Unconscious," he said without looking at me. Leaning forward, he probed Aber's head with his fingers. "A shallow scalp wound. It looks worse than it really is. Unless he has some other injuries I can't see, he should be fine in a few days. Your family heals fast."

Suddenly Aber stirred and moaned and tried to sit up. One hand went up to his head, but the doctor caught it and pressed it down at his side.

"Lie still," he said to my brother. "You need stitches."

"Wha—" Aber muttered.

The doctor called for needle and thread, and his assistant produced both. Then, as I watched, he peeled back a loose flap of Aber's scalp and plucked dirt and sand from the wound. It must have hurt; Aber began to thrash. At the doctor's command, six soldiers sit on my brother to keep him down. Two more held his head in place.

"Healing salve!" the doctor called.

He accepted a small jar from his assistant and smeared a greasy yellow-gray concoction liberally onto the wound. Without a second's pause, he began sewing the piece of scalp back in place. His stitches, I noticed, were small and neat.

My brother's wound, I saw, extended across the forehead, just above the hairline. It would leave an impressive scar after it healed.

Unfortunately, he would have to go bald or shave his head to show it off.

I glanced over at the open door. The sky, a dusky gray color that boiled like a soup cauldron, flickered constantly with lightning. I had never seen a such a fierce display of nature's fury. Tongues of light reaching halfway across the sky. Others leaped down and hit the ground, sometimes close and sometimes distant.

The doctor tied off the thread and motioned to the soldiers, who released Aber.

"Anything else hurt?" the doctor asked him.

"Everything!" my brother groaned.

The doctor snorted. "Rest for ten minutes. If you can't walk, these men will carry you to your bed."

"Thanks for caring." Slowly and carefully, Aber sat up and felt his head. "Ow!"

"If it hurts, don't touch it," the doctor said without sympathy. "Let the salve do its work."

"How many stitches?" I asked.

"Thirty-two."

Aber groaned again.

"Don't complain," I told him. "*You* didn't get struck by lightning!"

"I wasn't the target," he said.

"Then you think . . . ?"

"It might have been an attack. On you."

"I was afraid of that," I said. I had a feeling the serpent-creature in the tower of bones might be to blame. After all, I'd killed four of his men and ruined his assassination attempt. That had to bother him. What better way to retaliate than with a lightning storm?

"Or it might not have been," Aber said, sighing. "How will we ever know?"

"Quiet, my lord," the doctor said briskly to me before I could answer.

Like all army doctors, he had the bedside manner of a half-wild goat. "Let me look you over."

I lay unflinching as he poked and prodded me from skull to shinbones. Nothing seemed to be broken, though my skin felt raw. He commented on the number of heat blisters on my hands and face.

"I was lucky," I said.

"Damned bad sort of luck, if you ask me," he said. The words sounded clear and close by. My sense of hearing had almost returned to normal. "A lucky man would not have been hit. You do have your father's constitution, though. Any lesser man would be dead now."

I raised my hands and studied them. Tiny white blisters covered the palms and backs. Not good, but it could have been a lot worse. From the pain I'd felt, I had half expected my hands to be burnt to ash and bone.

"See?" the doctor went on, standing and dusting himself off. "You're barely hurt. A little salve, a few days' rest, and you'll be all right."

"Thanks."

"Can you get up by yourself?"

"I think so."

A little unsteadily, I climbed to my feet. Neole helped steady my arm. I twisted left and right, testing my muscles. My whole body tingled with pins and needles as though circulation had been cut off and was only now returning.

"Good," he said. He took my right hand and began applying a soothing yellow salve to it. Almost instantly the stinging, burning sensation went away. "This will do wonders for those blisters."

Aber grinned feebly up at me. "And with your pretty face messed up for a few days, I'll have a better chance with the ladies," he said.

"It's nice to see you haven't lost your sense of humor," I said.

He gave me a puzzled look. "Oh?"

I concentrated for a moment, willing my face and hands to change, and from the gasps of the doctor and the soldiers, I knew it had worked. My own meager shape-shifting ability had successfully hidden the blisters. I still felt them, though.

"Damned fast healers," the doctor muttered to himself. "Don't know why they bother to call me if—"

"I'll keep that salve, if you don't mind," I said. I plucked the little jar from his hand. "I'll put more on later, when I'm in my room."

"Don't bother," he said. "The blisters are gone now."

"Just in case," I insisted. "I'm sure they'll be back."

"As you wish, my lord." He shrugged, then peered intently at Aber as if expecting my brother to heal instantly, too. When Aber didn't, he just shook his head.

Taking a deep breath, Aber sat up.

"I'll be fine," he told the doctor.

"As you say, Lord Aber." Motioning to his assistant, they headed down the hallway.

Taking a deep breath, I stepped over to the open door and stood gazing out into the darkness. Occasional flickers of lightning crossed the sky, then thunder rolled noisily. Gods, I hated this place.

And something else bothered me. I had a feeling we were being watched . . . that whoever had directed the lightning blast at me was now spying on us through magical means. It might have been the serpent-creature, or it could have been someone else entirely. It might even have been the king's guards. The only sure thing I knew was that I wasn't happy about it.

Well, let them all look. I *wanted* them to see me. I *wanted* them to know we had survived unscathed. Let them do their worse! They were powerless against a son of Dworkin.

With a mocking grin, I gave a casual wave into the darkness, then closed the door and bolted it. Aber's spells would have to keep us safe indoors.

"Do you need anything else?" Neole asked.

I shook my head. "Don't go back outside until the lightning has stopped for an hour," I told him.

"Yes, sir." He saluted, then led his men down the hall.

I offered Aber my hand, and pulled him to his feet.

"Check those tripwires," I told him. "Is the house still clear? Are we being watched?"

"Do you hear any screaming?" he asked.

I listened intently, but heard nothing.

"No."

"You'd hear a scream if someone got in who's not of our blood. A loud, piercing scream that doesn't stop."

"Good." I chuckled. "That should discourage visitors."

Keeping up my shape-shifted appearance began to wear on me, so I let my body slide back to its injured form.

"You said the lightning struck me," I said. "How did you get hurt?"

"I tried to grab you and pull you free. When I got close, it knocked me flying. It felt like a horse kicked me."

"You were lucky," I said.

"We both were. Despite the doctor's opinion."

He went to the door and opened it a crack, peeking out. Over his shoulder, I saw that still more clouds, pierced by the blue lightning, filled the heavens with a crackling, roaring light show like nothing I had ever seen. Bolts continued to strike the ground, and not just inside the wall but outside it as well. The attack appeared to be continuing. If anything, the storm seemed to be gaining strength.

"Is there any way to tell who caused the storm?" I asked. "Or who's controlling it?"

"Dad might be able to . . . or someone as powerful. If someone did cause it. We still don't know for sure."

"What do you mean?" I demanded. "Of course someone caused it!"

"I don't know . . . stranger things have come out of Shadow over the last forty years. We have all seen storms that can travel between worlds. Some of them looked like this, with dangerous blue lightning."

"Maybe you were being attacked, only nobody realized it at the time."

He hesitated. "I suppose that's possible. Though the first such storm came up years ago, before I was born. It killed seventy-six people."

"This one has to be an attack," I said, shaking my head. "If the first three bolts hadn't come so close to me, I might have doubts. But that lightning was aimed at me. Considering everything that's happened, it can't be a coincidence."

He thought about it, nodded, turned back to watch the storm. If anything, the lightning grew more intense, sheets of it flashing across the sky and lighting up the wall and courtyard before us as though it were noon.

"I wish they would hurry up," I murmured to myself.

"Who?" he asked.

"Everyone. Dad if he's still at court. The hell-creatures if they're coming back. King Uthor if he's sending word of Dad's arrest—"

For our father still hadn't returned from his audience with King Uthor.

FIFTEEN

The storm raged on throughout the day. Every time I went to the door and looked outside, the dark sky roiled more violently than before. With a high wind that whistled over the wall and whipped through the house, this clearly wasn't the weather for travel. I pushed back my half-formed plan of visiting King Uthor's court and trying to find out what had happened to our father.

Clearly, I wasn't the only one who found this sudden storm unnerving. A strange hush had descended over the servants. I could not help but notice how they watched Aber and me from the corners of their eyes, how they silenced their voices when we entered a room, then swiftly found duties elsewhere.

They, too, must be remembering our last days in Juniper, when a strange storm had descended on us and lightning bolts began to blast the highest towers to rubble. Fortunately, the lightning here now seemed to be staying high among the clouds. But the similarities still disturbed me. I did not like it that our enemies could control the weather.

I stayed close to Aber as we wandered through the house, checking on the servants and guards, poking into unused corners to see what damage the hell-creatures had done. Although I still became confused by the odd turnings and switchbacks in the halls, I began to sense an order in the seeming randomness. Too, there were landmarks to learn—statues in alcoves, faces of doors, lots of other points from which I could get my bearings.

Aber stayed with me, and I found myself drawing strength and reassurance from his presence. We both needed to plan for the future . . . to find out what had happened to our father. Somehow, I thought I wouldn't feel so helpless if I had a goal to work toward.

We had talked about trying to contact my father and Taine via Trumps. After a hasty lunch of cold meat pies and ale, I broached the subject with Aber once more.

"I'm not contacting Dad," he said. "I don't mind bringing out any Trumps you want, but more than that—no. I've learned better."

"Fine," I said. "I don't mind doing the work. Get me Trumps for Dad and Taine. I'll see what I can do."

"Let's move into the library," he said, glancing pointedly around the dining room. No servants were in evidence, but they could easily walk in on us at any moment. "It's more private there."

"All right. I know where it is. I'll meet you there."

He gave me a puzzled look, but didn't ask how I knew. Pushing back from the table, he hurried from the room.

I drained my ale, then strolled out to the front hall. Extra lamps had been lit, reducing the gloom somewhat, and I went into the library. With its thousands of ancient scrolls and old, leather-bound volumes along the walls, it seemed the perfect place to try my first magical experiments.

Aber returned perhaps fifteen minutes later. He had taken the time to wash up and change into fresh clothes. He carried not just the two Trumps I'd asked for, but a deck of perhaps thirty cards.

"Why so many?" I asked.

"In case you want to talk to anyone else." He set them facedown on the table. "This is a family deck, no places just faces."

I picked up the top card. About the size and shape of the tarot cards used by fortune-tellers in Ilerium, it felt cool to the touch, like ancient ivory. A rampant lion had been painted on the back in gold.

"I recognize your work," I told him. "You painted this one."

"Years ago. Turn it over."

I did so, revealing the portrait of a dark-haired man of perhaps twenty-two, with a thin moustache and our father's piercing eyes. He had an almost mocking half-smile on his face. He dressed entirely in dark reds, from his shoes to his hose to his shirt with the puffed velvet sleeves, and he leaned casually on a long wooden staff. A thin white dueling scar showed on his left cheek.

"From the scar, this must be Taine," I said.

"That's right."

"He doesn't look much like this anymore."

"It will still work, if he's reachable. Try him first."

I chuckled. "Don't think you can fool me. You're avoiding Dad."

"Damn right."

Raising the card, I stared at Taine's picture. The few times I'd used Trumps previously, simply picking them up and concentrating on the picture had been enough to bring the person or scene to life before me. First would come a sense of contact and motion, then the figure would seem to become three-dimensional and lifelike, and we would be able to talk.

This time, however, I sensed nothing from the card. I might have been staring at a blank piece of paper, for all the good it did.

"Well?" Aber finally asked.

"Nothing," I said. "He's not there."

Aber nodded. "It happens. He's either dead, unconscious, or in a place where Trumps don't work."

Of course, we had no way of telling which.

"The next card is Dad's," he said, "if you still want to talk to him."

"I do. What's the worst that can happen?"

"Plague, pestilence, death . . ." He shrugged. "Dad can be pretty creative."

"So can I."

"Yes, but you haven't promised to throttle me if I bother you with a Trump again."

"Not yet, anyway." I had to laugh at his sour expression. "But I am thinking about it, the way you keep popping into my bedroom unannounced."

"Go on, then. Call him."

I drew the next Trump from the stack and turned it over. It showed our father, all right, but dressed rather comically in a jester's outfit—complete with bells on his pointy-toed purple slippers. His image gazed up with an idiotic grin frozen on its face.

"If this is how you paint him, no wonder he's annoyed."

Aber chuckled. "You know it's the subject that matters, not how he's dressed. I made this one when I was mad at him."

"It shows."

"Well, he deserved it as the time. He has never been fair with me."

"You complain too much about it."

He sighed. "You don't understand."

I raised my eyebrows, but he didn't elaborate. Probably ashamed of whatever incident brought on this bout of petty annoyance. He certainly had a problem with our father . . . but wasn't that something all sons worked through? Perhaps in some ways I'd been the lucky one, growing up believing myself an orphan.

"Go on, call him."

"In good time," I said. "One bit of advice first. Don't let him see this Trump."

"Oh, he's already seen it. He found it amusing."

I just shook my head. Sometimes I thought I'd never understand my new-found family. If someone drew me that way, I'd have his head on a silver platter . . . not that it mattered now. We had more important work.

Taking a deep breath, I raised Dad's Trump and stared into the jester's intense blue eyes. Almost immediately I sensed a consciousness, and the image stirred slightly, but no direct contact followed. I stared harder, *willing* a connection between us. I knew he was out there.

Finally I heard a distant, almost petulant voice say: "*Not now,* my boy."

"But—" I started. He had to know what had happened for his

own safety.

"Not now!"

Contact broke off. My instructions were clear, but I had no intention of following them. This was more important. Holding up the Trump, I tried several times to reach him again, but could not. Something prevented me from reaching him.

Tossing the card onto the table, I leaned back in my chair and steepled my fingers, thinking. What could be so important he couldn't spare two minutes?

"Well?" Aber demanded.

I glanced over at my brother. For once, he seemed genuinely concerned, so I told him what Dad had said.

"Not now," I went on, warming to the subject, "has to be the most frustrating phrase ever invented. I hated it as a child, and I hate it more today. *'Not now!'*"

He chuckled and gave me an I-told-you-so look.

"'Not now,'" he repeated. "Is more helpful than you realize. At least we know he's alive."

"True," I said.

"Did you hear any screaming while you talked to him?"

"No. Why?"

"The dungeons under the palace are filled with prisoners. If he were locked up inside, I'm sure you'd hear screaming."

I chuckled. "You don't have to sound so hopeful. No, he isn't being tortured, nor is anyone around him. It's like you said—he's in the middle of something and doesn't want to be disturbed, no matter how important it might be. Arrogant, conceited little—"

He held up a hand for silence, so I ended my tirade before it had really begun.

"What if," he said, "he's being watched too closely to talk to us right now?"

"What do you mean?"

"Think about it. If someone is holding a knife to his throat, he won't be in any position to communicate."

"True," I said, conceding his point. "But does he have to be so rude, arrogant, and conceited about it?"

"You're getting a taste of what I went through. And he *likes* you!"

"I'll count myself lucky to have learned anything," I said. "Dad's still alive. That's more than we knew before."

"I suppose," he said.

Actually, it created more questions than in answered. What had he been doing? Why couldn't he talk? And why hadn't he come back here after his audience with King Uthor?

Sighing, I picked up the deck of Trumps and flipped through them quickly, not letting my attention rest on any single card longer than necessary. Freda . . . Blaise . . . Davin . . . Pella . . . all my half-brothers and half-sisters were there, plus several other people I didn't recognize. For a second I toyed with the idea of contacting Freda to tell her what had happened and get her advice, but then I decided against it. She had orders not to talk to anyone via Trump to protect her location. I didn't want to endanger her. Considering how many relatives we had already lost, and how determined our enemies seemed to be, leaving her alone seemed like the safest plan for now. For all I knew, that serpent-creature might be spying on us again.

"Is this an extra set of Trumps?" I asked.

"Yes. Why?"

"I'd like to keep it for a few days, if that's all right."

He shrugged. "Fine."

We stayed in the library for a few hours longer, talking more like two old friends catching up with each other than brothers. It felt good to sit and take a moment to catch my thoughts.

"How did you come to know so much about magic and Shadows?" I asked him at one point. "Dad doesn't seem to be the best teacher . . ."

Aber gave a derisive snort. "The only thing I learned from *him* was how to make Trumps—and I mostly taught myself after watching him make one. I used trial-and-error until I got it to work. It was my Aunt Lanara who taught me the most, though. A true Lady of Chaos. Very strong, though she didn't approve of Shadow worlds, or of Dad. Still doesn't, I suppose."

"I thought only Locke's mother came from Chaos—"

"That sounds like Locke, all right," he said sarcastically. "He thought that only *his* mother was good enough. She is a first cousin to King Uthor, you know. It broke her heart when Locke sided with Dad and ran off to have adventures in Shadow."

"And your mother?" I asked. "What about her?"

"Not nearly so grand or well connected as Locke's. But she loved Dad, though he tossed her aside and vanished into Shadow shortly after I was born. She's dead now, and I don't remember much of her."

"What happened?"

"She tried to follow Dad into Shadow, and she couldn't handle it . . ." His voice broke a little. "They found her dead. Strangled. For a while everyone thought Dad did it, but it turned out to be a cult of volcano-worshippers. They made her a sacrifice."

"I'm sorry," I said, nodding sympathetically. Her end must not have been a pretty one. I remembered how, on my first trip to Juniper, Dad had laid traps—ranging from tornadoes to giant carnivorous bats—for anyone following us. If Aber's mother had run into one of those, I didn't wonder that she had lost her life.

He sighed philosophically. "It was a long time ago. Shadows were new back then. People weren't as experienced with them as they are now, nor as wary."

"What do you mean?" I said. "Shadows were new? What are you talking about?"

He looked at me oddly. "Just what I said."

"How can they be new?"

"Well . . . they just suddenly appeared one day. All these Shadow worlds . . . Juniper, your Ilerium, all the others . . . they haven't existed long. One day, they simply sprang into existence. I thought everyone knew that."

"Not me," I said. Once more I found myself rearranging my mental view of the universe. "I assumed they always existed. Everyone kept calling them Shadows . . . I thought they were shadows cast by the Courts of Chaos. At least, that's what Freda told me, I think . . ."

"It's one theory," he said with a shrug. "Chaos does cast Shadows. We're in one now—the Beyond. It's the closest shadow to the Courts, and it's always been here, as far as I know. It's so close it's considered part of the Courts of Chaos. But the other Shadows . . . the nice ones, where Dad and everyone else likes to roam . . . they didn't exist when my mother was young."

"When did they appear?"

He thought for a minute. "I don't quite know. Maybe fifty years ago, as Chaos counts time. Maybe a little more."

"And they just suddenly appeared?"

"Well . . . it wasn't quite that simple, or so I'm told. I wasn't there, after all. According to my grandmother, a huge storm descended on the Courts of Chaos. No one had ever seen anything like it before. The sky went black and quiet. The stars disappeared. Then the ground began to shake and split apart, and whole cities were destroyed. Thousands died. Only afterward did things begin to return to normal . . . though—at least according to my grandmother—nothing was ever quite as good as it had been before."

"How old is our father?" I asked, feeling a strange prickling sense of foreboding.

He shrugged. "I'm not sure anymore. Time runs differently in Shadows. He's been out there a long time. But his oldest child—as Chaos reckons time—must be thirty-five or forty now."

"Then he's old enough to have lived through that storm—the one that came before these new Shadows appeared?"

"Sure. I know he is. Why?"

"Oh . . . no reason. Just curious."

I did not voice my sudden suspicion. He was old enough. He

was interested in science and experiments. What if our father not only enjoyed these new Shadows . . . but had actually done something to *create* them?

No, that was impossible—how could one man create thousands upon thousands of worlds? No single person could possibly wield so much power. He would be like a god. And if our father *did* have god-like powers, he certainly hadn't shown them. He had allowed us all to be trapped in Juniper. He had let his children die at the hands of unknown enemies. No, it was a crazy idea, and I pushed it to the back of my mind.

And yet, some distant part of me noted, such power would make him a man to be feared. It *would* explain why someone was trying to kill him . . . and the rest of us too . . . wouldn't it?

SIXTEEN

everal hours later, the storm still raged outside, and it seemed to be growing worse. I heard wind constantly now, howling like a wild animal. This time at least I knew it was real, not something imagined or hallucinated. Thunder growled constantly, too, a low, steady rumble.

Twice Aber and I walked back to the courtyard door and looked out, and the last time we saw three distant tornadoes over the wall, their funnels black as night as they twisted and turned. And yet they did not seem to be gliding across the land, the way tornadoes did in Ilerium . . . these seemed rooted in place, swaying back and forth like the pendulums of some enormous clock.

"Have you ever seen tornadoes here before?" I asked Aber.

"No," he said, "and I don't think it's a good sign."

"Can you do anything about them?"

He gave me a funny look. "I think you have an exaggerated idea of my magical abilities."

At that, I laughed. "It seems I've always underestimated people. About time I started overestimating them!"

He laughed too, but uncertainly.

After a long break, when it seemed they wouldn't be able to go back outside because of the storms, the guards asked for permission to resume their exercises in the front entry hall.

"Go ahead," I told Captain Neole, looking at Aber for guidance. As I expected, he gave a subtle half nod. "Just don't break anything."

They made room by moving the lamps, braziers, and odd bits of furniture to one side. I had to admit the chamber was big enough, and as long as they watched out for the rows of tall stone columns running down the center, they seemed in no immediate danger.

They worked through a series of exercises, then began pairing up to practice swordplay. I found myself watching from the library door, a bit enviously. Part of me longed to join them, to forget myself for at least the next few hours in grueling physical exertion, but I didn't feel up to it. Tired and sore, with a headache that threatened to split my skull, I wanted nothing more than to curl up in bed and sleep for the next few days.

"That's it," I told Aber. "I'm going to bed."

He seemed surprised. "Already?"

"I've had it," I said. "Between visions and lightning bolts, my head feels like it's going to explode. Wake me if we're being attacked and slaughtered, or if Dad shows up. If it's anything else, solve the problem yourself!"

"Can you find your way back to your room?"

"Sure." I felt certain I could, at least from the main staircase. I'd been up it often enough to get my bearings. "What about you? Your day has been just as hard."

"True. But I have some work to do first," he said.

"Oh?"

He laughed. "Nothing you'd find exciting or interesting. Just some letters to write."

"To anyone I know?"

"Distant cousins, whom I'm hoping will prove sympathetic to our situation."

"Good idea," I said. For once, he was thinking like a soldier: find allies and bring them into the fight on your side. If I knew anyone here, I wouldn't have hesitated to summon their help.

He went to the desk and retrieved quills, a short-bladed knife for cutting down the point, and writing paper, all of which he arranged within easy reach.

I left him there bent over the table, pen in hand, and the scritch-scratch noises followed me out into the hall.

Safely back in my room, I undressed and gave my clothes to Horace, who made as if to leave with them. Then he paused.

"Sir?"

"What is it?"

"Do you need me to watch your sleep tonight?"

I thought about it, then shook my head.

"No need. I'll be fine. Go to bed and catch up on your own rest."

"Yes, sir!" I didn't have to tell him twice—he hurried into his room and shut the door before I could change my mind.

Then I turned toward my bed. A subtle movement of the bedclothes warned me that they weren't empty. An assassin? Or was it another trick of this accursed place, where down was up and everything moved on its own?

I couldn't take any chances. Softly I crept over to the chair where I'd so carelessly hung my swordbelt moments before. Drawing the blade slowly and silently, I inched closer to the bed, reached out, and flipped back the covers.

A familiar and quite beautiful face peeked out at me.

"Rèalla!" I said with delight, relaxing.

"A sword?" She lowered her eyes, then smiled up at me. "Is this the way you welcome lovers to your bed, Lord Oberon?"

"Not usually."

I returned my sword to its scabbard at the desk. Then I joined her in bed. We kissed, and made love frantically, as though it might be the last thing either one of us did.

Far too early the next morning—at least, I assumed it was morning—I awakened from a deep and dreamless sleep to Aber's annoyingly chipper voice.

"Wake up, Oberon. Too many hours in bed will make you weak!"

"Go away!"

"I'm hungry, and I see no reason to eat alone with you in the house. Time to get up."

I groaned, then closed my eyes again.

"Port, throw him out!" I called

"Sorry, Oberon," my door replied. "I am not a bouncer. You will have to throw him out yourself."

"Don't be a slug-a-bed!" he told me. I heard him open the wardrobe's doors and rummage around inside. "You've got plenty of clothes here. Pick something or I'll pick it for you."

I sighed. So much for a quiet morning in bed. All I wanted to do was go back to sleep. After making love to Rèalla half the night, exhaustion threatened to overwhelm me.

"Is Dad back yet?" I asked, eyes still closed.

"No."

"How about the hell-creatures?"

"No sign of them, either."

"Then what's the rush?"

"I'm hungry!"

I rolled over, opening one eye. Golden light bubbled up from the lamp by the door. He stood before me with arms folded, tapping one foot impatiently. He had gray silk pants and shirt tucked under his arm.

"Ready to get dressed?" he said. "Where's your valet?"

"Sleeping, like any sensible person!" I told him. "Now, go back to bed. I need my sleep. I'll have lunch with you later."

"Afraid not. We have too much to do today. I'm expecting replies to my letters. And don't you want to try Dad's Trump again?"

I gave a huge sigh. Clearly he wasn't taking no for an answer. Sitting up, I swung my legs over the side of the bed, then pulled the sheet across my lap to cover my nakedness.

"All right, pest. Give me the clothes."

"Here." He held them out, and I took them.

Behind me, still buried in the covers, Rèalla stirred and murmured a sleepy question.

"It's just my brother Aber," I told her. I rubbed her back through the quilt. "Go to sleep."

"Who's that—" Aber began, leaning forward to see.

"Don't be nosy," I told him. "I know you won't approve, but I couldn't help myself. She's beautiful and smart . . ."

Without warning, my brother sucked in a panicked breath and leaped back, looking desperately around the room. He motioned frantically for me to stay silent and get out of bed. Running to the desk, he began to fumble with my swordbelt.

"What *is* it?" I said impatiently, yawning.

"Oberon," he said. Something in the quiet tone he used set my nerves on edge. *"Get away from the bed.* Don't argue. Do it quickly. You're in danger."

My breath caught in my throat. Danger? What had he seen?

Suddenly wide awake, I stood and took two quick steps toward the door. Port's face appeared there, staring at us with concern.

"What is it?" I demanded.

Rèalla stirred again and rolled over, half opening her eyes.

"Oberon?" she asked.

"Don't move," I told her. I scanned the covers, looking for anything dangerous—snakes, spiders, some Chaos-born monster—but saw nothing unusual or out of place.

Rèalla, head pillowed on her arm, blinked and looked up at me. She was even more beautiful by day—not that you could tell from the lack of windows.

Aber drew my sword and turned toward the bed, a grim expression on his face.

Chaos and Amber

"Hey!" I told him. "What are you doing?"

"Get out of the way, Oberon."

"What is it?" I demanded. "What do you see?"

"A succubus!"

In one swift motion, he leaped toward my lover.

SEVENTEEN

ait!" I cried, leaping in front of him. "What do you think you're doing?"

Rèalla screamed. I knew Aber meant to kill her, and I couldn't allow that. What had she done to provoke him? Why this half crazed, half desperate response?

He skidded to a stop. Rèalla gave another ear-piercing shriek and threw herself behind the bed, trying to hide in the bedclothes.

"Stand aside!" Aber said. He tried to dance around me.

I blocked his way. With a feint, then a quick punch to his stomach, I took the air and the fight out of him. He doubled over, and I took the opportunity to pry my sword from his fingers.

"Have you gone you insane?" I demanded. Crossing to the desk, I returned my blade to its scabbard.

"She's—" he gasped.

"She's mine," I said fiercely.

"She's—a—succubus!"

"A what?" I demanded.

"A female demon." He glared at her. "They feed on the blood of their lovers. Look at yourself, Oberon!" His finger stabbed at my chest. "You're marked! She's been feeding on you!"

Involuntarily, my hand rose to touch my chest. The welt I'd dis-

166

covered yesterday was still there, though smaller. But now I felt a second one next to it.

A chill swept through me. Rèalla had been drinking my blood? No wonder I had twice awakened to find her in my bed. No wonder she wanted to be with me. I could not believe what a fool I had been.

"Rèalla," I said, voice very calm. I wouldn't let her see how unnerved I had become. "I don't believe you've met my brother. This is Aber."

"No, Oberon," she said, peeking out at us. "I have not had that pleasure."

"Come here," I told her.

Silently she rose and came around, covering herself with the sheet. I put my arm around her shoulders in a protective gesture.

"How can you keep that *thing* in your bed?" Aber demanded, staring from me to Rèalla and back again. "Kill it! Kill it and be done, before it kills you!"

"Rèalla is a good woman. I enjoy her company." I turned and gazed down at her, allowing myself a wistful smile. That much at least was true. And she was startlingly beautiful, which didn't hurt.

"Not as much as she enjoys yours." He jerked his chin toward my chest. "You are nothing to her but food!"

"No!" Rèalla cried. "Those are love bites! I would not hurt him—"

"Shh," I told her. I gave her hand a reassuring squeeze. "You don't need to explain yourself to him. Or to me. If you need blood, you may take as much of mine as you need to live, but no more."

Aber howled, "*Oberon!* You don't know what you're saying! You don't know what you're offering! She'll drink you dry!"

"Never!" Rèalla vowed fiercely. "I will take only what I need, no more!"

"I believe her," I said.

"Her kind has a barbed tongue," Aber went on, glaring up at us. "They drink the blood of men who take them to bed. She will feed on you every night until you are too weak to resist, then she will reveal her true form."

"True form?" I asked.

"You would not like it," she said, and for once she refused to meet my gaze. "I much prefer this one. It is . . . elegant."

Aber climbed to his feet. "I never thought a succubus would dare to feed on a Lord of Chaos—you *must* kill her, for that insult alone!"

I looked at Rèalla again, and this time she turned her eyes toward mine. In those depths I thought I saw a warmth, a spark of love for me. I believed she really *did* care for me. Just as I had begun to care for her . . .

She said, "Oberon . . . you must believe me . . . I mean you no harm."

"Why not?" Aber demanded, voice shrill. "You're an assassin! You were sent to kill him! Admit it!"

"Go on," I told her softly. I took her hand and pressed it to my lips. "Tell me the truth. It doesn't matter if you came to kill me. My feelings for you won't change. But I must know."

"If I wanted him dead, he would be dead already!" she snapped at Aber. "I had plenty of time to kill him . . . but I did not."

"Your mark is on him!" he said.

"I mark all who take me to bed. It is a sign of love!"

"Love? Hah! Your kind cannot love!"

She spat at him. "We love more fiercely than you will ever know. You are unworthy of such love!"

Aber's face grew flushed, and his hands knotted into fists. "How dare you—" he began. I had never seen him so lost for words. "How dare you—"

"Don't spit on the carpets," I murmured to Rèalla. "They're expensive." Then, turning to Aber, I said, "And you're exaggerating the problem."

Aber shook his head. "You're mad," he said in a hurt voice. "She has you bewitched. When Dad finds out—"

"I know what I'm doing," I said. "I'm not a child in the first flush of love."

"You're acting that way!"

"Trust me."

He shook his head, and his voice dropped to a whisper. "Let me kill her, if you can't do it. She's a spy and an assassin. She's dangerous. She *will* kill you in your sleep. It is her nature."

"We all have to die sometime," I said, "and I can think of many worse ways than in bed with a beautiful woman."

"This isn't a game, Oberon."

"No," I said firmly, "it *is* a game—a very dangerous game. But it's necessary if we're going to find out what's really going on." I put my arm around Rèalla's shoulders. "She told you she will not kill me. I believe her. That's the end of it."

"Thank you," Rèalla said.

Aber stared from one of us to the other. "You *are* mad. Both of you. This cannot be permitted—"

I kissed Rèalla. "Go into the next room. Let me speak to my brother alone."

"Yes, Oberon," she said demurely. With a triumphant glance in his direction, she turned and hurried through the little door at the back of the room.

Aber stared at me like I'd just grown a second head. "Don't do this, Oberon. She's toying with you. She wants something, and it's not your love. She'll kill you when she's ready."

"If I were so easy to kill," I said, "I would have died years ago. That which doesn't kill you makes you stronger, they say."

"No. I've seen her kind before, Oberon. She will work on you slowly. You'll grow pale and weak, you'll lose your will to fight, and then you'll die." He set his feet stubbornly. "I'm not going to let that happen!"

"She can no longer be a lover to me," I said in a low voice, glancing at the door. It was firmly shut; I knew she couldn't hear us talking. "I know that. You've ruined her for me. Now she is just a tool . . . and I will use her to get to our enemies."

He shook his head, and I could tell he didn't believe me. "I don't want to have to explain to Dad how you ended up with a succubus in your bed," he said. "I know I can't stop you. But be careful, okay? Watch who you let into your room and your bed."

"I'll tell Dad everything myself when he gets back," I promised. Then I cleared my throat. "And, speaking of letting people into my room . . . I don't recall Port announcing you. How did *you* get in here?"

Aber stared at me like I had sprouted two extra heads. "How can you care when—"

"I do." I smiled pointedly. "Just taking your advice to heart, dear brother. I can't have people barging in on me at all hours of the day and night, after all. Now, where's that Trump? I want it. *Now.*"

He crossed back to the spot by the door where I'd first noticed him. There, he bent and picked up what looked like a small Tarot card. He must have dropped it when he saw Rèalla.

He returned and silently handed it to me. It was smaller than the other Trumps I had seen, but like the others it felt cool and smooth, as though carved from bone or ivory. Though the rendering was crude, one side showed my bedroom to the smallest detail, from the high canopied bed to the wash stand and looking glass. The back had been painted a simple gold color, without the rampant lion design in the middle. I had never seen a Trump like this one before.

"Whose is it?" I asked.

"Mine."

I raised my eyebrows. "It doesn't match your other Trumps." I flipped it over and held it up. "And you're a better artist than this."

"It was one of the very first I made, when I was ten or so. I used to use it to sneak in here and visit Mattus late at night. I dug it out when I wanted to check on you—it's the only one I had for this room." He shrugged. "For all the thanks I got . . ."

I snorted, then tossed the Trump onto my bed. "Yes, I'm ungrateful. I'll keep it, if you don't mind."

"I do mind. Dad won't be happy," he said, folding his arms stubbornly. "I'm supposed to be watching you."

"You're not doing a very good job of it, and a Trump of my bedroom isn't going to help. Besides, I value my privacy. You can have it back when I'm not sleeping here any more."

"But how can I watch you if you lock the door?"

"I have to have some way to keep the monsters out."

"Or in!"

I chuckled. "That, too."

"You're the most conceited brother I've got. And that's saying a lot."

"Port!" I called.

The face appeared in the middle of the door. "Yes, Lord Oberon?"

"My brother is not to be admitted inside my rooms unannounced," I said. "If you see him appear inside through magical means, give a warning shout, will you?"

"Very good, sir."

"And open up for him, will you? He's just leaving."

Aber sighed and shook his head in frustration.

"It's all right," I told him. Stepping forward, I clasped his shoulder and gently turned him toward the door. "Neither Rèalla nor I meant any insult to you. I know you're trying to look out for me. Go downstairs. I'll join you for breakfast in five minutes. Wait for me."

As my door unlocked itself and swung open, he stomped out into the hallway, muttering about insanity running in our family.

He was probably right. Every member of our family seemed to have more than his fair share of problems. Our father was a compulsive liar. Aber felt a constant need to prove himself. My sisters Blaise and Freda were obsessed with spying on each other—and on everyone else. Even Locke, supposedly such a great and noble warrior, the best of us all, had been a petty, paranoid, jealous, and thoroughly obnoxious prig, unwilling to accept anyone who might threaten his favored status as firstborn son. That's why he had hated me. That's why he had prevented our father from bringing me to Juniper to join the rest of our family until it was almost too late.

Feeling tired and old, I retrieved Aber's Trump from the bed and put it on the desk, next to my sword. I'd take it with me when I went out, in case I needed to find my way back here quickly. Then I began to get dressed.

Rèalla returned just as I finishing pulling on my boots. She looked splendid again, in a pale, shimmering green gown. I smiled and pulled her to me, feeling nothing but regret. Why did the beautiful ones always mean trouble?

"You are angry?" she asked.

"At you? No." To my surprise, I found I honestly wasn't angry at her. I wished she had told me the truth at once, but she could not help her nature.

"Good." She buried her head in my shoulder. "I thought I had lost you."

"No." I hugged her tight, but I could feel a new tension between us. Our perfect moment had passed.

The door to the hall still stood open. My valet poked his head in, saw us, smirked, and had the good sense to withdraw—closing the door in the process. At least someone here had manners.

As I held Rèalla, I could feel the flutter of her heart. A dangerous game indeed, I knew, leaning forward and breathing her musky scent. She had to think nothing had changed between us, at least for now.

There was an old saying . . . hold your friends close, and your enemies closer. I thought of that as I cupped her chin in my hand, and kissed her long and passionately. So beautiful . . . and she had come to betray me. To suck my blood, my strength, my life.

When we came apart for air, she took both my hands and gazed into my eyes.

"I trust you, Oberon," she said, searching my face. "I do not trust many men. Do not let me down."

"I won't," I said.

And yet I felt my love for her slipping away. I had been a fool, a childish, impulsive fool. I never should have trusted anyone in this place. I should have let Aber kill her. I should have done anything other than what I had done . . . and what I knew I would continue to do.

Women had always been my one great weakness. Years ago, in Ilerium, when I was sixteen and a raw recruit in King Elnar's army, I spent a night whoring with my friends after a particularly bloody campaign against the Nazarians. That night a much-scarred old captain named Mezeer pulled me aside.

"You have real promise," Captain Mazeer had said to me, and I saw then that he was very, very drunk. "Don't . . . don't throw it all away."

"What do you mean?" I asked him.

"I've seen the way you look at women . . . I've seen the way they

look at you. . . . You're too handsome . . . too trusting." He hic-
cupped. "It's a bad combination. So . . . my young friend . . . watch
your step. A woman . . . a woman will get you killed if you don't."

It had been good advice. And I had never taken it.

Instead of running for my life, I kissed Rèalla again. She leaned
into my arms, body lightly thrust against mine, lips warm and soft,
the smell of her filling my nostrils.

Kissing her this way, my anger disappeared. I had nothing to
fear from her, I thought, as I felt her body responding to mine. True,
she had been using me. And yet, in my own way, I had been using her
as well. She had been an anchor to normality for me, a way to hold
onto my old life.

I no longer needed such a support. Instead, I would turn her to
my own purposes.

"Tell me why you really came here," I said.

"Because . . ." She hesitated, searching my face, and I saw the
shame of betrayal in her eyes. I nodded slightly, encouraging her; I
could use that emotion—bend it, reshape it to my needs, and make it
serve me.

I said, "Because you love me."

She nodded.

"For us to continue," I said, "I must know everything. We cannot have secrets. Tell me, who sent you here?"

"Lord, I must not! None of us will be safe!"

"No one will harm you. I promise."

She bowed her head. "It was Lord Ulyanash," she whispered.

Ulyanash . . . the name meant nothing to me. Could he be the serpent I had seen in my visions, torturing my brothers and spying on me?

"Describe him," I said.

"He is tall and dark, with long black hair, two small white horns, and red eyes, like coals." She hesitated. "He was born of a minor house, I know, but his ambitions are well known. He has many friends and supporters in King Uthor's court these days . . ."

"Is that where you met him?"

"Yes. I was in the employ of Lady Elan. He . . . persuaded her to place me into his service."

I nodded; the stealing of servants was a much-practiced tradition in Ilerium among the nobility. It seemed little different here.

"What else can you tell me about him?" I asked.

"I think he does not care about you. He did not know who you were before he sent me here—all he had was your name. He could not even tell me what you looked like."

"That's why you asked who I was in the hallway, the first time we met?"

"Yes. But this plan was not of Lord Ulyanash's design. He does not have the imagination."

"You were to kill me, weren't you?"

She could not meet my gaze. Head down, she nodded.

"Why didn't you?" I asked.

"I could not! You were so kind to me . . . you treated me like an equal, not a servant." She hesitated. "And . . . I liked you. Even though it will cost me my life when he finds out, I could not obey. I could not kill you."

"Thank you for that." I hugged her close. Her heart fluttered in her chest; I could feel it as our skins touched. Then, as I nuzzled her neck, wondering how much more she knew, I felt her shiver.

"Why does he want *me* dead?" I asked. That was the one thing I did not understand. "Why not my father, or my brother Aber? I have no power here. They are the ones who matter, not me."

"I do not know, Oberon." She pulled away and perched on the edge of the bed, sighing deeply. "For some reason, Ulyanash fears you, and that makes him dangerous. You must be careful in all things. Your enemies here are powerful."

I sat beside her, and a plan began to take form in my imagination. I put my arm around her shoulder, comforting.

"You must go back to Ulyanash," I said.

"No!"

"You must," I said firmly. "Tell him you've done your job and I'm dead. Then see what else you can find out. I need to know whose plan this was, and *why* they want me out of the way. Otherwise their next attempt to kill me may well succeed." I gave her another quick kiss. "Talk to no one else about me. And . . . come back as soon as you can?"

She smiled wistfully. "Yes, Oberon. I will come back. But . . ." She glanced pointedly at the door, and I read her expression.

"Aber won't hurt you. I won't let him—or anyone else here. You are under my protection now, for whatever good that does."

She brightened noticeably. "Thank you, Oberon."

"I'll talk to my brother after you're gone. All right?"

She smiled, squeezed my hand, and gave me a kiss on the cheek.

Then, without a backward glance, she let herself out into the hallway.

Somehow, I had a feeling I would never see her again. Too much could go wrong with my plans. If Ulyanash had other spies in our household, or had other ways of spying on us, he would soon discover Rèalla's deception. And if that happened . . .

Sighing, I headed downstairs to find Aber.

EIGHTEEN

Throughout breakfast, Aber pretended to pout and hold a grudge. Course after course arrived, was served, and then carted away by attentive servants. At last, depositing vast trays of fruit and cheese on the table, they left us alone.

Aber sighed. "Sometimes," he said, addressing no one in particular though I knew he meant it for me, "I think I'm the only one left in this family with any sense."

"Sense, but no vision."

He turned his head in my direction. "What's that supposed to mean?"

"Had we done the sensible thing in Juniper, we would all be dead now. We have to do the unexpected, the courageous, the daring. It's the only way we can hope to win. You need to see the proper path. It's not always the safe one."

He snorted. "You sound like Dad now."

"That's a good thing."

I leaned forward, looking him in the eye, and bluntly told him of my plans for Rèalla . . . how she would claim to have killed me, then spy on her master and report back whatever she learned. A little to my surprise, Aber seemed pleased.

"Who is her master?" he asked. "Who sent her here?"

"Some minor Lord of Chaos. His name is Ulyanash."

He paled. "Ulyanash?"

"Do you know him?" I demanded.

"Lord Ulyanash is . . . not a friend. To any of us." His expression hardened.

"Could he be behind it all? The murders? The attack on Juniper?"

"What did your succubus say?"

"She didn't think it was him."

He shook his head slowly. "I don't think so, either. He's an idiot. If he weren't such a good fighter, no one would pay any attention to him. There must be someone else, someone more powerful who's working quietly to control and direct him."

"That's exactly what Rèalla said."

He gave me an odd look. "You found out quite a lot from her, didn't you?"

I shrugged. "You get more from women with kisses than threats. Take a lesson from that."

"Maybe I *was* wrong about her," he admitted. I knew how hard that must have been for him to say. "Just don't promise her too much, okay, Brother? I don't want a succubus for a sister-in-law."

I smiled, letting my eyes go distant. "She *is* beautiful . . ."

"She came to *kill* you!"

I chuckled. "You're too easy to tease. Don't worry, I know what she is and why she came to me. I won't forget. Once her work is done . . ." I shrugged. "Our family and our safety, in that order, is what matters."

He nodded, studying me. I could almost read his thoughts: Perhaps I wasn't quite the naïve and trusting young soldier I appeared. I had the impression he had unexpectedly raised his estimation of me.

"You'll kill her after all?" he asked. "For feeding on you?"

"I never said that."

"No, but . . ."

I went on, "You're too bloodthirsty for your own good. Let me worry about Rèalla. I'll take care of her in my own way, and in my own time."

He gave a half groan. "You're going to end up marrying her, I know it!"

"Forget about her. She doesn't matter. We have important things to talk about."

"All right. Where do we start?"

"With Lord Ulyanash. Tell me everything you know about him."

My brother took a deep breath. "If I recall correctly, his full name is Demaro il Dara von Sartre Ulyanash, Baron of the House of Tanatar and Lord of the Far Reaches. I'm sure there ought to be a couple dozen more titles in that list, too, but I can't remember them."

"Sounds impressive," I said. "Lord of the Far Reaches . . ." I imagined a sprawling castle with vast estates stretching farther than the eye could see.

Aber half sneered. "The Far Reaches are a distant swamp-land, and the House of Tanatar is about as far as you can get from King

Uthor and still qualify as a blood relation. Like I said, it's a minor house."

"Then . . . why attack us?" I asked. "What have we done to him?"

"Nothing, that I know of."

"From what you and Locke told me, we're no threat to him . . . or to anyone else here. So why bother with us? We were all off in Shadow, minding our own business. How can killing us possibly advance Ulyanash's standing—or anyone's?"

"He has always had ambitions beyond his station," Aber said. "His rise in court has been—for lack of a better word—surprising."

"How so?"

"The first time I saw him, he reminded me of a bear strolling through a crystal shop. He didn't know how to act, or who to flatter. He made mistake after mistake, and everyone laughed at him. Finally Lord Dyor decided to make an example of him for other distant relatives to learn from. Dyor arranged a duel by custom methods, and they fought."

"Did you see it?"

"Yes. The whole court did."

"What happened?"

He swallowed hard. "Ulyanash killed him—slowly and brutally. He would not accept satisfaction after first or second blood. If anything, he turned the fight into a brutal, bloody circus. Women were crying. Men begged them to stop. But Ulyanash would not yield his right, and he made an example of Lord Dyor that no one who saw it will ever forget."

"Was Dyor a good fighter?" I asked.

"One of the best in the Courts."

"What happened next?"

"Everyone said Ulyanash was finished. Rumor said King Uthor planned to strip him of his titles and throw him into the Pit of Ghômar for what he'd done. And yet, despite that, nothing happened. Instead of being punished for his effrontery, Ulyanash began attending the best parties and social gatherings, from the Blood Festival to the Feast of the Seven Dials. You couldn't escape him. He moved into the center of everything, and the best men and women stood cheerfully beside him as equals." He shook his head. "They shouldn't have paid any attention to him, considering his family and what he did to Lord Dyor, and yet . . . there he was. Still is, I suppose."

Slowly I nodded. It made sense to me now. Someone powerful had seen what Ulyanash could do and decided to use him. And part of that use had been against our family.

I asked, "Who is his patron?"

"I don't know. He must have one, or he wouldn't have gotten as far as he has. But I never heard anyone speak of it."

"Perhaps they were frightened."

"That's possible. I know he frightens me!"

"Can you guess who might be supporting Ulyanash?"

"No." He shook his head. "I never heard before, and I've been away too long now to make discreet inquiries. My few friends in court have all drifted away and aligned themselves elsewhere. I haven't heard any gossip in years. None of us has, not Freda nor Blaise nor even Locke, though he would have been the best bet. He probably could have found out through his mother's side of the family . . . they have strong connections."

"Death is never convenient," I said. "Forget about Locke. Any other ideas?"

Shaking his head, he said, "Our family has never been very popular. Once Dad inherited his titles, that pretty much finished off our influence in the court. Dad never cared enough to bother making any friends or allies who could help us . . . he was too busy experimenting and building his little toys."

Somehow, considering our family, I wasn't terribly surprised. I sighed. I must have gotten it from my mother's side of the family, but I had never had trouble making friends. I would have to work on building up our list of allies in the Courts of Chaos . . . assuming I lived long enough.

Despite Aber's lack of immediately useful information, I had a feeling I could still learn a few things from him. I decided to try a different approach.

"Let's work backwards," I said. "How many people here have enough power and influence that they *could* raise Ulyanash to his present favored position?"

"That's hard." He frowned, thinking. "King Uthor, of course. Perhaps a few of his ministers. Maybe a dozen Lords of Chaos who are central to the throne and its power."

"Then we have a fairly short list. We'll need to work through it one at a time, trying to eliminate them. I don't suppose any of them look like giant serpents?"

"Afraid not. At least, not the last time I saw them. But that was years ago."

I nodded. "What's Ulyanash like in person? Charming?"

"Boorish and obvious. He never has a good thing to say about anyone but himself. How great a swordsman he is, how many duels he's fought, how many kills he's made."

"He must have *some* useful traits."

"He's a good fighter. Other than that . . ."

That was pretty much what Rèalla had said.

"What else can you tell me about him? Is he vain? Conceited?"

"Both, I'd say. Ulyanash thinks he's better than everyone else, and he's quick to take offense at any slight—real or imagined. He likes to force duels. The one with Taine—"

"What!" I sat up straighter. "He fought Taine?"

"Years ago. He gave Taine that scar on his cheek."

"I didn't know that," I said.

"Is it important?"

"I don't know." I considered the possibilities. "Why didn't he kill Taine, if he had the chance? If he's got it in for our family, he missed a good opportunity."

"Maybe he had no reason to kill Taine at the time."

I mulled it over. It sounded plausible. If they fought their duel before the plot against our family had begun, Ulyanash would have had no reason to kill Taine. A dueling scar to mark his victory would have been enough.

"Did you see the duel?" I asked.

"No, but Blaise did. She was there."

"Of course she was." I sighed. Another dead end, with Blaise off in Shadow, hiding out. She wouldn't be able to tell me anything about Ulyanash's fighting technique.

Aber went on. "I got all the details from her, though. She said it was a game for Ulyanash. He toyed with Taine for ten minutes, making him lunge and stagger, then swatting him on the ass and making his squeal. By the end of the duel, Taine was gasping for breath, dripping in sweat, and horribly embarrassed. Everyone was laughing at him."

"Blaise included," I guessed.

"She said she couldn't help it. Taine looked ridiculous. And Ulyanash . . . well, he loved every moment."

I sighed, envisioning the fight. Clearly it hadn't been pleasant for Taine. There had been more than a couple of men in Ilerium's army who liked to show off their skills with a blade by humiliating lesser fighters in our ranks. I had never put up with it . . . as a common soldier or as an officer.

"And afterwards?" I prompted. "What happened to Taine?"

"He slunk off. I guess he couldn't face anyone in the Courts of Chaos after what happened. I haven't seen him since."

A terrible thought struck me. "Did he leave . . . or was he kidnapped?"

"Kidnapped!" Aber stared at me, a shocked expression on his face. "What do you mean?"

"Think about it," I said, my thoughts reeling through the possibilities. "Suppose someone powerful wanted to capture him and question him about us. And he didn't want anyone in our family to miss him. The duel could have been a ruse, forced on Taine so everyone would think he'd run away. It made his disappearance seem reasonable."

"And all this time he's been a prisoner?"

"Yes."

Aber looked away. Clearly the idea had not occurred to him before. And clearly he did not like it.

"Well?" I prompted. "What do you think?"

"It's unbelievable. You're seeing conspiracies where there can't possible be any."

"I'm not paranoid. People *really are* trying to kill us—"

"Okay, okay." He stood and began to pace. "But if someone wants us dead, why start with a kidnapping? Why not force Locke or Davin into a duel . . . or Dad, for that matter?"

"I don't know. Maybe they wanted to find out more about us first. Maybe they have been attacking us for years, but subtly. No one realized it because no one knew to look for the signs. We may never know the whole truth."

He stopped and looked at me. "Let's assume you're right. Let's assume they've held Taine prisoner since the fight."

"Torturing him, questioning him, and now bleeding him to spy on us. He's been helping them—"

Aber shook his head. "No. I don't believe it. Taine would never betray us. He has a stubborn streak like you wouldn't believe. I *know*."

I considered how defiant our brother had been, even half dead on that altar slab, and conceded the point. No, Taine would not talk—at least, not knowingly.

"The serpent used his blood to spy on us," I pointed out. "He didn't need to talk."

Aber nodded. "Magic is sympathetic. Like is drawn to like. That's why the serpent could use Taine's blood. We—you and I, everyone in our family—are all the same in many ways." He paused. "But I still don't understand why anyone would start a war by kidnapping Taine. He was fairly harmless. Nobody really hated him. Why put him through this?"

"They had to start somewhere," I said. "Maybe Ulyanash considered him the easiest target."

"Easier than me?" Aber laughed. "I don't think so!"

"How many duels have you gotten into?" I asked.

"Well . . . none." He shifted uncomfortably. "I'm not much of a fighter, after all. I'm more of an artist, philosopher, and poet."

"As I'm sure everyone in court knows."

"Yes." He nodded. "I've made Trumps for a lot of people . . . not just family members."

"But what about Taine? Had he fought duels before?"

"Yes." Aber sighed unhappily, as if guessing my thoughts. "He had his share of scrapes and misadventures. It didn't come as a huge surprise to anyone when he got into an argument with Ulyanash."

"Exactly. Ulyanash wouldn't goad you into a duel because you don't fight. He might be stupid, but he knows better than to force a duel with someone like you . . . someone his peers view as weak and defenseless. There's nothing worse than being thought of as a bully. People would turn their backs on him, even his patron. He's not that stupid."

Aber's brow furrowed. "So Ulyanash could take his time with Taine, make sport of him, and really rub it in because everyone knew Taine could defend himself."

"Exactly. It was all in fun, after all. For his trouble, Taine got nothing worse than a scratch on the cheek. The only permanently damage came to his pride. If he couldn't defend himself . . . well, tough luck, everyone thought."

Aber was nodding. "Yes, I understand."

He started to say something more, but at that moment, Captain Neole burst into the room.

"Lords!" the captain cried. "There has been a murder!"

NINETEEN

 leaped to my feet.

"Who is it?" I demanded. Could it be our father? I glanced at Aber, who gulped, eyes growing wide with alarm.

"A demon," Neole said. "Someone threw its body over the back wall a few minutes ago—one of the guards saw it fall. By the time he got outside, whoever did it had gone."

"A demon?"

I didn't know whether to feel horrified or relieved. At least it wasn't a family member this time.

Aber, shaking his head, looking distinctly uneasy.

"What's bothering you about it?" I demanded.

"Rèalla," he said. "It has to be her. You only saw her human form . . . but a succubus is a demon. In death, she would have changed back to her true self."

"But she just left!" I said. It didn't see how it could possible be her. "There wasn't enough time!"

"We don't know that. If Ulyanash found out . . ."

"How could he? You set up those magical tripwires last night. There shouldn't be any more spying."

"I warned you I wasn't very good at it." He looked uneasy.

"Maybe they found a way through or around my spells!"

I took a sharp breath. It couldn't be Rèalla. And yet . . .

"There's an easy way to settle this," I said. Turning to Neole, I added, "Show us."

He saluted. "Yes, sir. This way."

We left through a different door into a strangely desolate garden, filled with twisted, ugly plants the like of which I had never seen. Some bore spiked reddish-orange fruit, and some had nothing but thorns. Among them, moss-covered stones slowly wandered, looking old and tired compared to the ones penned on the other side of the house.

I kept looking up at the sky. As before, masses of clouds swirled wildly overhead, but this time no lightning flickered.

Aber caught up and walked beside me. "Spells take time to prepare," he said in answer to my unasked question. Shading his eyes, he stared toward the heavens. "The bigger the spell, the longer the time. That lightning storm must have been taken hours, maybe days to set properly. Whoever made it was lying in wait for you. It won't happen the same way twice."

"Is that supposed to make me feel safe?" I asked.

"Well . . . in a way, yes."

"It doesn't."

Captain Neole led us to the back wall, which towered twenty feet high. Made of yellow stone, it seemed to completely circle the house. Guards patrolled the top now, gazing out over whatever lay beyond.

Two more guards stood at the base of the wall, next to the body. I swallowed hard as I stared at it. A flat face with jutting cheekbones and round mouth . . . red eyes staring blankly . . . hands like claws . . . skin as dark as old leather . . . none of it looked familiar. The only thing at all familiar, however, was the pale, shimmering green gown. It matched the one Rèalla had been wearing, and I knew at once that this creature, this demon, had to be her.

"Not a woman, but definitely female," Captain Neole was saying. Bending, he tilted her head back so we could see her odd features better.

"Congratulations," I said flatly to Aber. "You got your wish."

"I'm sorry," Aber said softly. When I looked at his face, he seemed genuinely upset. "I would not wish this on anyone, least of all you."

Captain Neole said to me, "Do you know this demon, sir?"

"Yes, I knew her," I said. "Her name was Rèalla. Bury her here, on the grounds, with all appropriate ceremony. She is to be treated with respect. Is that understood?"

"Yes, sir," he said. He motioned to the two guards, and they picked her up and carried her off around the side of the house, following the wall.

"We have a mausoleum," Aber said. "That's where they will take her."

I nodded, feeling cold and numb inside.

Then I looked up at the wall. It had to be three or four feet thick at the top. Whoever had dumped her here had either thrown her over the wall, flown the body up and over, or sent it over by magical means. None of the options left me feeling very safe at the moment. And thunder rumbled distantly, reminding me of our enemies' power to control the weather.

"I doubled the patrols immediately," Captain Neole said to me. "Do you have any other instructions, sir?"

"No. Stay vigilant."

"Yes, sir."

"We will be inside. If anything else happens, summon us at once."

He saluted. I motioned for Aber to follow me and turned toward the house. Head high, I strolled through the twisted garden at a leisurely pace. I had to assume Aber's spells had failed and that our every move was now being observed. Well, let them look! Let them think me unmoved by Rèalla's murder! The creatures of this world seemed to think only of hate and violence and death. First Helda in Ilerium, and now Rèalla here in the Beyond. Our enemies had taken too much from me. It had to stop.

"Oberon," Aber said from behind me, "I'm sorry."

"Me too," I whispered.

I looked up at the seething clouds, then at the sprawling house, which still oozed color from every seam and every crack. At that moment, I knew their deaths would not go unavenged. If I had to make it my life's work, I would find and destroy everyone involved in this conspiracy, from the greatest Lord of Chaos to the least of their minions.

I sucked in a deep breath, and everything suddenly came clear for me. *Bold. Daring. Unexpected.* Our mysterious enemy kept making the first move against us. That would change. From now on, we would act instead of react. If Ulyanash and his masters wanted a fight, I would give it to them. And I would win . . . or die trying.

"Get your Trumps," I told Aber as soon as we entered the house. "Bring them to the library."

"Why?"

"Because," I said, "we're going to be busy. You're going to announce me to all and sundry as Dworkin's new heir, come to the Courts of Chaos to walk the Logrus and claim my birthright."

"But you can't—"

"Can't I?"

He nodded. "It is your right."

"Play it up. Sell me to them. My name must be on everyone's lips. They must all know who I am before this day is over!"

"You're insane!" he said, staring at me.

"Maybe I am." I smiled, lips thin and hard. "First, though, there will be a party for me, hosted by . . . I don't know. Someone you know and trust."

"Who?" he demanded.

"It doesn't matter." I waved my hand grandly. "Pick someone. Anyone. Make sure they accept. Don't take no for an answer."

"But Dad—"

"Has nothing to do with this," I interrupted. "I want to be seen tonight by everyone who matters in the Courts of Chaos. I want each and every one of them, from the highest noble to the lowest slave, to know I've arrived here . . . and that I'm not afraid of them!"

"This isn't wise."

"Wise?" I laughed. "If you're afraid to live, you're already dead!"

"Then I must be dead," he muttered.

"Oh, no." I seized his arm and propelled him toward the stairs and his room. "You've just awakened, dear brother. We've all been asleep far too long here. I'm not going to sit in this house and wait for death to find me. It's time to move—time to leap feet-first into King Uthor's court. We will renew ourselves . . . and our family."

"I don't understand," he said.

"You don't have to. Leave everything to me. Now, get those Trumps, and be quick about it! We have lots of work to do before the party."

My enthusiasm seemed to be catching. Taking a deep breath, he bounded up the stairs three at a time.

We would need new alliances to replace the ones Dad had let slip away. If Ulyanash could do it, why not me? New friends and new allies . . . yes, I could play this game. And I would win.

TWENTY

ou realize," Aber said, "that your plan won't work."

"Why not?" I asked.

We sat in the library, surrounded by books and scrolls. He had brought down a large, intricately carved wooden box packed to the top with Trumps, many showing people and places I had never seen before. Most were distant relatives, he assured me—cousins, aunts and uncles, and grandparents from our father's various marriages. Aber had drawn them over the years and squirreled them in his room until needed.

"Who is this?" I held up a Trump showing a handsome man with moustache and beard. His eyes reminded me of Freda's.

"Vladius Infenum," he said. "Isadora's grandfather on her mother's side. He's dead, I think."

"Murdered?"

"By his wife." He pulled out a different Trump, this one showing a skeletal woman with upturned tusks. "Here, Lady Lanara Doxara de Fenetis. I think she'll do."

"Who is she?"

I regarded her image casually, trying not to stare too hard lest I make contact with her. Her small black eyes had a ravenous quality that made me uneasy.

"Our great-aunt. Dad's mother's oldest sister."

"That's right—you mentioned her before. She taught you to paint, didn't she?"

"Yes."

"Is she well connected?"

"She used to be," Aber said. "She stopped entertaining a decade or so ago, due to frail health . . . though I think that was just an excuse. Her guests tended to overstay their welcomes and eat her out of house and home. She's still well remembered at court, and I think retirement has bored her enough that she might well leap at the chance to help you. Family is important to her." He smiled fondly; I could tell he liked her. "She was a great painter in her day, and she used to give me lessons . . ."

"I thought Dad was to blame for that."

"I inherited his talent. Aunt Lan taught me how to use it. She always said I was her favorite nephew. Dad would more happily have drowned me than taught me anything."

"She sounds ideal for our purposes," I said, changing the subject before he could complain about our father. He seemed to be doing that a lot lately. "Go ahead and ask her."

This just might work. There would be a certain novelty value in dragging an aging Lady back into the social light. People who might normally pass on such an invitation—especially to launch someone unknown into society—would attend just to see her.

He picked up the card, moved to the far side of the room, and stared at it. Over his shoulder, I saw the old woman's picture ripple and start to move. Her hair whitened; her tusks yellowed, and her skin grew as wrinkled as a raisin.

"Aunt Lan!" he said. "It's your nephew, Aber. May I visit you for a few minutes?"

She replied with something I couldn't quite catch, and as I watched, he reached toward her image. In the wink of an eye he disappeared, taking the card with him.

I sat impatiently, hoping it wouldn't take long. I had a feeling our enemies wouldn't be sitting around waiting for us to move. Finally, after perhaps ten minutes, I felt a nagging at the back of my mind and knew someone was trying to reach me via a Trump. It had to be Aber. Opening my thoughts, I looked up.

An image appeared before me, only it wasn't my brother. It was Great Aunt Lanara herself, dressed all in black, regarding me with those dark and hungry eyes set deep in that much-wrinkled face. Her upturned tusks, if anything, had grown longer since Aber had painted her.

"So you are Oberon," she said. Her lightly accented voice held a mild quaver. Slowly her gaze traveled down to my boots and back up again. She seemed to be looking through me to my soul, and I found her scrutiny made me distinctly uneasy. I tried not to show it.

"That's right," I said. I folded my arms and returned her frank stare. "I'm pleased to finally meet you. Aber speaks very highly of you and your work."

"My . . . work?"

"Your paintings."

"He is a good boy." She smiled, lips pulling back in an awful rictus. "He informs me of your own ambitions in court, and that you need an introduction into society. He says you aspire to great-ness and wish to be known in the Courts, to wield power and influ-ence as, in fact, *I* once did."

"As you *still do*," I said politely. "Or we would not have come to you."

Turning her head slightly, she addressed someone I couldn't see: "You were right. I rather like him." I assumed she spoke to Aber.

"I knew you would," came the reply. "He's clearly the prize of Dad's offspring."

She turned back to me.

"Tell me two things first, and tell me honestly. I will know if you are lying. If I like your answers, I will do more than you have asked. Much more."

"Very well." I regarded her impassively. "I will answer truth-fully."

"Who is your mother?"

"My mother was a woman from a Shadow world. Her name was Eilea Santise, if that is important to you."

"It is. Names hold power. Your mother is now dead?"

"Yes. A long time ago."

Lanara nodded slightly. "You are not lying," she said. "And yet you are not telling me all."

"What more do you want?"

"Everything."

I shifted uncomfortably. "I am a bastard, born out of wedlock. Dworkin did not acknowledge me as his son—though in fact he stayed to help raise me—for many years. My mother lied to me her whole life. So did Dworkin . . . Dad. They claimed my father was a sailor who died at the hands of pirates from Saliir."

"Interesting," she said, with a mysterious half smile. "So your link to the throne is only through your father. A pity. Two blood lines are always stronger than one."

"I am as I am," I said. "I make no apologies."

"I did not ask for any. You have spirit. I like that . . . in moderation. I accept your answer."

I inclined my head. "And your second question?"

"How will you pay me for this service?"

I regarded her thoughtfully. "That is the harder question of the two," I said. "You have no need of gold or jewels, so I will not insult you by offering them. Nor do I believe you would put much store in promises of lifelong affection from a bastard grand-nephew whom you have never met before."

"True," she said. "Go on."

"Therefore," I said, "I offer you nothing."

"Nothing?" she asked, as though hardly able to believe it. She threw back her head and howled with laughter. "Nothing! The whelp offers me *nothing!*"

"Nothing," I continued, "except the excitement your actions will bring you." I leaned forward, staring into her eyes. "Think of it, Auntie! A house of ravenous guests, plots and intrigue spinning wildly before you, and the very real possibility of a murderer in your company! I have been marked for death, Aunt Lanara, and so has Aber. Rather than hiding in Shadow, we will seek out our enemies so we may destroy them! Help me, Lanara, and you will help us both!"

"Well spoken," she said, "and I believe you have told me the truth—at least as you see it, for truth is a flexible thing, with many meanings and many edges. Yes, I will help you, Oberon, but you may well come to regret it for the rest of your life. The price for my help will be quite high."

"Name it," I said.

"One of my many nieces, born of my sister Desponda and her husband, Yanar, is named Braxara. To be brutally honest, Braxara is ugly, dull, and stupid. Finding a suitable mate for her proved too difficult for her parents, so now the task has fallen to me."

I swallowed, not liking the direction this conversation had headed. Aunt Lanara smiled like a spider that had just discovered a plump fly in its web. Slowly, she linked her fingers under her chin and leaned forward. I thought it made her look more than a little sinister.

She continued, "If I help you in this matter, I will expect you to marry Braxara in one year's time. That will give you ample opportunity for courtship."

"Perhaps she would be happier with someone like Aber," I suggested meekly.

"I could never wish such a fate on my darling nephew," Lanara said, smiling pointedly. "And it is you, not Aber, who craves my assistance."

One year . . . it seemed forever. Much could change in that time. I could be dead. Braxara could be dead . . . or even promised elsewhere, if a better suitor came along. Better to promise now and reap the benefits immediately of such an alliance.

I bowed my head. "Assuming I live to see my wedding day," I said before she could change her mind, "I accept your terms."

"Good." She smiled again. "I will prepare everything for tonight. The time is short, but it can be done. Aber, dear boy?"

"Yes, Aunt Lan?" I heard him say from somewhere to the side.

"Go back and help Oberon prepare. Come fashionably late, but not *too* late. And Oberon . . ." She turned back to me. "I may be old, but my friends are numerous and their weapons are sharp. Your betrothal will be announced tonight, with vows that cannot be broken. Do not embarrass me, or you will not live to regret it."

She beckoned Aber to her side, and I stretched out my hand to him. When he grasped it, I pulled him back through to the library.

"Do not forget, Oberon!" Lanara said to me, voice distant now and fading. "One year!"

She made a curt gesture, and our contact was broken.

Aber flopped down in the chair next to me.

"That was too easy," he said. He put his feet up on the table and folded his hands over his belly. "Just the sort of plan I like."

"Easy!" I snapped. "You just got me betrothed to an ugly, half-witted cousin!"

"She's not that bad!" He laughed. "At least, not since she got her tails bobbed!"

"Tails? Bobbed?"

"Hers were a little too skinny and ratlike for my taste." He shrugged. "But I'm sure you'll both be very happy together. Her family are always good breeders. Lots of kids will calm you down. Say, thirty or forty to start with. They do tend toward big litters . . ."

I groaned. Somehow, I didn't think he was joking this time.

"And," he went on brightly, "Every time you complain about her, you'll hear a little voice in your head saying, 'At least she's not a succubus!'"

"Thanks . . . I think!"

He shrugged. "Oh, you'll be happy enough. You'll get your introduction to society. And thanks to Aunt Lan, you've got your first allies."

"I do? Who?"

"Why, she and her husband. She liked you a lot."

"How can you tell?"

"She's doing everything you asked. If she didn't like you, she would have said, 'No!'—and not quite so politely. Think of it as a present from her. A wedding present."

"It's not a present if I'm paying for it!"

Aber sighed and shook his head. "You don't understand. She did you a bigger favor with that marriage than you realize. Lord Yanar is one of King Uthor's advisors. Marrying his daughter will confer immediate status on you within the court . . . not to mention a measure of protection. Yanar is powerful and influential."

"Braxara and I aren't married yet," I said with a grim little smile. "And a year is a long time to wait."

"Want me to see if Aunt Lan can move up the date a bit?"

"Not particularly!" I replied with a laugh.

He chuckled in return. "No, I guess you wouldn't!"

"I don't suppose you have a Trump showing Braxara, do you? I'd like to have at least some idea of what I'm getting into."

"Nope. She's not someone I'd ever want to know well enough to paint!"

"Wonderful," I muttered. How bad could my future bride be?

Port chose that moment to speak.

"Sir," he said, face appearing in the center of the door. "Anari wishes to enter."

"Let him in," I said.

Port swung open, and the elderly head of the household hurried inside, breathing hard. He must have run up the stairs, I realized with alarm.

"What's wrong?" I demanded.

"Lords—" he panted. "Lady Freda—has just arrived—and—"

Before he could say another word, I raced past him and into the hall. Freda, here? It could only mean the worst sort of news.

Our sister had been ordered to hide in Shadow until we found our enemy and straightened out this whole mess. Nothing short of disaster should have brought her home early.

TWENTY-ONE

ber raced after me, and side by side we pounded down the broad stone staircase to the cavernous entry hall. There, surrounded by a flurry of movement, stood our sister.

Freda wore a long red silk dress, red shoes, and a matching broad-brimmed hat, now perched at a steep angle atop her head. Heavy gold rings set with large rubies covered her slender fingers and flashed in the flickering light of the lamps. She looked tanned and well, as though returning from a month's vacation at the seaside.

Around her, more than a dozen servants, dressed in what looked like cloth spun from pure silver, were shifting twenty-five or thirty large wooden trunks. Several guards and household servants helped. All the while, six women similarly dressed in silver milled about Freda, some fussing with her hair, others with her clothes . . . she seemed more a pampered princess than the mystic fatalist I had known in Juniper.

"Freda?" I said, reaching the floor. I made way for the first of her trunks, which two men carried up the stairs with grunts and groans.

"Oberon!" She turned toward me with a cool smile. "I trust you are well."

"Yes, despite several assassination attempts."

She showed no surprise at that statement.

"And an impending marriage," Aber added.

That got her attention. "Who is the bride-to-be?"

"Cousin Braxara," Aber said.

"No, no." She shook her head. "That will not do at all."

"I promised our Aunt Lanara," I said.

"I will see it undone later, after I have unpacked." She beckoned Anari over. He had followed us down the stairs at a more dignified pace. "Have my usual rooms prepared. I will be staying."

"Yes, Lady Freda." He bowed.

"Hold on," I said to Anari. Then I turned to Freda. "You're not staying. It's not safe. People are still trying to kill us."

"Bosh," Freda said. "A well-raised Lady of Chaos does not get into such troubles. Not in the Courts, and not in the Beyond. Do you think me a common duelist?"

"Ladies of Chaos don't duel, they poison," said Aber from behind me, his voice a loud stage whisper.

Freda pretended not to hear him.

"I have come to see Father," she said. "Where is he? I have important news. It cannot wait."

"He's . . . not available." I swallowed. "In fact, he doesn't want to be found. He made it clear when I tried to contact him by Trump. He said he'll be back in a few days."

"That," she said, "is not acceptable."

"If you have a better plan . . ."

"Of course. Luckily for you, I came back early. Clearly *someone* with sense needs to take charge of things. How did you ever get trapped into marrying that cow Braxara?"

She clapped her hands sharply and waved away the women who had been fussing over her. They joined the men dressed in silver, helping shift some of the smaller packs and bags.

Noticing my nonplussed expression, she said:

"Good help is hard to find. You sent me to a Shadow where I am worshipped as a goddess; it is easy to get used to being pampered. So I brought a few of the faithful with me. They think this is the afterlife."

"A few?" I eyed the throng critically. They didn't seem to be having any trouble acclimatizing to the Beyond, I noticed somewhat enviously. In fact, they all seemed to be happily taking it in stride . . . though I supposed, if you served a goddess, you must be prepared for such things.

"Barely two dozen," she said.

"Your right, I'm sure." I sighed and drew her to one side, where they couldn't over hear our conversation. "What are you *really* doing here?" I asked. "Your instructions were clear. You were to stay in Shadow until the danger is past. Nothing has changed. We are still under attack."

"And," said Aber, trailing us, "Dad's going to be furious when he finds out. He picked that Shadow especially for you and Pella."

"Do not prattle on," she said to him. "This is neither the time nor the place for such a—"

With an expression of annoyance she turned and hurried back to her luggage. A servant had been about lifting a large crate one-handed, and she took in from him and set it down.

"Careful with this one, Sahin!" she said. "It is filled with glass!"

Aber rolled his eyes. "Perfume, I bet!"

"She hasn't changed a bit," I said with a smile.

Sahin threw himself to the floor. "Yes, my goddess," he whimpered. "Forgive me! Forgive me!"

"Rise. Finish your work. Take more care. You have my blessing."

"Thank you!"

Rising, he lifted the trunk with greater care. Freda watched him for a moment, then wandered back to join us.

"There is much yet to be done, I see," she said to me. Her eyes swept across the remaining trunks, then fixed on Aber. "Make us all drinks in the library, please. Travel is thirsty work, and there is still much I must do today."

"Yes, Freda," he said meekly, and he hurried into the library. He always ended up doing as she asked, I'd noticed, though sometimes his cooperation seemed grudging.

She waited until he was out of sight, then pulled me into a secluded alcove. It seemed she wanted a private talk. She had never confided in me before, and it took me a bit by surprise now.

"Where is Father, really?" she asked in a soft voice. "I must know!"

"He went for an audience with King Uthor. He didn't come back."

"I cannot believe—" she began. Then she stopped herself. "He did not tell you, did he?"

"Tell me what?"

"Where he went afterward? He would be back here by now; it

does not take so long to see the king. Who did he visit next? Where did he go?"

"I don't know—do you?"

"I . . . have a suspicion." She turned away, eyes distant. "There is a place he goes when he is unhappy or sad. A Shadow . . ."

"There's a woman involved?" I guessed. "His lover?"

"Yes."

"Who is she?"

"I do not know . . . only that she is a powerful sorceress. She has given him things . . . objects of power . . . and helped him to master the magics he now commands."

I frowned. "If she's so powerful, he should have gone to her as soon as war started in Juniper. Why didn't he?"

"I do not know. Perhaps she is not in a position to provide military assistance. Or perhaps he is guarding her safety."

So, a woman was involved . . . suddenly Dad's actions began to make sense. If he meant to protect her, then he certainly would make sure neither Aber nor I—nor anyone else—knew her location.

She continued: "What else has happened here? You mentioned several attacks?"

Quickly I filled her in, from Rèalla to the lightning in the garden to the serpent-creature scrying on my bedroom.

"I'm not sure what's happening outside," I added. "King Uthor's hell-creatures searched the house yesterday. They were looking for something specific, something small, but I don't think they found it. Any idea what it could be?"

"None. How about you?"

"No." I shook my head. "Now, what brought you back here, really?"

"That I must share with Aber, too. It concerns us all."

She turned and led the way to the library. After we entered, she closed and bolted the door behind us, then crossed to the far wall, pushed on a high-set sconce, and opened a small door that had been cunningly concealed as a wall panel. A hidden room or passage—I couldn't see which—lay beyond. She glanced in, then closed the panel; apparently it was empty. I heard a soft *click* as its latch caught.

I glanced at Aber.

"I didn't know it was there!" he said.

"There is a lot you do not know," Freda said.

"We have been spied on constantly since we arrived here," I told her. "Aber tried to put up spells to protect us, but we aren't sure they worked. What can you do to help?"

"Wait. I will check."

She gathered the folds of her dress and sat at the table. Then, taking a deep breath, she closed her eyes and seemed to go into a light trance. I saw her eyelashes flutter, and several times her hands jerked, but mostly she remained silent and still.

"Whiskey?" Aber asked me in hushed tones.

Nodding, I accepted a glass from him. He filled it, we clinked glasses in a silent toast, and then we both sat back, sipping, to wait for Freda. I had never seen her do anything like this before; how long would it take?

Finally, after what must have been ten or fifteen minutes, Freda suddenly opened her eyes.

"A nice job," she said to Aber. "I only found one hole, and I do not think it has been used."

He smiled with obvious relief. "Great!"

"Did you fix the hole?" I asked her.

"Yes. No one will spy on this house again without us finding out. That I can promise."

"I told you she was good!" Aber said smugly.

"Red wine, please," she told him.

Drawing a small deck of Trumps from the bag at her side, she shuffled them and began to deal them out in front of herself. I recognized my picture, Dad's, Aber's, and the rest of our family. She included her own, too. A circle began to form, with images looking in toward the center.

As she worked, Aber poured a goblet of red wine and set it to one side. Then he topped off my whiskey as well as his own.

"I hate to drink alone," he said.

I did not know how the Trumps worked for Freda, but they helped her see the future—or possible futures—and that was exactly the sort of information we needed. Leaning forward, I watched her flip the last Trump and set it in place in the exact center.

Drawn by Aber, it showed Locke in a quite unflattering portrait: a disagreeable-looking, puffed-up man in silvered chain mail, with a slight pot belly (he hadn't had one in real life) and a look of indigestion on his face.

"Well?" I said.

"It is . . . inconclusive. Let me cast the future again."

Frowning, Freda gathered up the cards. I got the impression she hadn't liked what she saw and shifted uneasily in my seat. She shuffled twice, had me cut the deck, and began to deal them out a second time.

Aber and I continued to watch in silence. This time, the cards played out slightly differently—though once more Locke ended up at the center.

"So?" I prompted, as I slid into the seat opposite hers. "What news? Any predictions?"

For a long moment she said nothing, studying the cards. I remained patient, though every fiber of my being demanded immediate answers.

"You do not know yet," she finally said, "do you?"

"Know what? Something you saw in your cards?"

"Locke. He is alive."

"Impossible!" Our brother died in Juniper, I knew. I had seen him in his tent after the battle, being tended by physicians. I had watched him die.

"Yes, I thought so too." She nodded slowly. "But the cards say you, Oberon, will meet him soon. Perhaps even tonight."

I shook my head. "I was with him when he died, Freda. You saw his body. Locke is dead. We burned his body, remember?"

"We all saw it," Aber agreed.

"I know," Freda whispered. "I remember."

"Then what makes you think he's alive?" I asked.

She picked up her wine and sipped it. "Because," she said, "I spoke with him this morning."

TWENTY-TWO

t's a trick!" I said. I rose and began to pace. "You know how devious our enemies are, Freda. They found a way to fool you."

"That's what I thought," she said. "But he knew things . . . things only the two of us had shared." Her voice dropped. "It *was* him. I swear it."

I took a deep breath. Enough impossible things had happened to me in the last month . . . maybe Lords of Chaos really *could* return from the dead.

"What do you think?" I asked Aber.

He might be childish at times, but he knew a lot, and without Dad here, he was my main source of information on all things magical. Although Freda probably knew more about magic than any of our other siblings, she had an infuriating mysterious streak, and I was always left with the impression that she kept back as much as she revealed.

"I don't know," he admitted. I suppose—"

A light knock sounded on the library door. I motioned to Aber, and he hurried over and opened it.

Anari stood there.

"My lords, Lady Freda," he said. "Lord Fenn is in the dining hall. He asked me to inform you. He wants to see your father."

"What about Isadora?" I asked. Fenn and Isadora had run off together before Juniper fell, in search of help for our armies. They had not returned, nor had we gotten any word from them, since that time.

"Lady Isadora is not with him, sir," Anari said.

I glanced at Freda. "You didn't bring him with you, I assume?"

"No," she said, looking puzzled. "I went into hiding with Pella, remember? She is still in Averoigne, awaiting my return. I have not seen Fenn since he disappeared."

"Thank you, Anari," I said. "Let him know where we are and ask him to join us."

Fenn nodded a somewhat sheepish greeting when he entered the library. He was taller than Dworkin but not as tall as me, with blue eyes, light brown hair, and a hesitant but honest smile. He wore dark blue leggings and tunic, with a simple belt and boots. A sword hung at his side. I had not gotten to know him well, but until his sudden disappearance in Juniper, right before the attacks began, he had struck me as trustworthy. Since then, I half suspected him of being the one spying on us.

"It's good to see you all," he said.

"And where were you when we needed you?" I folded my arms and glared. "You ran out on us."

"Where have you been?" Freda asked. "Where is Isadora?"

"She's in Juniper," he announced smugly. "We retook it yesterday."

"What!" Aber cried.

"How?" I demanded.

"I brought an army of my own . . . trolls. Half a million of them." He chuckled. "You should have seen the bloodbath! Enemy soldiers had occupied the castle and the lands around it. No more."

I shook my head. "Trolls? I don't understand."

"I do," Freda said. "He found a Shadow where trolls are breeding out of control. He offered them Juniper as a new colony in exchange for clearing out the enemy. Think of it . . . a whole new world for them. Of course, they jumped at the chance."

"Brilliant, right?" Grinning, Fenn took a seat next to me. "Isadora is back there now, helping mop up the last of the invaders. You should have seen her, Oberon! Bodies stacked fifty feet high, and her standing on top, screaming her battle cry, sword in hand! Magnificent!"

There was a reason, I reflected, that Aber had once called her the warrior-bitch from hell.

Now Aber slid a drink across the table to Fenn.

"So you've retaken Juniper," I said. "Doesn't that leave us with, ah, a slight troll problem?"

"Half a million troll problems," Freda said.

"We can bring in giants to take care of the trolls," Aber said.

"And then dragons, I suppose, to take care of the giants?" I said with a annoyed snort.

"Now you're getting the idea!" Aber said with mock seriousness. "And dragons . . . what eats dragons?" He looked at Freda, who only sighed.

"Maybe it wasn't the best idea," Fenn admitted, "but it solved the immediate problem and got rid of the attackers. We can always find another Shadow like Juniper."

I asked, "Were there any survivors from our men?"

"Maybe, hiding in the woods. If the trolls don't eat them, Isadora will bring them back."

"Fair enough, I guess."

"But," Fenn went on excitedly, "I have more important news than that!"

"Let me guess," I said. "Locke contacted you and told you to come here."

"That's right!"

"What did you tell him?"

"I was too busy—but the trolls worked faster than I thought they would, so I came straight here."

I shook my head. This whole conversation had an air of inevitability to it. Someone—or something—wanted us all in one place. It would make the murders easier. Fortunately, only Fenn and Freda has risen to the bait. The rest of our immediate family remained safely hidden.

Fenn searched our faces. "Has he been in touch with you, too, then?"

"Locke," I said firmly, "is dead."

"What!" He stared. "When? How?"

Quickly I filled him in on what had happened in Juniper, and then here. He shook his head stubbornly, though.

"You made a mistake," he insisted. "It *was* Locke, and he contacted me by Trump less than an hour ago! I know my own brother better than any of you. It *was* him!"

"This is a family of lunatics!" I said. "Locke is dead! We all—Aber, Freda, and I—saw his body! You can't deny it."

Fenn frowned. "But Locke said—" And then he paused. "But—" And he paused again.

"Trust me, Locke is dead." I glanced at Aber. "Unless you can think of some way for him to come back?"

"As far as I know," Aber said with a uncomfortable shrug, "death is final."

"It *is* hard to kill a Lord of Chaos," Freda said, "but once he is dead, he remains dead. I have never heard of one coming back to life. And some have been very powerful."

Aber said, "I supposed it could have been a ghost . . ."

"Are ghosts real?" I asked.

"Yes," Freda said. "I have spoken with a few of them, as the need arose. But they have no physical form. They could never use a Trump."

Fenn said, "Locke wasn't a ghost. I'm certain."

"Nor was my Locke a ghost," Freda said firmly. "He was as much flesh and blood as you or I. No, there must be another answer. And we will find it."

"Besides," Aber said to me, "where would a ghost get a set of Trumps? I have Locke's here. It's complete . . . I checked after I took them back from his room. Freda's Trump and Fenn's Trump are both there."

"Are you sure?" I asked. "Remember, hell-creatures searched our rooms. Have you checked his Trumps since then? Maybe they borrowed a few. Or maybe Locke, or whoever is impersonating him, used that Logrus trick of yours—the one where you pull items from distant Shadows—and has them now."

He gasped. "I hadn't thought of that! Let me check." Turning, he ran out into the entry hall.

"It was not a ghost," Freda repeated. "It was a man. I know the difference. And it *was* Locke. He always was an arrogant bastard. Who else would have dared order me about like a common servant, even through a Trump?"

"What did he ask you to do?"

"He told me to come here. Our father needs me, he said. Forget about hiding in Shadow, he said, and be a dutiful daughter. Come and help."

"So you came."

"Yes. How could I not?"

"It sounds like he tricked you into joining us here," I said.

"What about me?" Fenn asked. "Why would he contact me and tell me to come here? Freda is the powerful one, next to Dad."

"Get us into one place and it will be easier to kill us all."

"Let us assume it was neither Locke nor a ghost," Freda said. "What other possibilities remain?"

"Here's one," I said. I willed my features to change, and in a second I looked exactly like Locke, from arrogant sneer to haughty tilt of the head. I faced my sister.

"Get thee to the Courts of Chaos," I said in a fair imitation of Locke's voice. With a little practice, I think I could have matched it perfectly. "I command you!"

"You are not funny," she said flatly.

"I wasn't trying to be." I let my face fall back to its normal appearance. "Our enemies include shape-shifters. Remember the barber who tried to cut my throat?"

"Ivinius? Yes, I remember that unfortunate incident. But *you* are clearly *not* Locke, even when you take his form. I know my brother well enough to tell the difference. I was not taken in by a demon."

I sighed. She could be as inflexible as our father sometimes. And yet . . . she had a point.

"At least concede the possibility," I said. "The Courts of Chaos are full of shape-shifters, Aber tells me."

"True," Freda said, "but it is considered bad manners to impersonate people. Also, the one who spoke with me not only *looked* like Locke, he acted and sounded like Locke, and he had Locke's memories. He *knew* things . . ."

"What sort of things?"

She blushed and looked away. That was a first; he had known something personal, something embarrassing.

"It was . . . something that happened when we were children. No one else knows, or will ever know. He offered it as proof."

"Maybe it *was* him," Aber said from the doorway. I hadn't heard him return. "His Trumps are gone."

"Maybe the man who died in Juniper wasn't Locke after all!" Fenn suggested, sounding excited.

"What!" The possibility shocked me. "You mean . . . Locke might have been replaced by a demon?"

"Yes!"

It seemed impossible. And yet, our enemies had gone to fantastic effort and expense to destroy us. Would it be so hard for them to replace Locke with a shape-shifter? One who would lead our troops to defeat in Juniper?

"No," I said firmly, remembering Rèalla and how she had looked when we found her body outside. "A shape-shifter would have reverted to its true form after its death."

"Yes." Freda nodded. "We all saw Locke's body. It was not a demon."

"There are other possibilities," Fenn said.

I looked at him. "Such as . . . ?"

"Perhaps Locke found a double of himself in one of the Shadows," Fenn said, "and left him in charge while he slipped off to safety."

"That doesn't sound like Locke," I said. He was nothing if not duty-bound, valiantly defending Juniper and our family even in the face of impossible odds.

"No, it doesn't," said Freda. "And yet . . . if our father had ordered him to do this thing . . . if he had a greater mission, which might save us all . . . yes, I believe he would have left a double in charge of the army. At least for a short time."

"And he might have taken Davin with him!" Aber said excitedly. "You said he disappeared—"

"No," I said. "I said we never found his body. He and his men lost that battle. We assumed he went down fighting."

"But if he didn't—"

"If he is with Locke—" Freda added.

"We cannot assume it's Locke," I said.

"Nor can we assume it isn't him," Fenn said.

I looked at Freda, who leaned over to study her circle of cards, with Locke in the center. What did she see?

"Locke is pivotal to coming events," she said softly. "I have never seen a reading like this for a dead man."

We all grew silent, pondering the possibilities. If Locke and Davin lived, it changed everything. We had friends . . . fighters . . . men of strength to help us. And if they had a secret mission that could help—the possibilities sent my imagination soaring.

And yet, despite Freda's insistence, a nagging doubt remained. Locke and I had made peace between us in those last days before he fell. No double would have done that. No, the answer was obvious. Somehow, though this double had managed to fool Freda, it couldn't possibly be Locke.

"Who else do you suppose Locke contacted?" Aber asked me.

"My guess would be everyone," I said. I shook my head. "I still can't accept it, though. Our enemies want nothing more than to get us all in one place. Locke seems to be doing that for them. We must remain on guard. I don't think we can trust this person claiming to be Locke—or anyone else—until we find out the truth."

A grim silence followed. I looked around at my siblings' faces. Expressions of worry and unease were plain to see.

"I just hope the rest of our family has the sense to stay where they are," I grumbled half to myself.

TWENTY-THREE

ord Oberon," Port said. "You have a visitor."

An hour had passed since Fenn's return. I had retreated to my room, a powerful headache throbbing at my temples, to try to think things through.

I glanced at the carved wooden face in the door.

"Who is it?" I asked.

"A household servant; I do not know his name. Apparently a message has arrived for you. Shall I have him slip it under the door? You look tired."

"That's not the half of it." I sighed. "Let him in."

"Very good, sir."

Port unlocked himself and swung the door open. A man I vaguely recognized as one of the household servants stood outside.

"Yes?" I said.

"A runner brought this for you, sir." He held out a small white envelope.

"For me? Are you sure?"

"Yes, sir."

I motioned him forward. Who would be sending me messages here? It had to be our father. At least, I hoped so.

I took the message, waved him off, and returned to the desk.

Behind me, the man cleared his throat. I glanced at him.

"The messenger is waiting for your reply," he said.

"He can wait a few minutes more. Find Lord Aber and ask him to join me here, please. Tell him it's important."

"Yes, Lord." He bowed, then hurried out.

I stared down at the letter. The front said simply "Oberon" in careful script. When I turned it over, I found nothing more than a blob of dark red wax stamped by a seal in the shape of a griffin.

I broke the seal and unfolded the letter. Six lines of the most intricate and flowery penmanship I had ever seen cordially invited me to dine with Lord and Lady Ethshell the following night.

I turned the paper over, but that was it. Brief, to the point, no wasted words.

But . . . why me? I had never even heard of Lord Ethshell. Why should they invite me, of all people, to join them?

Aber rapped on the doorframe. "What is it?" he said, and swept in without being asked.

I held out the letter. He read it and gave a small, "Hmm."

"Is that good or bad?" I said.

"Oh, it's good. Very good. You must go, by all means."

"Why?"

"Because, dear brother, they want to take your measure." He gave an evil smile. "Unless I'm mistaken, they just received the invitation to Aunt Lan's engagement party tonight. Since their eldest daughter Honoria is still without a husband, and you are, shall we say, husbandly material . . ."

"But I'm engaged to Braxara."

"That's never stopped true love before."

Now it was my turn to "Hmm." I wasn't sure I liked the sound of that. We had so much going on—so many people trying to kill us, or worse—that I didn't want parents flinging their eligible daughters at me.

"You can bring me along," he told me, "as chaperone."

"Maybe she'd prefer your hand, since I'm spoken for."

"I've already been considered, and rejected, as unsuitable husbandly material. Too artistic, I fear. The Ethshells have a strong military tradition."

I looked at the invitation again. "It doesn't say anything about bringing a guest."

"It will be fine. Dad should be the one going with you, but in his absence, any male family member will do."

He took a piece of paper, wrote a brief reply, folded it up, and dribbled a bit of wax on it. Then he motioned for the servant who'd brought the message to approach.

"Here is our reply," he said.

"Very good, sir." He bowed and left.

The moment he was outside, Port closed himself. I turned to Aber.

"What's she like?"

"Honoria? Oh . . . she's hard to describe."

"Try."

"Two or three extra eyes, half a dozen arms, red hair, and very well rounded. Quite a . . . woman, I guess you'd say."

"Red hair?" I raised my eyebrows. Some of my favorite lovers had been redheads.

"That's right. Very red, very long, very thick, and all over her body." He chuckled at my expression. "Well, as much of her body as I've ever seen. I can only imagine the rest."

"This does not," I said, "sound promising."

"Dinner will be a small but traditionally formal affair with the Ethshells. No more than twenty people. I'm sure you'll impress them all."

"Traditionally formal? I'll guess that means fancy clothes, boring speeches, and pretentious old men and their wives?"

"You've dined with them before?"

I sighed. "With their counterparts in Ilerium, anyway."

"You'll see," he said with an encouraging nod, "the food alone will be worth the trip. Now, though, we have to get you cleaned up for Aunt Lan's party."

I tried on outfit after outfit, assisted by Horace and Aber. My brother kept summoning fancier garments using the Logrus, and each time I thought I looked magnificent, he would shake his head and try again. Fancy collars, shoes like golden hooves, hats of impossibly complex design—I tried them all on, then tore them all off. The stack of discarded silks, leather, and frilled lace grew high on top of my bed.

When I finally stood back and regarded myself in a looking glass, I had a hard time keeping from laughing. My final costume seemed ludicrous. Crimson leggings, a heavily ruffled red shirt with sleeves that puffed out like over-ripe melons, and a jaunty cap with long flowing red feathers that trailed down behind—I had never seen anything so outlandish in my life.

The sad thing was, Aber took it entirely too seriously. He adorned himself in dark blue, though his shirt had splashes of gold at the sleeves. His hat's feathers were longer and more spectacular than my own—not that I objected, of course.

I studied my reflection in the looking glass. Not bad, I finally decided. Once you got used to the puffiness and color, everything fit me well and flattered my appearance.

"If Helda could see me now," I murmured.

"What did you say?" Aber asked from across the room. He brought my swordbelt over.

"You're absolutely certain," I said for what must have been the tenth time, "that everyone will be dressed like this?"

"Of course."

By tradition, according to Aber, I could not arrive via Trump. I had to ride to Aunt Lanara's house in an open carriage, emerge in grand style, walk up the steps through a multitude of well-wishers, and finally enter the grand hall. There, a feast in my honor would commence, followed by dancing and entertainments into the small hours. I would get my first look at Braxara over dinner, when her father offered up a toast in our honor.

"Aunt Lan's parties are notorious for their excesses," Aber told me. "Everyone important will be there. Perhaps even King Uthor himself."

"What about Dad?"

He frowned. "He should be there. Everyone will talk about it if he isn't. Want to try his Trump again?"

I shrugged. "I suppose I'd better. Even if he doesn't show up, he ought to know what's going on."

He brought our father's Trump to me, and I concentrated on it. It took a long time, but finally his image began to stir, as if he were far away. A misty, blurry image came into view—Dad, with a dense forest of pine trees behind him.

"What is it?" he snapped at me.

"We were worried about you," I said. "The audience with King Uthor—"

"Never took place," he finished. "Forget about it. There are more important things happening. I will be back in a day or two. Guard your backs until then; our enemies are moving fast."

Suddenly he was gone. I never had a chance to tell him about the serpent scrying on me, the lightning attack, Rèalla being sent to assassinate me, or my engagement to Braxara. Moving fast, indeed!

I repeated what Dad has said to my brother.

"Very curious." Aber's brow furrowed.

"Very," I agreed.

"At least he's planning on coming back. Where do you think he was? Any clue?"

"Not in the Courts of Chaos, certainly. The forest behind him looked normal."

"More important things are happening . . . what do you think he meant?"

"I think insanity runs in our family."

I buckled on my swordbelt. Though it had served me well, I had to admit now it showed its age. Aber, of course, noticed too.

"You need a weapon suitable to your station," he said. "I'll get one of Dad's." He headed for the door.

"Anything special about them?" I asked, following.

"I'll pick one of the enchanted ones!" he called over his shoulder. Then he bounded down the hall, into an alcove, and up a small flight of steps.

I didn't have long to wait. In less than a minute, he returned with the most beautiful weapon I had ever seen in my life. It was longsword, with intricate scrollwork along the entire length of the blade. The hilt, inlaid with gold, silver, and precious stones, fit my hand as though it had been made for me. I hefted it. It felt curiously light—far lighter than it should have been, considering its size and workmanship.

"Well?" Aber asked.

"It will do."

"It will do? That's one of the finest swords ever forged. It belonged to our grandfather, Duke Esmorn. He carried it through the Logrus, and it gained magical powers as a result."

"What sort of powers?" I asked.

"I'm not sure. But that's what I've always been told. Dad refuses to use it."

"Why?"

Aber shrugged. "I don't know."

I regarded the flat of the blade more closely and noticed a small inscription: "The meek have no need of arms." Truly, this was a warrior's weapon. I would take good care of it.

Chaos and Amber

I raised the sword and took a few practice swings. The hilt seemed to turn slightly in my hand, almost as if it had a will of its own will. Interesting. I noted it for future study.

We left not long after, just Aber, Freda, and me—Fenn, pleading exhaustion, begged off—in a grand carriage drawn by white beasts. I hesitated to call them horses, for their necks stretched too long, their long, thin, bony tails had no hair, and their feet . . . well, six legs gave them speed, but somehow lacked the grace of thoroughbreds.

We left from the courtyard by the rock garden, and the driver circled the main building at a fast trot. With red skies boiling overhead, and purple lightning flickering constantly, guards swung open tall gates for us. We drove out, and madness surrounded us.

I did not know how to describe it. It was as though I stood at the edge of a great cliff, and before me streamed every nightmare known to mankind, pounding at my senses. Colors swirled in mid-air. The rush of wind, which had long died down to the merest whisper at the back of my mind, rose to a full-throated roar. Above, the clouds vanished, leaving a sky as black as midnight, but filled with stars that moved like fireflies.

The horse-creatures began to gallop, hooves pounding. The carriage lurched and jumped. Air screamed around me.

Standing in my seat, I threw back my head and laughed. So this was Chaos. So this was what I had feared!

I drank it all in, arms wide. My every sense raged. The noise and color and tastes and textures assaulted me. I felt hopelessly jumbled and no longer tried to find angles, familiar elements, or anything to cling to. I reveled in the wildness, and my heart knew no boundaries. Chaos! Yes, Chaos! It flowed around me, through me, *became* me.

Aber, laughing, pulled me down. I stared at him, beyond words, beyond emotions.

"You are drooling," Freda said. She wiped my mouth with the hem of her dress.

"Why didn't you *tell* me?" I cried.

"This is the Beyond!" Aber said. "It's why we have walls, or all would be washed away!"

The landscape outside had begun to change. I stared. I couldn't help myself. Every way I turned, I found something incredible. Colors that leapt and spurted like water from a fountain. Walking trees. Stones that roamed the land. Mountains that shook and heaved and abruptly flattened to prairies.

And demon-creatures moved everywhere, on foot, on horse-back, and in the air.

The ride, perhaps an hour long, proved a mesmerizing but ultimately uneventful spectacle. I wasn't entirely sure when we left the Beyond and entered the Courts of Chaos, but that we did so I had no doubt.

I had expected an assassination attempt on one or all of us, but it didn't happen. Perhaps Aunt Lanara's influence carried even this far: knowing I must attend her party, our enemies drew back. That, or they had another, more deadly plan in mind . . .

At last the lands grew more normal and less motive, and streets of huge walled estates appeared. We drove more slowly now, as we encountered traffic—carriages similar to our own, mounted riders, even a few pedestrians. Most looked as human as we did. I found that strangely comforting.

Slowing, our carriage turned in at a set of high iron gates. Behind it, towering over the wall, lay a house so immense it made ours look like a cottage in comparison. It blazed with light, inside and out, and I saw figures moving on a dozen different floors—many of them pressing up to windows to watch us.

Liveried servants, who looked more like frogs than men, stood everywhere at attention. A dozen of them bounded forward to take care of us.

"Announce Lord Oberon, Lady Freda, and Lord Aber," my sister said.

"You are expected, Lords and Lady!" one of the frog-servants said.

Freda motioned me out. "You must go through the motions of betrothal for now," she said softly, so only I could hear. "It is the honorable thing to do."

I nodded. Then trumpets sounded, and a cheer went up as half a hundred doors were flung open and guests began to stream outside. There must have been a thousand of them, as the throngs grew deep around us. They began to call out: "Oberon and Braxara! Oberon and Braxara! Oberon and Braxara!" over and over again.

"What should I do?" I asked Aber, as subtly as I could considering how many people were staring.

"Get out, walk in, find our aunt!" he whispered back.

I stood, raised one hand in a salute, and stepped down onto the steps which the frog-men had carried up to the carriage. The crowds parted for me, leaving a narrow passage up to the house's main entrance.

There, just outside, Aunt Lanara stood beaming down at me. She wore a tiara of diamonds that sparkled and gleamed, and her long gown shimmered with starlight. Even her tusks had been polished and their tips capped in gold.

Beside her stood an elderly man, white-haired, in gold and red pants and shirt. This had to be her husband, my uncle. Aber had told me his name: Leito.

I stopped before them and bowed. "Uncle Leito. Aunt Lanara."

"Welcome, Oberon. Come inside, my darling boy, and enjoy the hospitality of our house."

"Thank you."

A cheer went up from the men and women around me, and everyone began to file back inside. Turning, Leito and Lanara led the way.

Their house proved a cavernous shell, at least in the front. The party seemed to be taking place on more than one level of the house. Above us, people stood on huge flat stones that floated in mid air, drifting up and down, though never bumping into each other or crushing their riders. People stepped from one stone to another freely as they passed, mingling, talking. Laughter, bits of song and poetry, and comments about Aber, Freda, and especially me reached my ears.

"We must see to dinner preparations," Aunt Lanara said. "Stay here by the door, greet everyone who comes up to you, but commit to nothing. I will return for you shortly."

"Thank you," I said.

She patted my cheek and hurried across the floor, calling to servants. They began to spread out into the crowd on the ground floor, carrying trays of appetizers. Others stepped up onto the floating stones and began circulating among the guests overhead.

"Try not to stare," Aber said in a quiet voice. He had come up behind me.

"I can't help it!" I whispered back.

A heavyset woman with three eyes, greenish-gray skin, and a pair of short horns jutting from her forehead floated down to us, surrounded by four young women who held up corners of her heavily layered and more heavily bejeweled dress. I literally fought back nausea. I had never seen such a repulsive creature before.

"Countess Tsel," Aber said to her, bowing formally. After a second's hesitation, I did the same. "May I present my brother, Oberon?"

"Please do." She offered me a cool hand, scaled like a snake's. I kissed it unhappily.

"Enchanted," I said.

"This is my brother, Duke Urchok," she said, indicating the squat man with a face full of tentacles, who had just come up to join her. "And my niece, Lady Portia, and her husband, Baron Yorlum." She indicated a well-dressed couple to her left, both with horns and slightly too-elongated faces, but human enough looking overall.

"I am honored, Duke, Baron." I bowed to both men, then kissed Lady Portia's hand, my touch lingering for a moment. "And I am most delighted to meet you, my Lady." Would that she were my bride, instead of Braxara!

Portia blushed. The Baron, with a dark glance at me, took her elbow and escorted her away. They stepped onto one of the floating rocks and drifted toward the ceiling.

"Oberon," Duke Urchok said in a muffled voice filled with faint hisses and squeaks. He gave a nod. "Good to meet you. We have heard great things about you from your aunt."

"Your house is old with tradition," Countess Tsel said, regarding me, "and you might find it profitable to meet my daughter Eleane."

I glanced at Aber, who gave a slight nod of encouragement. These two must be important. Somehow, I didn't think Aunt Lanara would approve of my dining with them.

"I would be honored," I murmured, forcing a polite smile.

"Tomorrow?"

"Alas, I have a prior engagement."

"Then we will do it the following day. For dinner." He looked around the room. "Are any of your other brothers here? Locke, perhaps?"

"No," I said. "It's just Aber and me. Locke is dead."

"Dead! Oh dear. Poor boy, you're practically an orphan. Then you certainly must come to dinner. Bring Aber, but not your father. My dear Sikrad simply *cannot* have Dworkin in the house. They do not get along."

Then the countess spotted someone else she desperately needed to talk to and swept away, followed by her brother and entourage. I stared after her, not quite sure whether to be insulted, bewildered, or amused.

"Who is Sikrad?" I asked Aber.

"Her husband. No one has seen him in decades. Half the court thinks Countess Tsel killed and ate him."

"What!" I cried. "She's a—"

"Hush! A cannibal. She's probably eaten a dozen husbands over the years."

"And her daughter?"

"Nothing but rumors about her . . . so far." He grinned at my horrified expression. "I'm sure you're safe enough, at least until *after* the marriage, should you get that far. Now keep your voice down. It's not polite to shout about such things."

I swallowed hard. Monsters. Cannibals. Eligible daughters. What had I gotten myself into?

"You could do worse than her daughter," Aber said. "The countess owns many of the finest *krel* farms in the Beyond."

"In case you've forgotten," I said, "my engagement is about to be announced here!"

"Do you really think that would stop someone like Countess Tsel from trying to marry you off to one of her offspring? After all, if you're good enough for Aunt Lanara, you're certainly good enough for the Countess! They have been rivals for longer than I can remember."

"Why is it," I said, "that half the people here seem to have matrimony on their minds?"

"Why do you think Dad's been married so many times?" he said with a laugh. "Maybe now you're beginning to see the reason I like life in Shadows better. I fully think half the females in Chaos are in search of mates at any one time."

Then Aber's face hardened.

"Be on your guard," he said, gazing over my left shoulder. "Our enemies approach."

"Who?"

"Oberon," Aber said loudly. He swallowed hard. "May I present Lord Ulyanash?"

I turned, forcing a half smiling. Finally I would meet one of our enemies face to face. I would not let any fear or apprehension show.

Ulyanash looked much like Rèalla's description—long, straight black hair, red eyes, two white horns on top of his head—and he dressed all in black, from pants to shirt to boots. Silver buttons at his sleeves added a splash of color. Rather than large and muscular, as I had expected, he was smaller than me and thin almost to the point of skeletal. I found it hard to guess his age, but it couldn't have been much older than I was—no more than five or six years. To my surprise, he carried no weapons.

As we came face to face, his red eyes narrowed. I could tell he was sizing me up, too.

"I am delighted to finally meet you," I said, smiling with all my teeth. "We have several acquaintances in common."

"Oh?" He set his hands on his hips and looked me over with contempt. "I find that difficult to believe."

"Oh, it's true. Why, just this morning a friend told me how much she once admired you."

"Just so." He smirked and looked over his shoulders at his

friends. "A woman I've cast off has made her way to you."

His friends chuckled.

I folded my arms. "Her name was Rèalla."

"I don't remember her," Ulyanash sneered as he walked in a circle around Aber and me. I pivoted on my right foot, keeping us face to face. "Shows how good she is in bed."

Once more his friends laughed.

"Actually," I said, "her complaints were all about your skills in bed. And . . . certain other areas, where you don't measure up."

He threw back his head and laughed.

"So, Oberon thinks himself a quick wit. The one great hope for that pitiful House Barimen—"

"Lord Dworkin," I said. "I believe his titles are older and more respected than your own, few though they are."

Ulyanash's face hardened suddenly. Apparently he wasn't used to being insulted.

"You are playing a dangerous game," he said. "Want to raise the wager?"

Aber dropped his voice to a whisper:

"Ignore him. He's looking for a duel."

"Then," I said, as I looked Ulyanash up and down with a dismissive glance, "he's welcome to have one!"

TWENTY-FOUR

lyanash's followers formed a circle around us. A hush fell over the party guests. They began hurrying toward our side. I spotted Aunt Lan, looking down and wringing her hands, atop a floating stone three stories above us. She motioned frantically for us to stop. I ignored her.

"Time and place?" I asked. If I let him pick them, I would have choice of weapons . . . and the advantage, as I saw it.

"Here," Ulyanash said smugly. "Now." With one hand he reached out to the side and plucked from the air some sort of three-clawed weapon, the like of which I had never seen before. "Your trisp and fandon?"

Aber looked at me. "You've never used a trisp," he said. I remembered our earlier conversation—people fought with them while standing on moving stones? "It's that blade he's holding. It extends magically outward, like rays of light—but sharp, and you control the length at the grip."

I didn't like the sound of it. "And a fandan?"

"Like a shield, kind of. You use it to parry the trisp, but you can attack with its edges as well."

Since I had never trained using them—or even seen them used before—I knew I couldn't accept them as our weapons. If I did, I wouldn't last ten seconds.

"No," I said loudly to Ulyanash.

"What do you mean—no?" Ulyanash demanded.

"It's my choice of weapons. I'm unfamiliar with these, so I choose knives."

"Knives!" He sneered. "What are we, children?"

"If you're afraid . . ." I shrugged and half turned away, playing to our audience. "A simple apology will do." A titter came from the crowd around us.

He hesitated, glancing uncertainly at the faces around us.

"Very well," he said, trying to sound more certain. "It does not matter. I am equally adept at all weapons. Your fate is assured, son of Dworkin, whether you fight me with toys or a man's weapon."

I took off the swordbelt Aber had given me and passed it to my brother.

"Why not use swords?" Aber asked me softly. "This one is enchanted. It would help you . . ."

"I remember," I replied in a low voice. "And if I won with it, everyone will say it was the blade and not me. Forget magic. When I kill him, everyone will know it was the strength of my arm and the keenness of my eye."

Everyone moved back a few feet, forming a ring around us. Ulyanash untied his cloak, threw it to one of his friends, then unlaced his collar and pulled his shirt off. His chest was narrow and bony, covered with a fine silken white hair.

I too stripped to the waist and stretched the kinks from my muscles. There would be no chance of our blades catching in clothing.

On the surface, judging by our appearances, it looked like an uneven match—with me the likely winner.

Aber, using the Logrus, produced a mahogany box with a glass lid. It contained a set of matched dueling knives. He opened the lid and gave first choice to my opponent. Ulyanash picked up both blades, hefting them, examining them, before finally selecting one. He put the other one back. Aber turned to me, and I accepted it.

About seven inches long, its blade had been etched with intricate designs of dragons. Its handle, wrapped in strips of black leather, fit my hand perfectly. I noticed that Ulyanash had to adjust his own grip several times trying to get comfortable with it.

Aber grinned, watching Ulyanash fumble with his weapon, and I realized he had chosen these knives specifically for our duel. They fit my larger hands, not my opponent's.

"Begin!" Aber said, snapping the box shut and stepping back into the circle of watchers.

We squared off against each other, and then Ulyanash's face and body rippled and began to change, muscles and bristled spikes popping out all over his skin. He seemed to grow several feet taller and several hundred pounds heavier, until the knife looked like a toy in his hand. He could have crushed me just by falling on me.

I gulped. I hadn't planned on magical tricks. Somehow, this fight no longer seemed like such a good idea.

I glanced at my brother desperately, hoping shape-shifting might be illegal, but he made no objections. Like everyone else in the crowd, his eyes were fixed on Ulyanash. Everyone seemed to be watching him, waiting for him to make his move against me. They thought he would win handily.

Not without a struggle, though. Taking a deep breath, I stepped forward and made a tentative slash at his right shoulder, feeling him out.

He ducked and thrust, and our blades locking together for an instant. Then, with a surge of powerful muscles, he threw me back. I skidded ten feet and almost fell. Breathing lightly, I regained my balance and moved forward once more.

He had me on strength, that much was clear. What about speed, though?

I circled, parrying a couple of his jabs, then tried darting forward. A dive and a quick roll took me under his guard. He looked startled as I came up under his left side. As he whirled—too late!—I rolled again, left, keeping low and fast.

He tried to stomp on my arm, missed, and teetered for a second, off-balance. I saw my chance.

With a lightning thrust, I stabbed upwards and nicked his forearm—unfortunately, not the one that held the knife. A narrow ribbon of blood spun out and upward, toward the ceiling. It spattered watchers on the floating stones above.

I rolled again and came up on the balls of my feet, poised to strike.

"First blood!" Aber called, stepping forward. "Are you satisfied, Oberon?"

I gave a quick nod. "Yes." The sooner this duel ended, the better as far as I was concerned.

"What about you, Ulyanash?"

"No," he snarled.

A startled murmur went up from the crowd. Clearly they had expected him to yield. Unfortunately, this was personal for him—not only had he made himself my enemy, I had humiliated him by drawing first blood. Pride wouldn't let him end the battle here.

"Then—continue!" Aber backed away.

Once more Ulyanash and I circled. He moved more slowly and cautiously this time. My taking first blood had done a little good—it had unnerved him. I would have to use that to my advantage.

I tried to close, and this time he danced back, slashing hard. He just missed my face; I felt the wind of his blade scarcely a finger's width from my cheek.

Careful, careful. Pressing forward, I worked to the left, making him turn. That seemed to be his weaker side; I noticed a slight hesitation every time I thrust toward his left cheek. Maybe he had a little trouble seeing with his left eye?

Suddenly he pressed a savage attack. He slashed again and again, knife a blur, putting me on the defensive. I parried and evaded as best I could, dodging and retreating in a circle. Our blades whistled. He grunted, and I noticed sweat starting to bead on his chest. Surely he couldn't keep up that frantic pace long—he would exhaust himself!

I waited patiently, backing in a wide circle, letting him press the attack, doing my best to stay clear.

Deliberately letting my foot slip a bit, I leaned to the left. He thought he saw an opening and lunged with a lightning blow. It came faster and lower than I expected, and I had to spin to the side, barely avoid having my belly punctured.

As I'd hoped, he had overextended his reach. I grabbed his right wrist in my left hand and squeezed as hard as I could.

I had crushed men's bones in combat before. Any normal human would have cried out and dropped the knife, hopelessly crippled. But Ulyanash's bones felt like iron. Instead of dropping the knife, he half turned, jerked his arm up—and sent me flying twenty feet high into the air.

The fall probably would have ended the fight—not from any injury I might have sustained, but because he would have been waiting for me on the floor below. A quick knife thrust, and I would have been dead.

Luckily one of the floating stones saved me. I came within a foot of it, grabbed it with my left hand, swung there a second, then pulled myself on board. The dozen men and women standing there pressed back, giving me room.

I turned, knife ready. But Ulyanash didn't follow me.

"Coward!" Ulyanash cried, pointing at me with his knife. "Look how he runs from the fight!"

"You threw him up there," Aber said. "Give him a chance to get back down."

"Or," I said, "you can come up."

People began stepping off the stone on which I stood. Panting, I waited and thought about the fight so far. Clearly I needed a new strategy. He was stronger and faster than me.

My stone began to drift toward the floor. Ulyanash moved back, giving it room. He smirked. Clearly he thought he had me.

When the stone was two feet off the floor, I hopped down and faced him. He approached me carefully, circling, knife out and ready.

Then, with a triple feint and a blindingly fast thrust, he caught me off balance and cut my chest. It was a shallow wound, little more than a scratch really, but it stung and bled openly. Blood flowed up into my eyes, and I blinked through a red curtain suddenly.

"Wait!" Aber called. "Second blood!"

Wincing, I drew back. Good—I needed a moment's rest. Grinning, Ulyanash moved back a few paces.

"Are you satisfied?" my brother asked Ulyanash.

"No."

"Are you satisfied?" he asked me.

"No," I said calmly. I began a slight shapeshift, closing my wound and stopping the blood flow. I noticed Ulyanash staring at my chest. He frowned. Clearly he wasn't used to opponents healing so quickly and effortlessly.

That gave me an idea. Shapeshifting might be a weapon he wasn't used to—if the rules permitted it. Or even if they didn't.

"So be it," said Aber. "Continue!"

I circled to the left, keeping my guard up, while Ulyanash sprang forward like a wolf scenting blood. I retreated before him, concentrating not on the fight, but on my body, on the change I wanted. Timing, timing, wait—wait—

I saw my opening. He lunged, and I let him catch my right arm with the tip of his knife. It pierced me so fast, I barely felt it, and his body continued on and over me. His left hand caught my right forearm so I couldn't counter. I could have driven the blade into his belly or chest otherwise.

I pulled him close, chest to chest.

"Big mistake," I whispered in his ear.

I saw startled confusion in his eyes.

"What—" he began.

Then the shapeshift I'd already begun took place. My forearm lengthened, extending a foot, driving the blade of my knife up under his chin, into his skull.

His eyes widened. His mouth opened, and I saw steel inside, piercing his tongue as it reached straight through his palate and into his brain. He screamed soundlessly.

Like a tree toppling, he began to fall on top of me. I tried to pull back, but his weight bore me down. I moaned as the knife drove more deeply into my arm.

His shape-shift began to unravel. As he became lighter and smaller, what seemed like a hundred different hands pulled him off me, began helping me up. I let my own forearm return to normal.

A dozen voices were commenting at once:

"Incredible fight—"

"I can't believe you beat *Ulyanash*—"

"—never seen the like—"

"How did he—"

"Well done," Aber said, crouching beside me.

Someone handed him a goblet of wine, which he passed to me. I took a deep swallow.

Freda was suddenly at my side.

Freda said, "The knife must come out."

I glanced down. Its blade was still buried in my arm nearly to the hilt. Tiny drops of blood beaded and rose into the air around it.

"Do it fast," I said.

"Not here," she said. She looked around. "Aunt Lanara—I need a quiet place to work."

"This way," our aunt said. She had just reached us. Looking concerned, she led the way through the crowd—which parted for her—to the far wall. There, she opened a door to a small sitting room.

"We'll be out as soon as possible," Aber promised her. "Oberon will be fine."

"I promised you excitement," I said, grinning.

"Yes." She frowned. "But I cannot tolerate such behavior. No more dueling at my parties!'"

I nodded. "I'm sorry. It was forced upon me."

She ushered us inside, then closed the door on her way out.

"Don't worry," Aber said, "she loved every minute of it. Her party's going to be the talk of society for the next month. And so are you."

"Just what I need . . ." I muttered.

"Sit down," Freda said.

Finding a small overstuffed cassock, I did so. Aber used the Logrus to fetch bandages, needle and thread, and a small jar, which seemed to have salve of some kind inside.

"This is going to hurt," Freda said.

"I've had worse," I told her.

"Oberon," Aber said. He was trying to distract me, I realized with a smile. "You let him stab you, didn't you?"

"Not something I'd normally do, but . . ." I gave a little shrug and winced as pain shot the length of my left arm. My fingertips began to tingle with pins and needles.

"Why?" he asked.

"Did you see what happened?" I asked.

"Just that you suddenly closed and stabbed him."

I chuckled. "There was . . . a little more to it than that."

"He did something with magic," Freda said.

Aber stared at her. "What?"

"I . . . do not know. I was looking at him through the Logrus as they fought. I thought I might learn something about Ulyanash from it."

"Did you?" I asked.

"Almost. He was using magic even before you fought. He had a faint red glow all over. Then, when you killed him, you suddenly glowed a brilliant white. I have never seen anything like it before. What did you do?"

"I shape-shifted, too," I said.

"To what?" Aber demanded.

"I think I'll keep that part to myself," I said. If no one had seen what I'd done, I didn't want word of it to get out. I might have to use that trick again someday.

Freda began to mumble something as she applied the salve. I felt better almost immediately. When I glanced back down to see what she had done, I realized she had applied the salve to the knife rather than to me. And, bubbling and frothing, the metal dissolved as I watched. Blood ran freely now, washing a few bits of steel from my wound. Even the leather handle fell off and bounced across the tiled floor, coming to rest against Aber's boots.

"Neat trick," I said. I wished we'd had that salve in Ilerium.

"It is the best way," she said. "Sewing the wound shut will hurt more. But I have a salve for the pain."

She began sewing the wound closed. Her stitches were quick and precise.

Aber said, "Ulyanash shouldn't have forced the duel on you. Nobody fights to the death anymore. It's . . . frowned upon."

"Why?"

"It's too easy for such fights to escape control."

I shrugged, winced.

"Sit still," Freda said. She had almost finished.

I continued, "I didn't want to kill him, but if I hadn't, he would have killed me."

"Yes." Aber's gaze was distant. "He had two chances to call the fight over, but he wouldn't. He had second blood, so there wouldn't have been any lost honor. It's clearly his own fault. No one who saw it will blame you."

"Good."

"His family, though . . . You're likely to have a blood feud on your hands. We all are."

"Done," Freda, tying up the wound with a length of bandage. "No more fighting tonight, Oberon. Promise me."

I rose. "I'll try not to," I said.

Aber said, "That trick aside . . . honestly, I don't think you should have been able to kill him."

I raised my eyebrows. "I'm pretty good with a blade, you know."

"He was a Lord of Chaos. A *full-blooded lord*. You don't know what that means."

"We are not as powerful as once we were," Freda said. "You know that."

Aber sighed. "Not that again . . ."

I looked from one to another. "Will someone tell me what you're talking about?"

"There are a lot of important people at this party," Freda said. "I have been talking and listening. I believe I know what has happened to Father."

I faced her. "What?"

"It is about the Shadows. King Uthor says they have weakened Chaos and everyone here. He wants them destroyed."

I looked from one to another. "What does that have to do with Dad?"

She hesitated. "There are forces in the universe that are equal and opposite to Chaos and the Logrus. They work to strengthen themselves and undermine our power. King Uthor's investigation into the cause of the Shadows' appearance has somehow focused on Dad. They think he's responsible."

"How?" I demanded.

"Nobody quite knows. But if he somehow allied himself with another power, something different from the Logrus, he may have found a way. He was arrested when he reached King Uthor's palace two days ago. Somehow, he . . . simply vanished from his cell. It should not have been possible. The Logrus sealed him inside, without access to magic."

Something different from the Logrus . . . I thought of the Pattern within me and swallowed hard.

Suddenly, it all began to make sense.

TWENTY-FIVE

f King Uthor is behind the attacks on our family, we must flee into Shadow!" Aber said. "I'm going now, before we're arrested next!"

Freda gave him a withering stare. "Nothing has been proved about Father," she said. "He is merely suspected. *We* are not—because we have done nothing wrong. We may fall under scrutiny, but we have nothing to hide. If you run, they will assume you are guilty and take action accordingly."

"Someone else knows about Dad," I said, frowning. Rising, I paced the room. "That's why we have all been targets. Someone other than King Uthor is trying to kill us for what Dad did."

"Then you're saying it's true—" Aber began.

"Yes! I . . . feel it." I swallowed, the image of the Pattern rising in my mind. Whatever deal our father had made with this *thing*, this power that was not the Logrus, I saw now that it involved me. Somehow, it had to do with the Pattern within me. If anyone else realized what I knew, what I could draw upon, I would be marked for death.

Aber sat heavily. "I . . . hoped it was all a mistake," he said. "Someone pursuing a blood feud against Dad. But if he has betrayed us . . . betrayed King Uthor and the Logrus . . ."

"Do not talk that way!" Freda said. "We do not know what he

has or has not done."

Aber raised his head. "You know. So does Oberon."

I swallowed. But I could not reply. Neither could Freda.

Finally I said, "We will talk more about this later."

"We cannot leave Aunt Lanara waiting," Freda said, gathering her skirts and rising. "Say nothing. I will see what else can be discovered."

The rest of the evening passed relatively uneventfully. We moved from the social hour to a huge dining hall. My uncle sat at the head of the table, with my aunt to his right and me to his left, opposite her. Aber and Freda sat at the middle of the table. A large section sat empty . . . I assumed Ulyanash and his followers would have been seated there. They had left early, taking his body with them.

Two seats down from me sat my bride-to-be, Braxara.

I had seldom seen a more unappealing woman. From her bald, three-horned head to her fanged mouth, from her pallid skin to her deathlike stare, every element repulsed me. Although I had fully intended to go through with the marriage to keep my word—it could be a marriage in name only, after all—upon catching sight of the bride-to-be I knew I had to find a way out.

Still, a year was a very long time, and many things could happen . . .

"A toast!" cried my Uncle Leito, standing. He raised his goblet. "To Oberon and Braxara!"

"To Oberon and Braxara!" everyone cried, raising their own goblets.

Glancing at my bride-to-be, I found her coolly studying me. I forced a smile. She did the same. Somehow, I got the feeling she disliked me nearly as much as I disliked her.

It was late by the time the party began to wind down. I had seen little of Freda and Aber all evening—they had been busy gathering news and gossip—and I missed them. Aunt Lanara and Uncle Leito kept close guard on me after the feast, introducing me to such a steady stream of dukes, duchesses, barons, lords, and ladies that I couldn't keep the names straight or tell one from another after the first dozen.

Finally, though, they saw fit to give Braxara and me a few moments together in the gardens just outside the ballroom. Here, strolling through the odd plants and small moving rocks, under the curious glow of three moons, we had a moment to talk.

"You are not what I expected," she told me.

"Nor you," I replied.

"Why did you accept this marriage?"

"I needed something from Lanara. This was her price. I'm sorry . . . it was not for love."

She laughed, and the moonlight glinted off her horns. "When has love ever had much to do with marriage?"

I shrugged. "I had hoped . . ."

"You have much to learn."

We walked together in an uncomfortable silence. We had not said another word by the time we returned to the ballroom. I hadn't known what to say to her; she hadn't offered anything more.

She made her departure not long after that, and the other guests took that as their cue to leave. When we bade farewell to the last of the guests, only my aunt, uncle, Freda, Aber, and a small army of servants remained. The servants busied themselves cleaning up.

"The evening has been a great success," Aunt Lanara proclaimed, "marred only by that unfortunate incident with Lord Ulyanash."

"It could not be avoided," I said. "I take some small consolation from the fact that he won't ruin any future parties."

She gave me an odd look. "He was well regarded, you know."

"Despite his family."

"True . . ." She sighed. "Still, what is done cannot be undone. We must concentrate on the triumphs of the evening. You and Braxara made a handsome couple."

Freda said, "I have never seen a finer gathering, Aunt Lanara."

"Thank you, my dear!" she positively beamed.

"We ought to be getting home," Aber said. "It's late, and I already sent our carriage on ahead."

"Thank you for everything, Aunt Lanara." I kissed her cheek. "Uncle Leito." I shook his hand.

He gave me a hug, and whispered in my ear: "Guard yourself, boy. I am hearing many rumors of your father, and his name is linked to treason."

I gave a quick nod. "Thank you."

Aber produced a Trump, and the three of us returned home directly.

*   *   *

We were all tired, but took a moment to linger in Aber's bedroom, where his Trump had brought us. I looked around at the clutter. Half-painted Trumps lay out on the desk, several dozen full-sized paintings, including several portraits of Freda, leaned up against the walls, and stacks of brushes and jars of paint and pigment lay everywhere. Even the carpets underfoot were dotted with spots and spills of paint. It had a very comfortable, lived-in feeling.

Aber cleared paintings off two chairs for Freda and me while he perched on the edge of the bed. When we all had our seats, Freda was the first to speak.

"The situation does not look good for Father," she said. "His flight has only served to convince one and all of his guilt."

"I imagine so," I said. "Do they have any idea where he went?"

"None," Freda said with a sigh. "He can apparently mask his trail. I also received a warning. If Father returns, we must notify King Uthor's counselors immediately. If we do not, we will be judged accomplices and dealt with accordingly."

Aber swallowed audibly. "Then it's settled," he said. "It's going to be Dad or us. We have to choose."

"No we don't," I said. "At least . . . not yet. He hasn't come home yet. And if he never returns . . ."

"Then all we have to worry about is whoever is trying to kill the rest of us," Aber said. "Great."

"Perhaps the death of Ulyanash will end the attacks," Freda said. "If he planned them—"

"He *was* involved," I said, thinking back to the tower of skulls, "but he was not the one in charge. Our main enemy is still out there."

Later, in my room, as I was preparing for bed, I felt a strange presence. Someone was trying to contact me via Trump. I figured it had to be Aber, so I opened my mind.

"What is it?" I asked. The image before me flickered, but did not come clear, as though something interfered with our connection. "Who's there?"

A low, unpleasant, and somehow familiar chuckle followed. "Don't you recognize your brother? You left me behind in Juniper."

"Locke?" I guessed.

"Very good." His voice had a mocking quality. I shivered; it sounded exactly as I remembered it.

"Locke is dead," I said, wary now. "Who are you?"

The mists between us parted a little, and I saw my dead brother standing there.

TWENTY-SIX

My eyes narrowed. It certainly *looked* like my half-brother, from the arrogant turn of the lips to the swaggering stride. He took two steps forward, staring at me in turn.

"Locke is dead," I said. "I saw him die. We burned his body on a funeral pyre."

"And your head is made of thicker stone than I'd thought. If anyone else there had a shred of sense, I'd be talking to them now. But you're the one who can help. Do you want to find out who's killing off our family, or not?"

I bit back an angry reply. This person certainly sounded like Locke. When we first met in Juniper, I had wanted to pound him into the ground with my fists. He had been rude, arrogant, and dismissive of me—a typical Lord of Chaos, apparently.

"Of course I do," I said. "But I need proof you're who you say you are."

"Ask Freda. She will tell you."

I shrugged. "She is convinced. I am not. I was with Locke when he died."

"That wasn't me."

I paused. "Then who was it?"

"I don't know. I was drugged, taken from Juniper, and held prisoner. Those who took me . . . well, to make a long story short, I escaped and most of them are dead. I've been preparing to act. I'm going to need help, though—your help, Freda's, everyone's. The time is almost right."

"Right for what?"

"An attack. I know who our enemy is. It's King Uthor."

I hesitated. That mostly matched my own theory. If Locke *was* telling the truth—if this really *was* Locke—then a lot of changes were coming. And I wasn't sure they'd be for the better.

"Where are you?" I said.

"I'm in a distant Shadow. Time moves faster here . . . much faster. I've had six months to raise an army. We can help each other, Oberon. I'm going to conquer the Chaos and make myself king."

"Is Davin with you?" I asked suddenly.

He hesitated. "No. He's in the field with our troops. Why?"

"We lost him in battle . . . his body was never recovered."

"He helped me escape."

"And Fenn and Isadore? They left to get help in Juniper, but never made it to the Courts of Chaos—"

"I don't know where they are."

A chill suddenly went through me. I knew he had contacted Fenn. Therefore, he was lying. This couldn't be my brother. If he knew personal details about Freda, then Locke must have shared them with someone . . . perhaps Taine or Mattus. The information could have been gotten from either of them through torture. Which meant he was in league with the serpent in the tower of skulls.

"Very well," I said without a bit of hesitation. I couldn't let him know I suspected anything. "Where shall we meet? Here?"

"No. Your house is being watched." He frowned, forehead wrinkling. "I have to go to the Courts of Chaos tonight. Maybe you can meet me then. I have allies who are going to help me seize power when the time is right."

I nodded. "That's right, you're a full-blooded Lord of Chaos, aren't you? So you can make a legitimate claim on the throne?"

"Yes."

I nodded. "Where?"

"Tsagoth Square. Do you know it?"

"No, but I'll find it."

"Here." His hand jerked, and something white flew threw the air at me. Instinctively I caught it—a Trump, showing an unfamiliar courtyard, surrounded by dark and foreboding buildings.

"Tsagoth Square," he said. "Come alone in one hour."

Alone . . . so I would be an easy target. I forced a smile and nodded. And then contact was gone.

I brooded on what to do and finally decided to do nothing for the moment. The fake Locke said our house was being watched. That couldn't be true, or he would have known about Fenn being here. Aber's protection spells must be working.

I would go, and I would have answers—or kill him trying to get them.

Then a question occurred to me. He had contacted my by Trump. Where had he obtained it? I frowned. As far as I knew, Aber had only made two, one for Freda and one for his own use. Though if Dad and Aber could make Trumps, perhaps others in our family could, too. . . . I would have to ask Aber about it later.

Taking out the set of Trumps my brother had loaned me, I pulled out our father's. Slowly I focused on it. I felt a distant stirring, and then contact . . . a voice, but no image came to life.

"What is it?" he said.

"It's Oberon. I need to talk to you."

"This is not a good time."

"I may be about to walk into an ambush. I need your advice."

"Wait—"

And then there was nothing. I couldn't tell if he had deliberately severed our connection, or if something else had interrupted it.

After trying twice more to contact him without success, I went downstairs, got a small crossbow from the guards' armory on the ground floor, loaded it with a bolt, and returned to my room. I stayed long enough to write a note explaining what had happened and where I was going. If Dad showed up, he'd be able to follow me; if Aber and Freda found it, they would know what had happened . . . and that the man who was almost certainly impersonating Locke had probably betrayed and killed me. Then I buckled on the enchanted sword that Aber had swiped for me from our father's rooms.

"I'm going out," I said to Port. "The next time Freda or Aber come past, let them in. Tell them I left a note for them on my desk."

"Very good, sir!"

I took two Trumps, Dad's and the one of my bedroom that Aber had made, and put them into a pouch at my belt. Then I used the

Trump that fake-Locke had sent and went through to Tsagoth Square half an hour early.

As the picture had indicated, Tsagoth Square was a small paved courtyard with huge flagstones underfoot. Dark buildings rose on all sides. Four moons moved through the heavens in different directions overhead, and stars swirled like fireflies. I looked around by the half-light they provided and spotted a few statues of hideously deformed men holding swords at the far end. They offered the only cover, so I hid behind them, where I could see the center of the square, but not be seen.

I drew out my father's Trump and stared at it. I felt a faint distant stirring, but no direct contact.

"I'm in Tsagoth Square," I said. "If you can hear me, I could really use your help now."

Nothing happened. No reply, no sense of his presence, not a word. I sighed and put the Trump away. So much for parental loyalty. I should have known better.

As I'd expected, I didn't have long to wait. Suddenly, the false Locke stepped into the square. He was alone. Drawing his sword, he stood ready to attack me when I tried to enter through the Trump he'd sent. Had I been on time, I would have been quickly killed.

That settled it. I rose silently, aimed, and fired the crossbow at his back.

He seemed to sense the bolt coming; whipping around, he batted it out of the air harmlessly.

"So," he said, stalking toward me, "you know."

"Yes." I drew my sword and bounded into the open. The blade

fit my hand like it had been made for me. I advanced on him, too. "Fenn gave you away. You spoke to him. He's in our house now."

He shook his head and sloughed off his face like a snake shedding its skin. I stopped and stared, bewildered and horrified. It wasn't Locke. I'd expected that. But the face underneath . . . Ulyanash?

"You're dead," I said. "I killed you!"

"You are as stupid as your father," Ulyanash sneered, wiping bits of skin away from the corners of his eyes. "You have no power here, unholy mongrel! You do not know our ways. You could not hope to stand against a Lord of Chaos who wants you dead."

"I did it once."

"That was my cousin Orole. I could not attend Lady Lanara's party and kill you myself, so I sent him in my place. We look much alike. Everyone is fooled whenever we switch places."

"I killed him, and I can kill you." I shrugged. "I can't imagine you're a much better fighter than he was."

"That shows how little you know." He raised his sword and advanced on me again.

"Explain it to me," I said, trying to draw out information. I circled, keeping twenty feet between us. "Don't let me die in ignorance."

"Born in ignorance. Raised in ignorance. What harm to die in ignorance?"

Leaping forward, he closed quickly, then lunged. I parried, still backing away. Best to keep him talking. He seemed as slow-witted as Aber and Rèalla had claimed. Why else take time to brag in the middle of a fight?

"I know more than you think," I said.

"Tell me something, then." He slowed his advance. "Maybe you can buy your life, if you have the information I want or need."

I chuckled. "Or maybe you can buy yours. How about we trade?"

He shrugged. "You are going to die anyway. Why not? There are things I want to know."

"I'll go first," I said. "Who is the serpent in the tower of skulls?"

He looked surprised. "Lord Zon, for all the good it will do you. My turn now. Does Dworkin really have the Jewel of Judgment?"

"I don't know," I said honestly.

"Wrong answer."

Without warning, he lunged. The silvered blade of his sword slid past my frantic parry, nicking my left shoulder. The wound was mi-nor—little more than a scratch, really—but it stung, then turned cold. An icy feeling began to spread down my arm toward my fingers. His blade was poisoned, I realized with shock.

"Want to change your answer?" he asked, drawing back a pace.

"I cannot change the truth. I have never heard of the Jewel of Judgment. What is it?"

"A ruby, a little smaller than a man's fist."

"Ah." I nodded, knowing the one to which he referred. When we were in Juniper, my father had somehow taken me inside the gem. It had opened up my mind to the Pattern within me.

"Then you *do* know the Jewel?"

"Yes. I didn't know it had a name."

"Where is it?"

263

"My father has it. Why is it important?"

I felt a strange warmth in my right hand. The sword's hilt . . . perhaps it was doing something to counteract the poison? I tightening my grew. The numbness no longer seemed to be spreading from my wound quite so quickly.

"It is . . . a key to controlling the Logrus. My turn. Where is it now?"

"I don't know. The last time I saw it, Dad had it in his workshop in Juniper. It may still be there."

Ulyanash regarded me silently for a moment, then nodded. "I believe you," he said. "Fair enough."

"My turn again," I said. "Who does Lord Zon work for? I know it's not King Uthor."

"Lord Zon works for himself. One day soon, he will be King of Chaos."

"And you'll be his right hand man? That sounds like a plot worse than my father's."

He smirked. "In a way, your father made all this possible. Uthor is weak because of him. His followers waver in their loyalty. When we strike . . ."

I saw movement over Ulyanash's left shoulder. A man was entering Tsagoth Square, stepping into it from empty air. Obviously he was using a Trump. Aber?

No—it was my father! And he had his sword drawn. It seemed he'd gotten my message and followed me here after all.

I took a deep breath. My whole left side felt heavy and cold. The warmth from the enchanted sword could not hold it back. Numbness spread into my chest. No wonder Ulyanash had won so many fights, if he poisoned his weapons. When the coldness reached my heart . . . I did not like to think what would happen.

"I seem to have run out of questions for you," he said. He raised his sword. "Prepare yourself, son of Dworkin!"

Dad began to creep up behind him, moving as softly as a cat. I had never been so happy in my life to see someone. I had to keep Ulyanash talking for just a few seconds more.

"I have one last thing to ask," I said. I let my sword sag down as if I couldn't hold it up any longer. "I need to know—who was behind the attack on our family in Juniper? Was it you?"

"Of course." He laughed.

I let my head fall to my chest. "I thought so."

He stepped forward, sword ready.

"Look behind you," I whispered.

He started to glance back, then thought better of it—it *was* an old trick, I had to admit. Instead, with his smirk growing broader, he raised his sword for a killing blow.

With one swing, my father struck Ulyanash's head from his shoulders. Blood sprayed across me, then began to drift up toward the sky. His body hit the ground with a dull thump.

"I came as soon as I could," my father said. He bent to clean his blade on Ulyanash's shirt. "Are you all right, my boy? Are you up for more work tonight? I need you."

"His sword was poisoned." I gave a pained grimace. "He nicked me. I think I'm . . ."

And I felt myself collapse.

TWENTY-SEVEN

I awoke slowly, feeling stiff. Sunlight came through an open window, showing a pleasant enough room. Whitewashed walls, long narrow bed, wooden floor. Outside, birds sang. We were in Shadow somewhere.

"Dad?" I called.

No answer. It seemed I'd been abandoned again.

My shoulder had been bandaged. I sat up and pulled away the dressing, discovering fresh pink skin over the wound. Apparently I'd been here a few days. The knife wound in my arm had also healed.

I washed up, dressed, and went into the next room. A small table sat waiting for me, along with a basket of cold bread, a bottle of red wine, and a note. The note said:

> *I have urgent business in another Shadow. Time runs very fast here, so it will probably be a few days before I return. Get your strength back. I need your help.*

The note wasn't signed.

I ate slowly. The crusty brown bread had gone a bit stale, but the wine more than made up for it.

As I chewed, I began to have a strange sensation of being watched. I remembered the serpent-creature who had used Taine's blood to scry upon me . . . Lord Zon, Ulyanash had named him. Zon might well be spying on me now and cursing the day I had come to the Courts of Chaos. Hopefully he had lost one of his chief lieutenants in Ulyanash.

The Pattern within me seemed to have special properties. Let's see how I could use them.

With the bread knife, I began to carve an image of the Pattern into the table before me. As I did, my sight seemed to drift away from the reality of *here* and *now*. I saw dark lines, threads of energy, rising from the table. They formed an image of the Pattern, slowly spinning in mid air. I willed it up, up, larger and larger, surrounding and protecting me.

Suddenly, like a door closing, my sense of being watched came to and end. Whatever connection Lord Zon had made between Taine's blood and me, between the tower of skulls and this little cottage, had been broken.

I let the Pattern go, and it fell apart. The carving became just scratches on the tabletop, no more. My breathing relaxed. Good— one problem had been taken care of.

It seemed I, too, could command some real magic—untrained though I might be. I could at the very least protect myself from being spied upon.

My use of the Pattern further confirmed my suspicions . . . Dad *had* allied himself with some power other than the Logrus. And he had given the gift of its Pattern to me . . . though where the Jewel of Judgment fit into it all, I couldn't yet say.

I sighed. Our enemies wouldn't wait. I couldn't sit around this cottage waiting for Dad to return. My every action had been well re-warded thus far . . . from the party at Aunt Lanara's house to the fight with Ulyanash. Of course, I reminded myself, I would have died if not for Dad's timely intervention . . . but wasn't that what parents were for?

It was time to take the battle to Lord Zon and his tower. I had been there often enough in my dreams. I knew what it looked like. Now it was my turn to try drawing a Trump.

Bending, I dipped my index finger into my cup of wine, then rose and crossed to the nearest whitewashed wall. My brother Aber always drew a representation of the Logrus beneath the images he painted on Trumps. Our father had told me it wasn't necessary; he could do it by simply keeping the Logrus fixed in his mind while he worked. I could not draw on the Logrus, as I had never ventured into it, but the Pattern within me seemed to have many of the same powers.

I summoned a mental image of the Pattern and began to sketch the tower of skulls . . . from the inside. I showed the altar slab, the winding staircase of leg bones, the doorway through which hell-creatures had dragged my brothers to be tortured. The image took on an *aliveness*, a sense of reality and immediacy, despite being pale pink lines on the wall. Whenever I willed it, I knew I could bring the image to life and step through.

Then, licking wine from my finger, I stepped back. Yes, it would do. Crude though it was, I really *had* created a Trump. I knew it would work.

Retrieving my sword from the bedroom, I found the pen and

ink my father had used, left him my thanks on the back of the note he'd left me, and told him I had gone to rescue Taine from the tower of skulls. I would return home to our house in the Beyond if successful. If not . . . he should try to contact me via Trump and bring me back directly.

Then I turned to the picture I had sketched on the wall, concentrating. Slowly, I felt it coming to life before me. It grew darker, blacks and browns emerging . . . lengthening shadows . . . the altar block . . . the circling stairway of bones . . . the entrance through which prisoners came . . .

Like a doorway, it filled the wall.

Hefting my sword, I stepped through.

The inside of the tower proved to be deserted. I knew it from the way my footsteps echoed; the shadows where I had previously seen Lord Zon remained empty. I no longer felt that malevolent presence there.

I crept up to the shadowy doorway and peered into a narrow corridor that circled down. A single torch lit the way, its light bubbling up to pool on the ceiling. Pausing, I listened, but heard nothing . . . no rustle of leather, no clink of armor, nor even the moans of prisoners.

I started forward, treading softly, sword ready. It couldn't possibly be this easy to rescue Taine.

The passageway descended. I came to a line of doors, all of them closed. Cells? I unbarred the first one and pushed it open, revealing a dark, tiny room scarcely large enough to lie down in. A skeleton lay chained in the far corner, its bones showing signs of having been gnawed. A few tatters of clothing remained, but nothing to tell me who it had been. Hopefully not one of my missing brothers or sisters.

The next two cells were empty.

The fourth cell held Taine. I rushed to his side. Still alive—?

He was not chained, but lay on a pile of straw against the far wall. His bare chest and arms were covered with scabbed-over sores and cuts, just as I had seen in my last spirit-voyage here. A yellow crust covered his eyes. For a second I thought he might be dead, but then as I bent over him and my shadow covered his face, he moaned and tried to push me away.

"Lie still," I said softly. "I'm your brother Oberon. I'm here to rescue you."

He began to thrash and cry out wordlessly. Clearly he was beyond reason. Luckily his strength was gone; his blows were like a child's. I pinned his arms with one hand, then picked him up and threw him over my shoulder. He was curiously light—he had to weigh less than a hundred pounds now, starved as he was to skin and bones—and I had no trouble carrying him.

When I turned to leave, however, the room darkened. Half a dozen guards filled the doorway, blocking out the torch light. They all held swords at the ready.

I swallowed and raised my own weapon. It would be a challenge to cut my way through them while protecting Taine.

Instead of trying to fight me, however, they slammed the door shut. I heard the bar dropping into place.

Darkness surrounded me. I had a terrible, sinking feeling inside. Taine moaned.

"Don't give up just yet," I told him.

He did not reply. I put him down on the pile of straw, then sat next to him, my back to the wall and my sword balanced across my knees.

I fished the first Trump out of the pouch at my belt, the one showing my room. A couple of thin blades of light came in through cracks in the door. I tilted the Trump until I could see I clearly and began to concentrate.

It should have come to life before me, but it didn't. I felt . . . *nothing*. Something, some spell of Lord Zon's, prevented the Logrus from working in here.

So much for my first backup plan. I put the Trump away. Before I could try creating a Pattern-Trump of my own, the light faded away, leaving me in complete darkness . . . no way to see or draw a new Trump.

I sighed. That just left my father.

It shouldn't be long now. It shouldn't be long at all . . .

TWENTY-EIGHT

After what seemed a lifetime, I felt the familiar sensation of someone trying to reach me via my Trump. I opened my mind and reached out.

Dworkin appeared before me, framed by the white walls of the cottage. My wine-sketched Trump lay behind his left shoulder.

"Where are you?" he asked.

"In a cell with Taine. Take us out?"

He nodded and extended his right hand. "Come on."

I picked up my brother's limp body, reached out to Dad, and he pulled us both through to the cottage. As the dark cell disappeared, I couldn't help but grin.

"Thanks," I said. "I've been waiting for you."

He glanced at the sword in my hand. "They did not disarm you, I see. What happened?"

"It was a trap," I said.

I carried Taine into the bedroom and set him down on the bed. He stirred a moment, then lay still. He looked worse in the bright light than he had in the cell. Still, he was tough or he would have died long before this.

"They locked me up when I went into Taine's cell," I continued.

"I tried to get out with one of Aber's Trumps, but they must have spells that prevent the Logrus from working, I think, like in Juniper."

"Interesting," he said.

"They haven't figured out yet that you're no longer using the Logrus."

Dworkin chuckled. "You know too much, my boy! Good thing they did not question you."

He looked over my brother's injuries briefly. "Dehydration and loss of blood, I think. Starvation. The wounds look worse than they really are. Get him something to drink."

"Water . . ." gasped Taine suddenly.

I looked in the next room, but only found the half bottle of wine I hadn't finished. I poured him a glass and held his head up while he took tiny sips.

He finished it all, then lay back and seemed to go to sleep—or pass out.

"What should we do with him?" I asked. "Do you know any safe Shadows, where they can't possibly reach him?"

"I have a better idea."

He produced a new Trump and handed it to me. It showed the library of our house in the Beyond. The paint glistened; it hadn't been made long before.

"Take him to Freda. She will nurse him back to health. Home may be the best place for them all right now. I can't think of a safer one."

"Aber and Freda put up spells to shield it," I said.

"I know," he said. "So have I. Get going."

"Then what? When will I see you again? You said you needed my help."

"I do. I will." He nodded. "I will contact you soon. I have one quick errand first . . ."

Scooping up Taine, I studied the Trump until the library grew before me. Scrolls, books, the table . . .

I stepped through and found myself in the room. Fenn and Aber were seated at the table, talking. They leaped to their feet, looking surprised—and happy.

"Is that Taine?" Aber cried.

"Yes."

"How—"

"I rescued him," I said simply.

I deliberately didn't mention our father's role in the adventure—if they knew too much, they might be considered conspirators with Dworkin and me, and punished accordingly. That was the moment I realized I *was* a conspirator, whether I wanted to be or not. Clearly, with that Pattern inside me, I could never hope to ally myself with King Uthor and the Courts of Chaos. They would destroy me at once if they ever found out. My future had to lie elsewhere . . . with this power to which Dad had allied himself.

"Let me give you a hand," Fenn said. He took Taine from my arms.

Aber and I followed him out and up the stairs to the floor where we all had rooms. He knew Taine's door, and the face carved in it let us all in without any question. It seemed they could adapt to emergencies when they had to.

Anari suddenly appeared in the doorway, looking concerned.

"Lord Taine?" he asked. "Is he—"

"Alive but unconscious," I said. "Find Freda and tell her to get in here. Then get us warm broth and lots of water. I don't think he's eaten in weeks."

"Yes, Lord." Anari turned and ran down the hall.

I returned to the bed. Taine began to stir and opened his eyes a little as Fenn put pillows behind his head.

"I dreamed . . ." he whispered.

"Try not to think about it," Aber said. "The important thing is that you're here and you're safe."

Freda appeared. "What is this about?" she demanded. Then she saw Taine and hurried forward, pushing Aber and Fenn to one side.

"I think," Aber said, drawing me out to the hall, "that you have a story to tell us."

I chuckled. "It's going to have to wait. I'm exhausted, and I'm going to bed. Call me if we're attacked, otherwise . . ."

"But your meeting with Locke! What happened?"

"It wasn't Locke," I said simply. "He told me where to find Taine before I killed him. Then I went and got him. It's that simple."

Port swung my door open as I approached.

"No one," I said after he closed, "is to come in here until I wake up. Especially not brothers, sisters, or beautiful half-dressed women!"

"A very wise decision," said Port, sounding happy at last.

I couldn't have been asleep for more than a few hours before I felt rough hands shaking me.

"What now?" I groaned. If this was Aber, using yet another of his seemingly endless supply of Trumps, I'd strangle him.

But it was not Aber. It was my father.

"Get dressed, quickly and quietly," he said. "We're leaving. I told you I needed your help. The time has come."

TWENTY-NINE

You keep telling me you need my help," I said, sitting up. "With what, exactly?"

"Oh, this and that," he said. "And I want your company, my boy. We should spend more time together. . . ."

I had a strange feeling he had no intention of telling me anything right now. The last time he had shown up like this and dragged me out of bed, it had been in Ilerium, and he had saved my life. Hell-creatures had hurled glowing green fire at my house, destroying it almost as I stepped through the door.

I began pulling on my pants.

"Is an attack coming?" I demanded. I pulled on my left boot, stamping my foot on the floor to force it comfortably into place. "If so, we have to get everyone out of the house."

"No one knows I am here," he said. "I do not think an attack will come. At least, not tonight."

"Will I need a sword?"

"Hopefully not. Bring one anyway."

Chuckling, I got my right boot on, then pulled on my shirt and laced up the front. I would have brought my sword whether he wanted me to or not; that he wanted me to bring it meant he expected fighting.

Finally, rising, I buckled on my swordbelt and loosened the blade in the scabbard.

"Ready," I announced.

"That sword—I meant to ask you where you got it."

"Aber borrowed it for me. I needed it for my engagement party. I'm supposed to marry my cousin Braxara next year."

He stared at me, shaking his head. "Oberon . . . how do you get yourself into these things? I will talk to her parents. We cannot have such a match."

"Not that they would let her marry the son of a traitor," I said.

He looked at me oddly. "Not a traitor . . . the founder of a new dynasty!"

"I'd be happy to make it through this whole mess alive."

He shook his head and pulled out a Trump I had never seen before. This one had been carefully finished, unlike the hastily sketched Trumps he had made in Juniper, and it looked old—a favorite place he had been many times before, I guessed.

It showed an ancient tavern with ivy-colored walls, small-paned glass windows glowing warmly from within, and a pair of huge brick chimneys from which smoke rose. The sign of a boar's head hung over the doorway.

"You're taking me drinking?" I asked, letting a hopeful note creep into my voice.

"I need help," he said, "to correct a great mistake I made many years ago. And this is where we are going to start."

"Aha," I said. "The theft of the Jewel of Judgment, I assume."

"What do you know about that?" he demanded, regarding me warily. Unconsciously, he touched his chest . . . just about the place a pendant would hang. Or the Jewel, if he had it on a chain around his neck. I studied him.

"It's all everyone is talking about in the Courts. People keep asking me if I know where you hid it."

Shaking his head, he forced a laugh. "Next time they do, tell them I never had it."

"All right," I agreed. No sense in tipping my hand any more than I already had. "Now, about this tavern . . ."

He smiled happily. "A friend of mine runs it," He said. "Come on. I do need a drink now!"

Taking my elbow, he raised the Trump and concentrated on the image. It seemed to come to life, rising and expanding before us, a low stone building with ivy running up the walls, plenty of open windows with curtains fluttering in the breeze. I heard voices raised in a cheerful drinking song, smelled baking bread and roasting meat on the faint wind that now touched my face.

He stepped forward, pulling me with him. My feet left the wooden floor, and I trod on hard-packed dirt.

It was early afternoon, and we stood in front of the tavern. A warm wind blew, heavy with the smells of trees and grass and summer. Birds sang and insects chirped.

Through the open doorway of the tavern came a minstrel's voice, accompanied by the strumming of a lute, and suddenly a dozen voices joined in on the chorus.

I smiled; this was the sort of place I liked. Leaving Chaos made it feel like a heavy weight had been lifted from my shoulders. I would not go back easily to that nightmare place.

Dad started forward, and I fell in step behind him, one hand dropping to the hilt of my sword. For all I knew, this might be a carefully constructed trap. If our enemies knew Dworkin frequented this place, what better spot for an ambush?

Fortunately, we found no hell-creatures inside—just a dozen men, who seemed to be locals in for a quiet evening of cards and gossip, plus a couple of serving maids and a portly man behind the bar, whose eyes lit up with honest pleasure as he spotted my father.

"Dworkin, my old friend!" he cried, coming around to greet us. "It has been far too long!"

Laughing, the two clapped each other on the back like old drinking buddies.

"This is my son, Oberon," Dworkin said with a nod to me. "Oberon, this is Ben Bayle. Not only is he a good friend, he is one of the best vintners I have ever found."

"One of the best?" said Bayle.

"All right," laughed Dworkin, "the best of them all!"

"That's more like it!"

"A tavern-keeper who makes his own wine?" I said, raising my eyebrows.

"And who better?" said Bayle, but he grinned happily. "You must try last year's red," he said to Dworkin. "It was a very dry year, and the wine has an extra piquancy. I think it's one of our best, on par with the red of '48."

"That good!" said my father. "Set us up." He glanced around the room; nobody paid us the slightest heed now, wrapped up in their own drinking and conversation and a couple of card games. "The corner table," he said to me, indicating the one he wanted with a quick jerk of his head.

I headed over and sat with my back to one wall, my sword on the chair next to me. Dworkin sat with his back to the other wall. We could both see the door.

"You should like this place," he said to me. "I spent a lot of time here when I was your age."

"I didn't think the Shadows were that old. How old were you when you created them?"

"You are fishing for information," he said.

"Better to get it from you," I said. "Provided you tell me the truth."

"There is truth in everything I say."

"You didn't bring me here to drink, did you?" I said.

"You look like you need it."

"It *has* been a difficult few days."

"What has happened?"

I told him, leaving nothing out—not even Rèalla. He chuckled a bit when I got to the part about the stinger in her mouth and the welts on my chest.

"Lucky Aber found her out—you might well have ended up her slave, or worse," he said with a chuckle. "They have powers over men. I hope she was worth it."

"I heal fast," I said. "And sometimes it's better not knowing everything about a woman."

Then I told him how she had turned against Ulyanash and been murdered for her trouble. He sighed sympathetically.

"Lords of Chaos do not take betrayal lightly," he said.

"I know. So why *did* you take the Jewel of Judgment, then? That seems like a pretty big betrayal."

He looked like he was about to answer, but Ben Bayle arrived first with two cups and a dark green bottle, which he uncorked and then poured for us. Dad took the first sip and gave a happy exclamation.

"Excellent!"

Bayle beamed.

I took a sip, too, and had to agree. It was among the finest wines I had ever tasted, and I had dined at King Elnar's table at more that one occasion. Elnar had fancied himself an expert on wines, though I found his favorite selections ran a little too sweet for my tastes.

"Did I tell you it would be worth the trip?" Dworkin said.

"Not really," I said. But I quickly added, "It is, though."

Dworkin drank deeply, let Bayle refill him, then raised his cup in a toast. "To Ben Bayle—always the best!"

I joined in enthusiastically. There were cries of, "Here! Here!" from other patrons.

"Now," said Dad, leaning forward and dropping his voice to a conspiratorial whisper. "I need two fast horses."

Bayle chuckled. "You always do. I'll get them. Anything else?"

"Wine and provisions for three days."

"Lots of wine," I added. "This red, if it travels well."

"Of course it does! My daughters will pack everything up for you. What else?"

Dworkin said, "That will do this time." He reached under the table, drew out a pouch that I knew he hadn't been carrying a moment before, and slipped it across to Bayle. I heard the clink of coins inside and guessed it held gold. Our host nodded, gave Dworkin a wink, tucked the money away, and headed for the small doorway behind the counter.

"I don't understand," I said. "Why bother with Bayle? If I understand the way Shadows work, you could get any horses you wanted just by traveling to a place that had them waiting for you."

"True," said Dworkin. "But I enjoy coming here, and I am a creature of habit. Also, Ben Bayle is a good man; I like him. I do not have many friends, but he is one."

"And the wine . . ."

"That too."

I had to agree, finishing mine and pouring more. If we ever returned to Juniper and rebuilt, assuming we could deal with the troll problem, we would have to persuade Bayle to join us.

It took nearly an hour for Bayle to get everything ready. I sat impatiently at the corner table, watching those around us, half expecting an army to come rushing through the door at any moment.

No army came, however, and I learned far more about hog breeding than I ever wanted to know from a lively discussion of that topic from the next table.

Dworkin laughed at me quietly.

"What's so funny?" I demanded.

"I will tell you later," he said.

Bayle finally reappeared at the back door and gave a small jerk of his head for us to join him. He seemed positively conspiratorial. He seemed to enjoy aiding us on our mission—whatever it was—and milked it for all it was worth.

"Our host also runs the local livery stable," Dworkin whispered *sotto voce* as we left.

"Quite the entrepreneur," I said.

He chuckled. "Create nothing but the very best," he said, "and you will never be disappointed."

"I don't understand," I said.

"Do not worry about it. Accept him for what he is, no more or less."

I puzzled over that. Out back, I discovered Bayle also ran several other businesses, all of which bore his name on the signs over their door: Bayle's Tannery, Bayle's Boots and Saddles, even Bayle's Fine Meats and Slaughterhouse. From the prosperous look of things, he seemed equally adept at all of them.

Now he stood before the stables, next to two boys who looked so much like him that they had to be his sons. They held the reins of two fine black geldings, long of leg with tall arched necks, braided manes, and long silky tails. Mine—I picked him on sight and came around front to let him smell my hands—had a splash of white on his forehead, Dworkin's a pair of white socks on the left. They had already been saddled, with packs and bedrolls tied behind. Several skins, which I assumed held wine, hung from the saddle.

I mounted, and Dworkin did the same.

"Thank you," he called to Bayle.

The tavern-keeper grinned. "Good luck, and good speed! Come back soon, old friend!"

Dworkin waved.

We rode.

THIRTY

t was a ride like no other.

Dworkin rode hard into the forest, leaving the tavern behind. He seemed to draw inspiration from the land around us, and I watched with awe as an outcropping of rock became the toe of a mountain, visible suddenly as we cleared the trees. Snow-capped heights towered, and just ahead, pines trees began to appear, singly, then rising into a forest as we rounded a boulder as big as a house.

The pass through this mountain chain led steadily upward. A winding trail, well traveled but empty at this moment, grew cold, as an icy wind swept down. I pulled the laces of my shirt collar tighter and hunkered down on my horse. The gelding trudged now, head down, breath pluming the air.

Dworkin called back: "Pick up the pace! There's going to be an avalanche!"

I kicked my horse in the ribs twice and got him to a trot. Boulders, tall as two men, blocked the trail, and the path skirted up and around them. As we rounded the second, I heard a deep rumble, like a dog's growl but lower, starting behind us. Turning in my saddle, I watched as the entire top of the mountain slid down to block the pass. No one would be following us through there before the spring melt.

Chaos and Amber

I looked ahead again. Already the landscape had begun to change, as scrub trees and yellowed patches of grass dotted the trail. We headed down now, and the air grew steadily warmer. The sky, touched by fingers of pink and yellow, brightened noticeably.

"Take a drink of wine," Dworkin said, raising his own wineskin. "Make sure you spill it on your shirt and your horse." He did just that, splashing it across his own shoulders, then across his mount's head, neck, and haunches.

I did the same, taking a swallow and splashing a good couple of swallows onto my shirt and onto my horse. I did not ask the why of it; I did not want to distract him from the journey before us. That he thought it important enough to tell me to do it told me all I needed to know: somehow, it would prove necessary.

The sky darkened to a deep purple as we entered a wood. In the twilight, strange noises surrounded us, chirps and peeps and a *wheep-wheep-wheep* sound that made my skin crawl. My horse quickened his pace without being told, staying right behind Dworkin.

Then huge dark-winged insects, some as large across as my hand, began to rise in swarms thick enough to blot out the sun. From the way they held their barbed tails, I suspected they were venomous. Yet they did not attack us.

"What are they afraid of?" I asked Dworkin.

"Wine," he said.

I pitied anyone trying to follow us through here.

We burst into the open, leaving the insects to their wood, and the sudden night sky seemed a carpet overhead, thick velvet studded with diamond stars. Three moons soared, the smaller two gliding quickly, the larger hovering over the treetops like an all-seeing eye.

That thought made me shiver.

Still we rode.

Silvered clouds came up from the east, obscuring the moons, and the temperature began to fall. As wind tossed the treetops, which grew taller still, a gray sort of wintery daylight broke over us. The land glistened with frost. My breath misted in the air.

Snorting and stomping, our horses plodded on. I found myself staring uneasily at the trees to either side. I had a strange feeling of being observed.

"Do you sense anything unusual here?" I asked.

Dworkin glanced back at me. "No. This world is a bridge between traps. There should be nothing here to bother us."

I hesitated, trying to put words to my uneasiness.

"The horses need rest," I said.

"Then we will replace them," he said.

Shortly, we came to a large grassy clearing, where two black horses identical to the geldings upon which we rode stood waiting. They even had saddles and bedrolls identical to ours.

I raised my eyebrows. "Just like that?" I said.

"Yes." Dworkin swung down from the saddle, changed to the next horse, and kept going. "Their owners are off hunting smirp in the grasslands and won't be back for a few hours."

"Smirp?" I asked.

"Same as rabbits."

I followed his example, then caught up with him.

"That was a neat trick," I said. "Whose horses were those?"

"Does it matter?" he asked.

I thought about it. "I guess not," I said. "They have the same horses they used to have—only theirs are tired."

"No." He made a dismissive gesture. "They are Shadows, not real. They spring full-grown from our minds. We create them with our thoughts; they are mere potentialities in an infinite universe until something real—something like us—gives them shape and substance."

"You sound like you've thought about this a great deal."

"Yes," he said, "I have."

And then the world changed around us again. The sky darkened as we climbed into foothills, and thunder rolled and cracked. Flashes of lightning lit up the sky directly ahead, and a stiff wind grew stronger. Looking up, I could see thick gray clouds gathering. A few drops of rain stung my face.

"Is this your doing, Dad?" I called.

"Yes!" he shouted then pointed ahead. "There's a cave! Get inside before the storm hits!"

We made our way up to the opening, perhaps fifteen feet high and ten feet wide, and rode inside. I saw marks on the walls from tools; it had been widened by men—or other creatures—at some point in its history. Behind us, the heavens opened up, letting go a torrent of rain like nothing I had ever seen before. Water fell in waves so thick, at times you couldn't see more than a few feet away. Grass, bushes, and trees alike came crashing down from the force.

Without looking back, Dad rode forward into the darkness. A

few torches, sputtering faintly, appeared to light our passage. I followed close behind.

Slowly, it grew light ahead, and then we rounded a corner and came into sight of another opening—this one leading out into a cheerful field filled with grass and clover. As we rode out into it, I heard another rumble as the mountain collapsed on top of the cave and tunnels we had just traversed.

Once outside, he reined in his horse; it had grown tired at this passage through so many worlds, as had mine. There was much to do to control them.

"Why don't we call it a night?" I suggested.

At first I thought Dworkin would refuse, but he sighed heavily, then gave a nod of assent. "There's a nice camping spot ahead," he said. "A clearing with a stream and plenty of wood for a fire. Lots of slow, stupid game, too."

"Sounds perfect," I asked.

"We can wait there," he said, "as long as it takes."

An interesting turn of phrase that said little but implied much—all of it different, depending on how you looked at the question.

"Are you expecting company?" I asked.

"I always expect someone," he said, "and I am seldom disappointed."

The trees around us grew taller, darker; pines replaced oaks. Then the path opened up, and ahead I saw the place he meant—a hundred yards of low-cropped grass, then a gentle incline that ended at a wall of stone, a steep cliff rising fifty feet or more above us. Pine trees overhung the top.

He reined in his horse. "Make camp here," he said.

"How long will we be here?" I asked.

"As long as it takes. I . . . am waiting for a guide."

"A guide? You mean you don't know where we're going?" I asked.

"I know. I am having a little difficulty finding it again, however."

"Tell me. Maybe I can help."

"You have been a help already, my boy. More than you realize. But this is not something you can do." He sighed. "I must do the last of it myself."

"Maybe, if you'd explain . . ."

He hesitated, as if not knowing how much he could safely reveal.

I said, "You're going to have to tell me, Dad. I know a lot of it already. Maybe I can help. Remember Juniper . . ."

He sighed, looked away for a long moment, took a deep breath.

"I have lived a long time, Oberon. I have done a lot of things of which I am not proud, and many of which I am." He swallowed. "You . . . you will be the first person besides myself to see the heart of the Shadows. The place where they begin."

"I don't understand," I said.

"All this—" His hand swept out, taking in the world around us. "All this is a Shadow. But what casts that Shadow?"

"It's not the Courts of Chaos, is it?"

"No!" He laughed. "The Courts cast their own shadows, true, but they are dim and dismal places, full of death and unpleasantness.

These Shadows—Juniper, Ilerium, all of them—are cast by something else . . . something greater."

I felt my heart beating in my throat.

"You did it," I said wonderingly. "It's the Pattern."

"That which casts these Shadows is a great Pattern, like the one inside you, but inscribed with my own hand at the very heart of the universe."

"That's why they're after you," I said, wonderingly. "King Uthor *knows*, somehow, and he wants to destroy the Pattern and the Shadows. Freda said they weakened Chaos—"

"Yes! It weakens *them*," he said, voice rising in a laugh. "But it made *you* stronger."

"How—where—" I stammered.

"It is close. But hidden . . . very carefully hidden, where no Lord of Chaos can ever hope to find it on his own."

"Then you hid it too well, if you can't find it either."

"I had . . . help."

My eyes narrowed. "Help? So they're right and you have allied yourself with another power. Who is it?"

"Not exactly a *who*," he said. "More of a *what*. But she is a good and loyal friend."

"A woman? Will she join us here?"

"I hope so." He swung down from his saddle, stretching. "We must wait until she comes."

A woman . . .

"What is her name?" I asked.

He didn't answer. Instead, he walked to the edge of the clearing and gazed off into the trees, lost in thought.

Sighing, I tethered both horses and began unloading their saddles and packs. Every time I looked up, my father had wandered a few steps farther, and now he was staring up at the cliffs as if trying to place them on some mental map.

"She has no name," he said. "At least, none that I know."

"Is she . . . human?" I asked.

"More so that most." He chuckled a bit to himself, as though at some private joke. Then he bent down and began gathering up handfuls of grass.

I had a feeling I wasn't going to get any more from him tonight, so I quit asking. He'd already told me more in the last five minutes than I'd learned from him since I'd found out he was my father.

I looked up at the cliff and thought I glimpsed a faint movement among the trees, a lighter shadow flitting past. Could that be his mysterious woman?

We spent an hour weaving grass into rope, like we'd done when I was a boy, and we used the rope to set snares along game trails running through the grass. While we waited for rabbits or quail or whatever the local equivalent might be, I went down to the stream and threw a couple of dozen rocks up onto the bank, then lugged them back to the clearing and set them in a circle.

Dworkin, meanwhile, had wandered off to the side by himself. I caught him gazing up at the cliff several times when he thought I wasn't paying attention. Whatever was up there, he'd seen it, too. Hopefully it was his mysterious woman.

I gathered wood and set a fire, lighting it with flint and steel that Bayle's daughter had kindly packed for us. Then, as the fire snapped and cracked, I spread out our blankets and sprawled on top of mine. Lying on my back with my fingers laced behind my head, staring up at unfamiliar constellations, I felt a deep contentment. This was the life I liked—roaming far from home, exploring unknown lands, getting to know myself and my father.

I had often gone camping like this with my "Uncle Dworkin" when I was a child. Side by side, we lay out under the stars, a crackling campfire at our feet. He would talk to me like a son and tell me stories of heroes long gone, of voyages and adventures, of treasures lost and found. Those had been the happiest days of my life. Once, even, we had come to a place much like this . . .

I sighed. Where had the time gone?

"Wine?" he asked me, holding out the skin.

"Thanks."

I sat up and took it from him, then took a long sip and passed it back.

"You brought me here before, when I was young," I said.

"You remember!" He seemed surprised.

"Of course."

I opened the basket Bayle's daughters had packed for us, discovering cheese, bread, and dried beef that looked more like army provisions than a picnic meal. It would keep. I wanted something fresh.

"I'll check the snares," I said, and I went and did so.

The first two had been broken by whatever they had caught, the third was empty, and the fourth and fifth both held something like a rabbit, but with short pointed ears and broad padded feet. The last two were empty.

I skinned the rabbits, spitted them, and brought them back. The fire had begun to die down to embers, so I laid the rabbits across the coals to cook. Then once more I sprawled back on my elbows to wait.

Dworkin was looking up at the cliff again, lost in thought.

"Is she up there again?" I asked.

"Eh? What?"

"This mysterious woman we're meeting. I saw movement up there before. Has she come back?"

"Oh . . . no, no women up there." He chuckled. "No women at all."

After we ate the rabbit with bread and cheese, washed down by more of Bayle's excellent wine, I felt tired and full. My thoughts turned to the rest of our family, and I wondered where they were and what they were doing right now.

"Should we call Freda and tell her where we are?" I asked.

"No," he said. "Time runs differently here. I doubt if it's been more than a few hours for her since we left the Beyond. We will be done and back before we have been missed."

"Good."

I lay back and closed my eyes, listening to the sounds of the night. Night-birds sang, insects chirped and buzzed in the grass, and the occasional bat or owl flitted past overhead.

As I drifted toward sleep, I heard my father shift and stand. That brought me back fully awake. What was he up to?

Slowly I opened one eye to a slit, watching him. Our fire had almost died out, but by its dull red glow I saw him creep off toward the trees.

I'd never find out anything if I waited for him to tell me. As soon as he vanished from sight, I rose and followed. Somehow, I knew he was heading for the top of the cliff and the mysterious visitor I'd glimpsed before.

THIRTY-ONE

angled branches poked at my eyes; leaves rustled underfoot. Quiet though I tried to be, I felt as though I made enough noise to wake the dead. Ahead of me, whenever I paused, I heard even louder crunching and snapping, so I knew I had headed in the right direction.

Finally I stumbled onto a game trail that led in the correct direction. I followed it faster now, bent almost double, watching the pale shape twenty yards to the side. It had to be my father.

The trail wound slightly, taking me first away, then closer, then away again. Always I tried to keep an eye on that pale blur. It seemed to be getting larger, but not closer, and then I heard a snort like a horse. Galloping hoofs thundered, and then it was on the trail ahead of me, not a man but something else, something animal. Tall, proud, with a billowing mane and tail.

For a second it paused, and I halted too, my heart beating in my throat. Not a horse, I saw now, but a unicorn—a single long horn rose from the center of its forehead.

With a cry that set my nerves on edge, it plunged ahead, up the trail, climbing higher. It leaped rocks, faster than a man could run, scrambling up toward the top of the cliff.

I couldn't help myself—I had to follow, had to see more. Giving up on following quietly, I ran as fast as I could. My shins banged on rocks., Branches whipped my face. Still I flew up the trail after it.

I reached the top of the trail, where the pine trees stood overlooking the cliff. The white unicorn I had followed joined a second unicorn, and together they melted into the trees and were gone. Panting, yet hardly daring to breathe, I lingered, hoping to glimpse them again. I had never seen anything so wondrous.

What had become of my father? Everyone in Chaos seemed to be a shape-shifter: could Dworkin himself be one of the unicorns? It was a lot to think about.

Slowly and carefully, I backtracked through the underbrush to our camp site—and drew up short.

It seemed we weren't quite so alone here after all. A man dressed in blue sat with his back to me, warming his hands at our campfire. How had he gotten here? I'd thought this world deserted. Had he somehow followed us, despite all those traps Dad had left behind?

I thought about drawing my sword, but the sound of steel leaving my scabbard might alert him. No, I'd have to take the intruder by surprise and from behind.

First, though, I had to make sure he'd come alone. Turning slowly, I stared into the shadowed woods surrounding our camp. I didn't see anyone else, but that didn't mean they weren't out there, lying in wait. That's what I would have done—sent one man forward to check things out, while covering him with a bow or crossbow.

When the man turned and threw the remnants of the rabbit I'd been saving for breakfast into the bushes, I heaved a heavy sigh. It was my brother, Aber.

"What are you doing here?" I demanded, standing and pushing my way out through the bushes.

He leaped to his feet, startled.

"I didn't hear you," he said.

"That's the idea when you sneak up on someone." I glared at him. "You're supposed to be home keeping an eye on Freda, Fenn, and Taine. Not to mention the house. So? What *are* you doing here?"

"I'm out for some fresh air?"

My glare grew more intense. "I'm tired of games. Dad's been playing them all day with me. I want the truth, and I want it *now!*" My tone left no room for argument.

He sighed. "All right. The *lai she'on* searched our house again, right after you went to bed, and this time they started torturing servants and guards, asking if any of them had seen the Jewel of Judgment."

"And you thought you'd be next?" I asked.

"Yes. Freda took Taine to visit Aunt Lanara. I . . . just left."

"What about Fenn? You just abandoned him?"

"He said he was going back to Juniper to help Isadora."

"How did you find us?" I asked. "We've been traveling through Shadows all day, and Dad left a series of traps behind for anyone trying to follow."

"So," Aber went on, "have you seen it? The Jewel of Judgment?"

I shook my head. "Not since Juniper. Dad had it in his workshop. At least, I *think* it was the Jewel of Judgment. He hasn't been exactly forthcoming with information."

"He never is." He swallowed. "Do you have any idea where it is now? If we can get it back to King Uthor safely, maybe—"

He broke off when I shook my head.

"No," I told him firmly. "It's impossible."

"Why?"

"I don't know where it is."

"Oh." He pondered that for a moment.

"For all we know, it's still in Juniper," I said. That was the truth. I didn't know with any certainty that it hung around Dad's neck on that silver chain.

"It can't be there," Aber said, "or the king would have recovered it by now."

"King Uthor's forces weren't the ones attacking us in Juniper."

"I pretty much knew that already." He looked puzzled. "I don't suppose you know who it was, do you?"

"Lord Zon. Have you heard of him?"

"No. But there are so many Lords of Chaos, no one can possibly have heard of them all. We could probably look him up in the genealogy if we went back. Do you think it's important?"

"I'm not sure. But I do think Lord Zon is a bigger threat to King Uthor than Dad ever could be. Ulyanash told me, before I killed him, that Lord Zon was planning to seize the throne. I think he's about to act . . . or would be, if I hadn't killed Ulyanash."

He frowned. "That's not possible. I was with you when you killed him. He said no such thing."

"It's a long story."

"Tell me."

I did so, leaving out only my suspicions about the Pattern and the Jewel of Judgment.

"This is the first time I'm glad I'm not the king," Aber said.

"What I don't understand," I said, "is why it's taken everyone this long to try to get this Jewel of Judgment back. Didn't someone notice it was missing years ago?"

"Apparently King Uthor's been trying to get it back ever since it disappeared, but quietly. Searching, trying to find out who took it, and what caused the Shadows to appear."

"If he's as powerful as you say, why can't he grab another one from a different Shadow? There must be plenty of rubies out there."

"Sure, but not like this one. Apparently it's got magical properties. At least, that's what they said."

"Oh?" That piqued my interest. Maybe I could find out more about it. "What does it do?"

"I'm not sure. But if Dad has it, you can bet he's been experimenting with it. That's probably what attracted King Uthor's attention. The king is . . . part of the Logrus, in ways I don't really understand. They're connected . . . a part of each other. And if the Jewel is connected to the Logrus too, then Dad's playing with it may have brought him under the King Uthor's scrutiny."

I nodded. It sounded like a plausible explanation.

"And how *did* you find us?" I asked.

"You're not hard to track. If one knows how."

"What do you mean?"

"I used your Trump."

I frowned. "I didn't sense anything . . ."

"There are other ways to use them. I've been around you more than anyone lately, we're blood relatives, and I drew the Trump, so perhaps I'm more attuned to you than most. By concentrating very lightly on your card, I can tell where you are . . . sometimes even look out through your eyes."

I shivered, not liking the sound of that. I'd have to practice keeping my mental defenses up. And it might mean using the Pattern to shield myself from any Logrus-spying.

"So . . . you're saying you looked through my eyes and drew a Trump of this clearing?"

"That's right." He pulled it out and showed me.

I took it and threw it into the fire.

"Hey!" he said.

"This is a special place for Dad and me. We used to go camping here when I was a boy. Dad won't be happy that you're here. And he'll be furious if he discovers you made a Trump to get here."

"Then we won't tell him." He shrugged.

"I'm not going to lie," I said.

He sighed. "Well, tell him whatever you want. I don't care." He rose and, using the Logrus, summoned a couple of blankets for himself, which he spread out on the ground next to mine.

I heard a crashing noise, as someone came through the forest towards our camp.

"Is that Dad?" Aber asked me.

"Probably."

A moment later Dworkin emerged from the bushes. When he spotted Aber and me sitting up by the fire, he frowned. He must have imagined he could quietly slip back into camp unnoticed.

"Hi, Dad," Aber said.

"What are you doing here?" he asked. "Why aren't you home?"

"It got a little unpleasant there, what with the searches and all the torturing King Uthor has ordered."

"Where have you been?" I asked Dad.

"Oh, here and there. Many people to see, many things to do."

"I saw you with her," I said to our father. "Tell me the truth."

"Answers will come in time. You are not ready for them."

"You're wrong."

Dworkin shrugged. "I have been wrong before."

"I need those answers!" I snapped. "I'm not a child anymore, and this isn't a game! All our lives are in danger! You say you need my help. Well, I'm not going another step with you until I get answers. And it better be the truth this time."

"Would I lie to you?" he asked.

"Yes!" He had lied to me constantly since he had swept back into my life.

He sighed. "Very well. Ask your questions, my boy. I will answer as best I can. I owe you that. I owe you *both* that."

THIRTY-TWO

or a second, I could not believe he'd finally given in. I almost expected to look around and see King Uthor's hell-creatures bearing down on us from all sides, Fate seemed so determined to keep me in ignorance. But it really *was* just the three of us here, sitting before the campfire, on a remote world far from home.

I licked my lips. "All right. Was that a unicorn I saw?"

"That was no unicorn," Dworkin said. "That was your mother."

"My—mother?" I felt my heart skip. Suddenly, everything began to make sense. My life in Ilerium—it had all been a lie. He had brought me there to keep me out of harm's way. The woman who had raised me as her own . . . she must have been paid. That's why Dworkin had taken care of her all those years. My mother—my *real* mother—had to be a shape-shifter . . . some lady of Chaos. But why not tell me the truth?

He let out his breath with an explosive sigh.

"Yes . . . I brought you here several times, long ago, so she could see you. You are her child . . . heir to all she represents."

"The Pattern . . ." I whispered.

"Yes," my father said simply.

Suddenly it all came clear. My mother couldn't be a lady of

Chaos. She had to come from somewhere else . . . and she must incorporate the Pattern into her being the way the people of Chaos incorporated the Logrus. That explained all Dad's secrecy. If anyone had known about me, about my true heritage, I probably would have been assassinated years ago. He had kept my true mother a secret to protect me.

"Where is she from?" I asked.

"I am not really sure," he said. "She found me, here, in this place."

I didn't know what to say or do. A thousand conflicting emotions ran through me. But mostly I felt relief. The largest part of the puzzle had come into place, and I thought all the other pieces would fall into position with a little more effort.

Aber stared at both of us. "A unicorn? What are you talking about?" he demanded.

I ignored him. "And the Jewel of Judgment?" I asked my father.

"It is a part of her . . . just as it is a part of the Logrus, and much else in the universe. I needed it to create the Great Pattern."

"Then you have the Jewel?" Aber demanded.

"Of course," he said.

My brother stood. "I want it," he said, and he held out his hand. "Give it to me."

"No," I said. I stood and put myself between them. We didn't have time for arguments now. "You're not returning it to King Uthor."

"It's for the good of everyone," he said. He peered around me at our father. "You stole it, Dad. It's weakened Chaos. It's going to cost

King Uthor his throne . . . and the lives of Freda and all your other children. Not to mention me. Hand it over, and I'll make sure you're spared."

I stared at him. "You sound like you mean it," I said.

"I do."

"But how can you offer a bargain like that? You're not the King—"

Our father struggled to his feet. "He's one one of them!"

"Yes," Aber told him.

I stared blankly at him. "One of what?"

"King Uthor's men," Dad said from behind me. I heard the whisper of his sword leaving its scabbard. "A spy, in the king's pay, prying into my affairs! Traitor!"

"You're the traitor," Aber retorted. "You've fooled Oberon with this nonsense about his mother and a Pattern, but you haven't fooled me. You're playing with forces beyond your understanding. I've tried to shield you—to protect you all—but I can't do it any longer."

"How long have you worked for King Uthor?" I asked.

"Since the party at Aunt Lanara's house," he told me. "One of his ministers pulled me aside and warned me what would happen if I didn't help. We would all—Freda, Dad, you, me, everyone in our family—be arrested, tried, and executed for treason. By helping them, I've made sure our family will continue. Now, give me the Jewel. I'll return it. It's not too late!"

Dworkin threw back his head and howled with laughter.

"What is it?" I demanded.

"I put it the one place no one will never get it!" he said. "Around the neck of the unicorn!"

Aber looked horrified. "You couldn't—"

"I *did*." He pointed his sword at Aber and advanced on him. "I ought to kill you here and now."

"No!" I held Dad back. "He meant well—"

"Me, a traitor!" Dworkin raged. He glared at my brother. "You are the only traitor here, Aber! A traitor to your own father!"

"It's *your own fault!*" I snapped. "If he knew what you planned, he might understand—"

"We do not have time for this!" He tried to push around me.

I blocked his way. "Then make time, Dad."

"I won't be branded a traitor back home!" Aber snapped.

"Damnable children!"

He tried to cuff me out of his way, but I caught his wrist. *Not this time.* He grunted, and I saw his neck muscles cord. My feet began to slide across the grass.

Two could play at that game. Setting my feet, I gritted my teeth and held him. Then, with a surge of my muscles, I threw him back ten feet. He staggered and came up panting, giving me an odd look.

"You are strong here," he said.

"Stronger than you."

"Maybe—"

Behind me, I heard Aber say, "Don't fight him, Oberon. I can take care of myself!"

I glanced over my shoulder. Aber folded his hands, and when he unfolded them, a ball of darkness writhed there.

"You would not dare—" our father began.

Aber said, "I didn't come here to fight. I came here to help—but if you try to hurt me, I *will* defend myself!"

The darkness began to grow larger. He cast it onto the ground between us, and it began to swell, consuming the earth, becoming a pit.

Dworkin took a few quick steps back. I did, too. I didn't like the look of that darkness. Aber stared down at it, mumbling words too fast and faint for me to catch. Could this be what he had called Primal Chaos?

"Saddle the horses," Dad said to me quietly, our disagreement seemingly forgotten. "I know the way now."

"What about Aber?" I asked as I heaved the saddle onto his gelding's back and began to tighten the cinch.

"Leave him. He dares not follow us."

"I *will* follow!" Aber shouted. "If you won't save our family, I have to try!"

The pit, I saw with growing horror, had become a yawning chasm, consuming everything it touched: our bedrolls, our campfire, our packs. We all stood on the edge of an abyss now.

"Then you are a fool," our father called to him.

He swung up onto his mount and turned its head away from our camp. I hesitated, gave a last look back at Aber, and did the same.

I had to give my brother credit. He had showed more spirit in the last five minutes than I ever would have expected.

We headed steadily away from the clearing for the next hour, following a trail I could not see. Again Dad shifted through the Shadows, bringing us to a world where day had already broken.

Then, as we rode, the air took on a strange, crystalline quality. Every branch on every tree stood out with a vividness of color and a sharpness of texture I had never seen before. No wind stirred; no insects chirped; no birds sang. Even the air itself seemed different—pure and energizing. I had never experienced anything like it.

When we finally left the wood and rode out across a grassy plain, I gaped at the sun directly ahead of us. It was half again as big as the sun in Ilerium, and it shone with a rich golden hue that sent a glow through everything it touched.

To our left lay an ocean, though it lay perfectly still, without the slightest wave to mar its surface. Nor did I see any sign of fish or water-fowl. Rays of sunlight touched the ocean and cast its shallows a brilliant blue-green color, deepening to azure farther from shore. I could have sat there and watched it for hours.

"We are close . . ." Dworkin murmured. "Yes . . ."

"To what?" I asked, still staring at the sea.

"To the Pattern, the *true* Pattern, the one at the center of everything. It is just ahead."

He dismounted and left his horse, just dropping its reins. I did the same. The geldings lowered their heads contentedly and began to feast on the grass.

Side by side, we walked to where a huge flat stone, which must have been a hundred and fifty yards across and a hundred yards long, rose just above the surface of the plain.

There, on the stone, like a ribbon of gold, I saw the familiar out-

line of the Pattern—the coils and turns, the elegant loops and switchbacks. It nearly matched the Pattern within me . . . almost, but not
quite. It more resembled that which the serpent in the tower of skulls
had raised from Taine's blood.

"It's flawed," I said.

"Yes," he said. "And that is why it must be destroyed. That is
why we are here. The problems must be fixed."

I looked at him. "When you made it, you had never seen the
whole Pattern, had you?"

"No."

"Wait!" cried a voice behind us.

I looked back. Aber was running through the grass to catch up.

"Go home," I told him. "You don't belong here. You tried to
save us. You did your best. King Uthor will understand."

"You're going to destroy it!" he said to Dad, ignoring me. "I
heard you say so. Why didn't you tell me? That's all King Uthor
wants! We've been fighting for the same thing, all this time!"

"Then you will help?" Dad asked him.

"Yes." He nodded quickly. "What must I do?"

"I am not quite sure what will happen," he said, "when I destroy
it. You must keep me safe until my work is done, no matter what happens."

Aber swallowed, glanced at me, and nodded again.

"What about everyone we sent into Shadows to hide?" I asked.
"What happens to them when the Shadows go away?"

Dworkin hesitated. "I cannot know," he finally admitted.
"Here. Use these." He drew out a small stack of Trumps he'd

been carrying inside his shirt. I flipped through them and removed the ones showing my brothers and sisters we had sent into Shadow to hide: Titus and Conner, identical twins, both as short as our father and both with his eyes and wary expressions; Isadora, in full battle dress, her red hair flowing; Syara, slender as a goddess, also red-haired; and Leona, sweet-faced and innocent; and Blaise, stunningly beautiful, but treacherous and manipulative. My family.

"Are these Pattern Trumps?" I asked, returning the others to my father.

He nodded. "Tell them to go back to Chaos," he said, "while they still may. That is the one place which I know will continue."

I handed half the Trumps to Aber and kept the other half myself. He raised Titus's Trump. I picked Isadora's and concentrated.

A moment later my sister's image rippled and became lifelike. She stood before me in chain link armor, a sword in her hand, red hair flowing in the wind, a smudge of blood across her chin. She looked fiercely beautiful. Beyond her, I saw Juniper Castle, its walls half tumbled. Smoke rose from two of the towers. Giant creatures, naked and hairy, carrying clubs and spears, roamed the walls. Those had to be the trolls.

"Oberon?" she said. "What do you want?"

"I'm with Dad," I asked.

"Good. We are almost done here. Our vengeance is nearly complete. Tell him."

"He's about to destroy all the Shadows. You must leave now."

"What!" she cried. "How—"

I shook my head. "We don't have time for that. You must return to Chaos as quickly as you can. We don't know what will happen to anyone still in Shadows when the end comes. Promise me you'll go?"

She hesitated, then nodded. "All right. But—"

"Thanks. I have others to reach." I put my hand over the Trump, and she disappeared, still calling questions. Hopefully she would hurry.

Next came Leona. I tried to contact her, concentrating as hard as I could, but though I sensed her out there, she refused to respond. Probably minding her orders, I thought unhappily. She had been told not to answer anyone, no matter what, until we settled the matter of whoever was trying to destroy our family.

"If you can hear me," I said, "this is Oberon. You aren't safe in Shadows anymore. Get to Dad's house in the Beyond as fast as you can."

I could do no more than that.

My last Trump showed Syara. I got no response from her, either. I tried sending the same message as the one I'd given Leona.

Then I put my trumps down and looked at Aber. He too had finished.

"Well?"

"I reached Titus," he said. "He and Conner are heading back. Blaise . . . sorry, she wouldn't answer me."

I nodded slowly. "I spoke with Isadora. I couldn't reach Leona or Syara."

"Let me try them," he said.

"And I'll try Blaise."

We traded Trumps, and he concentrated on first one, then the other. Then he shook his head.

"Nothing."

I raised Blaise's Trump and got only the faintest of stirring, as though she were far away. Still I concentrated, willing her to appear before me, *demanding* it.

Finally her image wavered and came to life, though not clearly. She lay on a padded bench sipping what looked like wine as scantily clad young men fanned her with enormous wicker paddles. In the distance, I saw an emerald sea, with languid waves splashing on a broad white beach. Gulls wheeled overhead, their calls raucous.

"Oberon . . ." she said. Her voice sounded like it came from the depths of a cave, flat and echoing.

"Get back to the Courts of Chaos as fast as you can," I told her. "You're in danger where you are."

"Danger?" She laughed and looked about. "Here?"

I frowned. "All the Shadows, including the one you're in, are about to be destroyed.

"Impossible!"

"This is the only warning you're going to get. Contact Fenn or Freda and join them in the Beyond. It's your only hope. If I'm wrong . . . well, you can always go back."

"Very well." She sat up, looking annoyed. How very like her. I covered the Trump and broke our connection.

"I told Blaise," I said to Aber. Then I told him about the decadent scene I had witnessed. We both had to laugh.

Our father, meanwhile, had finished his walk around the perimeter of the Pattern. He was nodding and mumbling to himself, gesturing in the air as if trying to do complicated calculations.

Standing, I climbed onto the immense flat rock and walked around its edge, avoiding the Pattern, to join him.

"Well? Can you destroy it?" I asked.

"That is not the problem," he said in a low voice, so Aber wouldn't hear. "It is only sand lying on top of the stone. It was . . . never meant to be permanent. The next one must be."

"Sand?"

I looked down at the Pattern; it looked like a solid gold ribbon on top of the rock. I reached out to touch it, but he caught my wrist.

"No."

"Why not?"

"To walk its length, you must start at the beginning. To enter anywhere else would kill you."

"I wasn't going to walk it," I said. "I just wanted to see what it's made of."

"Do not touch it."

"Dad?" Aber called. "Oberon?"

"What?" Dworkin said sharply.

"We've been followed!"

I followed my brother's pointing finger to see a line of hell-creatures—*lai she'on*—entering the grassland three hundred yards away. They wore full armor. Some carried pikes; two held red banners aloft, both of which blazed with a dragon crest. They advanced steadily on us.

"King Uthor's men," Dworkin said. He looked at Aber. "You brought them here!"

"No!" he cried. "They must have followed me! I didn't know—"

"Get me a staff," he said. "Then you both must keep them at bay as long as you can. I will do the rest."

"A staff . . ." Aber said.

He used the Logrus to reach into the air, feeling distantly for something. Then he pulled a wooden pole from mid air. It was a little bit longer than four feet from end to end—about the same height as Dworkin—and it looked familiar. With a measure of horror, I realized it was the pole that had held King Elnar's head in Ilerium after hell-creatures had killed him. My king's head had been ensorcelled . . . it had spoken to me and called me a traitor. Aber must not have realized where the pole had been, or what had been done to it.

Aber tossed the pole over to me, and with a shudder, I handed it to our father. We didn't have time to get another one.

Without hesitation, Dworkin turned and began to walk counter-clockwise around the Pattern, tapping his staff upon the stone, speaking words I could not understand. Magic, I assumed. Every now and then he gestured and waved the pole.

A wind suddenly came up, stirring the grass, then flattening it as it began to gust. Clouds appeared overhead, obscuring the sun. As darkness fell, lightning flickered like the tongues of serpents.

King Uthor's army of hell-creatures, marching into the wind, ducked their heads and leaned forward. First one, then the other banner broke and went flying off into the sky. Still they trudged on, advancing steadily, pikes held ready

I drew my sword.

Aber grabbed my arm. "Come back with me!" he cried. He held up a Trump showing the main hall in our house back in the Courts of Chaos. "We can't stay here!"

"We must!" I shouted. "Dad needs us!"

The winds seemed to be circling the stone, faster and faster. They swept up dust and dirt and grass and trees. Screaming, I saw one then the other of our geldings fly past. I could no longer see through the wall of wind to where King Uthor's army had been—and I did not know how they could have survived it.

I looked back to see what had become of Dad. He was still circling the Pattern, in the opposite direction of the wind. In the center of the stone, a golden whirlwind blew. As it touched the Pattern's lines, it swept away the sand, scouring the stone clean.

As the Pattern disappeared, I felt the stone underfoot begin to move. Surging up and down, like a boat on an ocean, I felt myself drifting.

Aber threw back his head and laughed, and I saw the true nature within him let loose.

"Feel it!" he cried. "Feel the power! Feel the strength of Chaos returning! This is what it must have felt like before the Shadows came!"

"No!" I screamed back, the howl of winds wild around me, noise in my head and blinding colors in my eyes. Beyond the stone, through the winds, I saw . . . stars. Stars that whirled and flew like fireflies in the night. The land and the ocean had vanished. The trees and grass—King Uthor's troops—all had disappeared. Only the stone remained, floating like an island in a sea of nothingness. The madness beyond howled through my body.

"This is the way it should be!" Aber said. He was in his element, a Lord of Chaos, born to revel in the constantly shifting universe.

"Now and forever! Come back with me, Oberon! It's over! Dad has destroyed the Shadows!"

He still held the Trump in one hand, and he held his other hand out to me. I took a step toward him, then stopped. I shook my head.

"No," I said. "My place is here, with Dad. You go."

He took a deep breath, then nodded. He looked down at the Trump . . . and vanished.

Dworkin continued to circle the stone. Horrorstruck by the nightmare surrounding us, I could do nothing but cling to the hope that this was not the end, but the start of something new and greater.

He reached me and held out the staff. I resheathed my sword, then took it.

"Look!" I pointed.

A tall white unicorn stood at the heart of the stone, her head raised defiantly high. A ruby dangled around her neck on a silver chain. Occasional gusts of winds whipped her mane and tail, and when she turned her head, her eyes glinted deep red, like rubies, like the Jewel of Judgment.

Dworkin saw the unicorn and grinned.

"She is holding this place together for us!" he shouted. "We must begin! There is not much time!"

"What must I do?"

"Use your knife!"

I drew it. He stuck out his arm.

"Cut me!" he screamed over the howl of the wind. "Open my vein! Let the blood flow!"

"No—"

"Do it!"

Taking a deep breath, I grabbed his wrist and gave it a quick slash—long but not deep. I did not want him to bleed to death. He must know what he was doing.

Dworkin grimaced, but made a fist. With blood pouring down his arm and dripping from his fingertips, slowly and steadily he began to walk backward, leaving a trail of blood. As it fell on the bare stone, sizzling and crackling like fat on a hot griddle, a glowing blue line began to appear. It burned with an inner fire, like nothing I had ever seen before.

I realized at once what he was doing . . . tracing a new Pattern, one that matched the Pattern within me, and within the Jewel of Judgment. He worked slowly and carefully, never slowing. And as he dripped blood, the Pattern burned deep into the stone.

Slowly the winds died. The storm abated. Still he walked slowly and calmly backwards, trailing blood, shaping the design. When at last he finished, when he stood in the center of the Pattern next to the unicorn, a terrible calm like nothing I had ever felt before came over the world.

Slowly, silently, Dworkin collapsed. In the blink of an eye, he was gone—and the unicorn with him.

Then the ground underfoot began to rumble and heave. I lost my balance and fell, over the side of the stone, into a darkness that never seemed to stop.

HERE ENDS BOOK TWO OF
THE DAWN OF AMBER

THE DAWN OF AMBER

concludes in September, 2004 . . .

Oberon, continuing his quest to learn the truth about his life and family, begins to master his new-found powers and build powerful alliances to protect his family. But enemies new and old rise before him, including a dark alliance that seeks nothing less than the complete destruction of the Pattern itself!

Survival is at stake, as Oberon races to build a kingdom. To do so, he must not only thwart the servants of Chaos, but cope with a father's who's gone mad, siblings who want him dead, and legions of invading soldiers! But first he must learn . . .

TO RULE IN AMBER

*The final volume of
the new Amber trilogy!*

JOHN GREGORY BETANCOURT is an editor, publisher, and bestselling author of science fiction and fantasy novels and short stories. He has had 37 books published, including the bestselling Star Trek novel, *Infection*, and three other Star Trek novels; a trilogy of mythic novels starring Hercules; the critically acclaimed *Born of Elven Blood*; *Rememory*; *Johnny Zed*; *The Blind Archer*; and many others. His fantasy novel *The Dragon Sorcerer* will be released by ibooks shortly. He is personally responsible for the revival of *Weird Tales*, the classic magazine of the fantastic, and has authored two critical works in conjunction with the Sci-Fi Channel: *The Sci-Fi Channel Trivia Book* and *The Sci-Fi Channel Encyclopedia of TV Science Fiction*. Visit his web site at: http://www.wildsidepress.com/jgb.htm

ROGER ZELAZNY authored many science fiction and fantasy classics, and won three Nebula Awards and six Hugo Awards over the course of his long and distinguished career. While he is best known for his ten-volume *Chronicles of Amber* series of novels (beginning with 1970's *Nine Princes in Amber*), Zelazny also wrote many other novels, short stories, and novellas, including *Psychoshop* (with Alfred Bester), *Damnation Alley*, the award-winning *The Doors of His Face, The Lamps of His Mouth* and *Lord of Light*, and the stories "24 Views of Mount Fuji, by Hokusai," "Permafrost," and "Home is the Hangman." Zelazny died in Santa Fe, New Mexico, in June 1995.